ISABELLE WEBB

ISABELLE WEBB

LEGEND of the JEWEL

a novel

N.C. ALLEN

Covenant Communications, Inc.

Covenant
Communications, Inc.

Cover image Yamuna River © Veer.com

Cover design copyrighted 2008 by Covenant Communications, Inc.

Published by Covenant Communications, Inc.
American Fork, Utah

Printed in Canada
First Printing: October 2008

15 14 13 12 11 10 09 08   10 9 8 7 6 5 4 3 2 1

ISBN-13 978-1-59811-618-2
ISBN-10 1-59811-618-5

To Josh—we cannot wait to see you again.
And to Enos, Deanne, Cody, and Nathan—we love you so very
much.

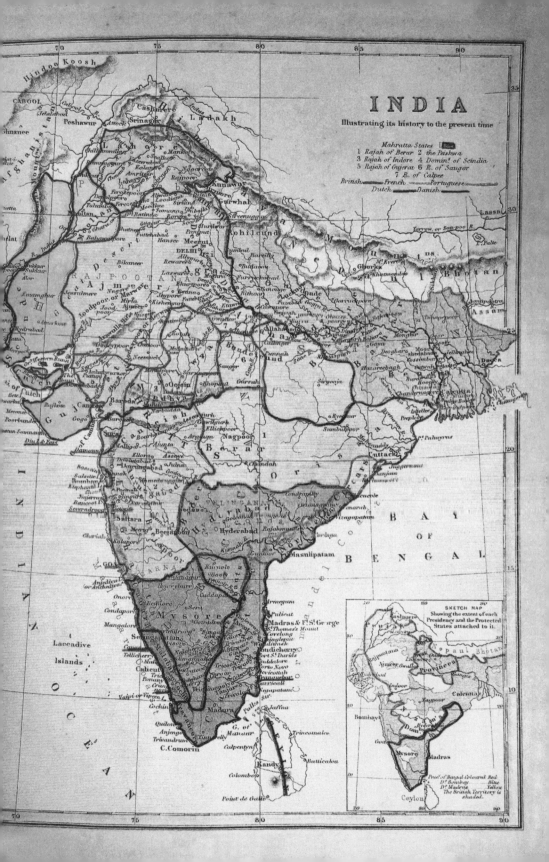

Prologue

.

I swear it, James, I thought I was doing something good, something smart that would make Mama proud and would give me a true accomplishment of my own, for once—something you didn't have to provide for me.

This man . . . how I loathe him, how I know now that he sees in me only something for his own gain. He believes that I am the key to his obscene quest. He told me I was wise and young and brave—all things he needed in a traveling companion. Now I know it is none of those things. His eyes almost seem to glow sometimes when he speaks of his treasure and how I am the one chosen to help him obtain it.

He stares at me with those green eyes, abnormally green. They glow. He lingers outside the tent in this place, this hot, stifling place with its strange people with their strange ways . . . unwilling to let me speak to anyone, to interact in any way, to let me send a letter to you or Mama. I wonder now if I will ever see my home again. I fear my life may end here, at the hands of a madman whom I dare not fight for fear of what he says he will do.

1

September 1865
London, England

"Not so very different from home, is it?" Isabelle Webb sat back slightly in her chair and surveyed the small London inn's patrons who were consuming their dinners, engaged in quiet, private conversation.

"No." Sixteen-year-old Sally Rhodes's disappointment was evident in the flat tone of her voice. "Except they all sound odd."

Isabelle smiled and brought her gaze back to rest on her young traveling companion. "They would say the same of you."

Sally cocked her head to one side. "I suppose they would. Still and all," she said, her expression brightening, "we are clear across the ocean now. That counts for something. And while this inn looks a bit like the other one we visited in Boston, there are a few differences."

"Such as?"

"It smells older."

Isabelle laughed. "Anything else?"

Sally's brow puckered and she toyed with her food. "Well, I know that several miles south of here, I won't find entire cities in shelled ruins." Her tone was deceptively calm to one who didn't know her well.

Isabelle's laughter faded and she cleared her throat. "That's true enough." She tapped her fingers in a soft but quick staccato on the tabletop and sighed. "But we're to forget all that for a time. No?"

"You're absolutely correct, Belle. How utterly gauche of me to mention it."

Isabelle's smile returned. "And how utterly Southern you sound when you speak so."

Sally sniffed. "You're nothing but an envious Yank."

Belle's smile widened. "Of course. You have driven right to the heart of my discontent."

"Posh." Sally folded her arms across her chest and turned her gaze to the room at large before tilting her head back slightly to glare at Isabelle. "Do I really sound so horribly out of place?"

"Don't I?"

"Yes."

"Then I'd say you're in good company." Isabelle nodded her thanks to the wife of the innkeeper who deposited a platter of food on the table.

"I'll be addin' the cost of your meals to your room," the woman said, wiping her hands on her apron.

"Very good, thank you," Isabelle said.

"And breakfast will be served promptly at seven in the morning."

"We'll be here scrubbed and pressed."

The woman nodded shortly, paused as though about to reply, and then turned on her heel and returned to a position behind a wooden bar worn smooth by many hands and resting arms through the years.

Sally shook her head as Isabelle handed her a plate heaped high with steaming meat and vegetables. "Your sarcasm never ceases," she said with a deep sniff of the delicious aroma.

"We won't be scrubbed and pressed?" Isabelle asked her as she looked down at her own plate and took appreciative stock of her food.

Sally waved a hand in Isabelle's direction as though the effort to reply was beyond the energy she was willing to exert. For several moments, the two lost themselves in the decadence of a simple, homespun meal. "I haven't tasted anything so good since my mother was alive, before the war started, really," Sally murmured after taking a sip from the goblet next to her plate.

Isabelle glanced at the young woman, wondering if Sally was feeling pangs of homesickness. But what was left at home? A house that had been stripped bare after seeing years of neglect and disrepair while Virginia had slowly starved herself. Parents whose bones rested in the earth and siblings who now resided with an aunt in West Virginia who couldn't be bothered with a girl who was on the brink of womanhood.

Isabelle herself had spent her adolescence on the streets of Chicago and had learned at an early age that to trust anyone but herself was folly. The haunted look she saw flash occasionally through Sally's eyes, however, reflected back to Isabelle an emotion she knew well. What could she say to the girl? *Don't think about it. Shut it away. Pretend you never had a mother—then it won't hurt so much.* Hardly comforting advice, even if it was the sort by which she'd lived her own life.

Finally, she merely nodded. "It is very good food. Did I ever tell you of the time I attended dinner with the president and his wife? Well, he wasn't the president at the time—we had just escorted him into the city, in disguise, of course, and—"

Sally's lips twitched, and Isabelle felt her nostrils flare.

"Say it. Go on, if you must."

"The disguise of an old woman with a shawl about her head?" Sally asked. "Oh, the newsmen had a jolly laugh at Lincoln's expense over that one."

"What would you have suggested, Miss Sally? The poor man was warding off assassination attempts before he even took office."

"Were you really there, then?" Sally's eyes lit with a spark of interest that she would undoubtedly have squelched had she seen it in herself, if only to deny Isabelle the satisfaction. "Did you escort him into Washington?"

Isabelle nodded. "I did. Met his train at Baltimore and traveled with him. A good diversion it was, too. Nobody shot him, did they?"

"No," Sally had to admit with a shrug. "Not then."

Isabelle's heart thudded hard against her ribs. Her mouth suddenly felt dry and she took a sip of her drink. When she set her goblet back on the table she had gained control of her expression. She hoped.

"Oh, Belle, I'm sorry." Sally reached for her hand and gave it a squeeze. "I didn't mean to be flip. I'm . . . sorry." Sally's throat worked as she tried to swallow her chagrin.

Isabelle returned the squeeze and pulled her fingers from Sally's grasp. "Nothing to be sorry for, silly."

Sally leveled her with a gaze that was sometimes altogether too perceptive. "You saved him once. You saved him more than once. You couldn't save him every time."

Isabelle waved her napkin at Sally as her eyes burned. When she saw that the napkin was white and that the gesture looked alarmingly like a sign of surrender, she clutched it in her lap and forced a smile. "A long, long time ago. It all feels like a very long time ago," she said.

"Not long ago enough," Sally muttered and turned her head to her left. Mercifully, she changed the subject. "That man over there," she said, turning back to Isabelle.

"What of him?" Isabelle asked, not looking.

"You're so very good at that," Sally said. "I tell you about someone and you never look right away."

"Sweetheart, I'm a spy. I should be very good at it."

"Former spy. We're leaving the entire old world behind."

"Some things are in the blood. Now," she said, "I assume you're speaking of the gentleman seated at the table near the bar who is handsome in a western-frontier sort of way, who stands well over six feet tall in his stocking feet and fills the shoulders of his suit coat near to straining."

Sally's mouth dropped open and she swiftly closed it. She leaned in slightly and hissed, "I don't suppose you've ascertained the color of his eyes yet?"

"Blue."

The young woman slowly sat back in her chair. "Why have you taken such notice of him?"

"Because should some sort of . . . ruckus . . . come upon us here in this dining room, he would probably be the only person I might have difficulty subduing. Why have *you* taken such notice of him?"

Sally snorted softly. "Not because I worried I couldn't subdue him. I thought I heard him speak with a distinctly American accent."

"You did. I'm willing to wager he comes from an area well west of the Mississippi."

"A *ruckus*?" Sally asked. "Do you assume a ruckus will follow you wherever you go?"

"One cannot be too careful."

"Isabelle, you're no taller than five and a half feet. How many men have you had to 'subdue' in your life?"

"You might find yourself surprised. And they're not always men. The innkeeper's wife, for example; she could give me a bit of a fight, thin though she is. Something tells me she's a scrappy sort."

"Well, isn't that wonderful," Sally said, her exasperation making her southern drawl all the more pronounced. "She's 'scrappy,' and you taunt her demand for punctuality at breakfast."

"I did not taunt her," Isabelle said, and stopped when she saw movement from the corner of her eye. The man who had been the focus of their interest was standing to leave the room. He exited through a door that led to a smaller parlor on the far side of the room.

"Let's follow him," Sally said, rising from her chair and placing her napkin on it.

"Why?"

"Because he's an American. And he's handsome. And I want to see if he'll raise a ruckus in the parlor."

"More likely than not he's gone in there to have a glass of after-dinner port and a smoke by the fire. Can't say I blame him," Isabelle said as she rose from her chair and followed Sally across the wooden floor, the flickering candlelight throwing gentle shadows about the room. "It's damp and cold tonight, especially for September."

* * *

James Ashby was well aware that the two American women had followed him into the parlor. It was not altogether unwelcome; the older of the two had caught his eye the moment he sat down to dinner. A pretty enough woman to look upon, there was something else about her presence that he couldn't define—something had drawn his attention to her while he had eaten.

The younger woman looked as though she should just now be coming out of the schoolroom and making her way into a debutante ball. She was exactly the sort his brother would have fancied, were he there. Petite, blond, sassy. Phillip had a knack for attracting and becoming attracted to young women who wanted large homes and rings on their fingers to match. He was sorely lacking in good judgment, and wasn't that just the reason for James's current predicament? James to the rescue. He always came to Phillip's rescue.

The Americans approached him, the younger in the lead, the elder staying a pace behind and looking at her charge as though quietly amused. Please, no games. Not tonight. He was weary from several weeks of Atlantic Ocean travel and wearier still from a delay that had held him in London for an additional four days. He had little time or inclination to be the object of a young woman's interest.

"Sir," the blond said as she approached and held out her hand, and he sighed under his breath in resignation. Rising from the comfortable wingback chair he'd claimed near the hearth, he took her gloved hand and bowed slightly over it. Ceremony, rules, society. Life was simpler in a shop with iron, fire, and a bellows. The tools of his trade cared little for niceties.

"Miss."

"Forgive my forward approach, but given that we have no common acquaintance to provide an introduction, I thought it best to throw convention to the wind."

When James remained silent, she plunged gamely onward, the only sign of her discomfort a fractional narrowing of her eyes. "I couldn't help overhearing your conversation with the innkeeper's wife in the dining room," the young woman said, "and figured you for an American. My companion agrees, and she even seems to believe she knows whence you hail."

"Is that so?" James took the hand of the older woman and bowed over it as well, noting a difference in the grip from the first woman to the second. For a moment, he wondered if the elder of the two would have been just as comfortable clasping his hand in a gentlemen's handshake. Her hair was dark, her complexion olive, and the intensity in her golden eyes only added to the impression that she was a woman sure of herself and comfortable in her own skin.

"Allow me to properly introduce the two of us," the older woman said. "I am Miss Isabelle Webb, formerly of Chicago, Illinois, and this is my traveling companion and ward, Miss Sally Rhodes, of Richmond, Virginia."

"A pleasure to meet the both of you," James said and indicated two chairs that flanked the fireplace in an intimate conversational setting. "My name is Mr. James Ashby, but I hardly think I need mention my hometown since you obviously know 'whence I hail.'"

"My friend exaggerates," Miss Webb said. "I merely mentioned that I should be surprised were you not from far west of the Mississippi."

"And indeed, you would be correct. Although I spent my extreme youth in Pennsylvania, I have lived the bulk of my life in the Utah Territory."

Miss Webb nodded. "I see. And were you drawn to the region for religious or mining purposes? Perhaps the railroad?"

He smiled. She was subtle, smooth, and obviously well informed. "I am a Mormon," he said.

Miss Rhodes's mouth formed a small *o*, which she hastily closed.

"Well, Mr. Ashby. Might I be so bold as to ask if you are visiting England for proselytizing purposes?" Miss Webb asked him.

"No, I regret my purpose for this journey isn't nearly so spiritually noble. I'm searching for my errant brother."

"A prodigal son?"

"Of sorts."

"Then I would say your journey is indeed very spiritually noble." Miss Webb smiled.

"For the time being, perhaps. But when I find him, I plan to kill him."

Miss Rhodes's mouth formed a bigger *o*, and Miss Webb laughed. "It seems to me it would be easier, then, to leave him lost. Unless, of course, your mother bid you find him."

He stared at her for a moment in spite of himself. She was startlingly accurate, and he knew the moment she realized it from reading his expression. Something flickered in her eyes. Knowledge? Satisfaction? It was as though she had surmised his whole existence with a few well-placed questions.

Was he so easily read, then, or was she merely extremely perceptive? Either way, he found himself irritated.

"We're very sorry to hear about your brother," Miss Rhodes said into the silence that had filled the room. "Will your search keep you here in London?"

"No," he said, pulling his gaze from the inscrutable Miss Webb. He took a deep breath. "No, I'll be leaving at the end of the week on a steamer for India. Bombay."

Miss Rhodes started in surprise. "As are we!"

"And what takes the two of you to India?" he asked, turning the attention away from himself.

"Escape, really," Miss Rhodes said. "The war finally being over and all, Isabelle needs to relax away from all of that, what with her wound still healing from—"

"Busy," Miss Webb interjected. "We've been extremely busy and need a holiday. India seemed as exotic as anything else on the map."

Miss Rhodes glanced at her companion and closed her mouth, her face flushing slightly.

He raised a brow at Miss Webb but refrained from comment. So the woman had secrets of her own she didn't want to share. He could respect that, as long as she didn't ferret out any more of his. "I've heard it is very exotic indeed—I'm sure you'll not be disappointed."

"Well, it was lovely to make your acquaintance, and now we'll leave you to your peace and quiet," Miss Webb said, rising from her chair. He rose as well and bowed slightly as the women took their leave.

"Perhaps we'll see you at breakfast," Miss Rhodes said with a smile.

"Seven o'clock sharp," he replied.

* * *

James retired to his room at the Pembroke Inn and slowly stripped off his overcoat, lost in thought. He tossed the coat over the back of a simple wooden chair that sat beside a simple wooden table and wandered over to an oval mirror that hung on the wall above a stand containing a pitcher of water and a basin. He watched his reflection as he loosened his tie and removed the cuff links from his wrists. They were his father's cuff links; they had been in James's possession since he was a young boy of thirteen and held his dead father in his arms.

He glanced up at his reflection again, clinking the cuff links together in the palm of his hand and turning them over with his fingers. He resembled his father now that he was a grown man—he had seen photographs of the first James Ashby, and he had his own memories. He couldn't honestly say, however, that he remembered his father looking as frustrated and stern as he usually did himself. His father had been a pleasant man who smiled and laughed often. James often felt the weight of his responsibilities heavily and resented it. It gave him a perpetually serious expression he rarely bothered to change.

It was because his father was gone that James bore so much responsibility and had ever since that awful death. James had looked down at his father's face as the man had drawn his last breath, his young heart pounding at the sight of so much blood. The blood kept coming and coming, spreading like a flood across his father's shirtfront and soaking onto his own small fingers.

His lips tightened fractionally against the vision, and he abruptly dropped the cuff links onto the stand that held the basin. That had happened a long time ago, and some memories were better left alone. Pulling his shirttails from his trousers, he walked the length of the room again to sit in the chair and look over his notes.

James's brother, Phillip, had crossed the ocean with one Thaddeus Sparks, a salesman of sorts who had apparently filled Phillip's head with all manner of stories about a lost treasure in India and incredible reward for the person who found it. James had been able to ascertain Phillip's arrival date in England, the fact that he'd stayed with Sparks at the Pembroke Inn, and then, only a scant few days before James's arrival, his departure on a steamship bound for India.

Miss Isabelle Webb had certainly had the right of it. James's mother had summoned him to her home and begged him tearfully to follow Phillip and save him from yet another foolish venture. Although he had steamed and balked and then returned to his own home to throw a few choice items about his parlor, in the end he had acquiesced and carefully followed the trail of his younger brother, who had been but an infant when their father had died.

When James had been twenty years old, he had established himself well as a successful blacksmith in Salt Lake City. Now Phillip was twenty years old and still hadn't a clue about what he wanted to do with his life. He spent his time fighting matches in the ring with his friends and generally gracing Salt Lake society as its darling boy, and James fumed about the fact that the young man might never find a solid profession for himself. He earned money doing the occasional odd job around town but only enough to satisfy the moment.

James withdrew a map of India from his stack of papers and smoothed the folds with his hand. Apparently, the steamer that carried his brother and Mr. Sparks was headed for Bombay, on the western coast of the country. James had been forced to wait for the next vessel traveling to India, which wouldn't be leaving for another three days. The delay frustrated him. The more the distance between him and his brother widened, the harder it would be to track him.

Where Sparks would take Phillip once they disembarked in Bombay was anyone's guess. James knew nothing of the so-called treasure that was the object of the quest—he had hopes that once he arrived in India he might find someone who could tell him more about it.

With a muttered oath, he retrieved a paper that had become the beginnings of a letter home to his mother. He now uncapped his fountain pen and tried to finish it.

I leave in three days for India, and I hope to find that Phillip is not too far ahead of me. Do not worry overmuch, Mother. I am concerned for your health. I'm certain I will find Phillip and will convince him to return home with me, and I do not want you unnecessarily stewing over the matter.

James paused in his writing and rubbed his eyes. It was his responsibility to reassure his mother that he would find Phillip and that all would be well. His jaw clenched, and he forced himself to take a breath and try to relax. He knew full well that if he allowed the anger to surface, he would awaken in the morning with an aching jaw and head. It was always the same; his life belonged to others, and the responsibilities had been his since his extreme youth. The guilt he felt for resenting it did nothing to ease his mind.

* * *

Scandalous, it might be, but Isabelle couldn't stay another minute in the inn. She needed some air, and her healing leg was throbbing. Women were unwise to walk about near dusk in an unfamiliar city, but telling Sally she'd take only a moment or two outside, she left the inn with her walking cane.

It was cool for September in London. The air hung heavy and damp. The streets had cleared of vendors, and the hustle and bustle of the daytime hours was fading. Isabelle drew a deep breath, taking in the smell of the oil from street lamps that had only just been lit.

She walked along the street, away from the inn, and turned a corner, heading toward the wharf as the shadows lengthened and the sun sank below the horizon. The water lapped in gentle waves against the seawall and the many ships that lined the docks. Even the seagulls were quiet, and the bulk of the night noise came from the taverns that stood along the quay.

Isabelle frowned a bit, her brows coming together in furrows as she looked out toward the horizon. Why was it so hard? She had thought herself immune and far enough distanced from Lincoln's death to be affected by the mere mention of him. Unbidden, the images of those final hours came to her mind, and she closed her eyes.

She was in a boarding house, the very same used by John Wilkes Booth and his associates. She finally knew of their plans, knew they were going to shoot the president at the theater. The window . . . she would have to go out the window because Mrs. Surrat had locked her in the room.

It was too far down, she felt the hideous crunch of the bone in her leg . . . someone was running toward her . . . she mumbled her message as the world went black . . .

Standing near the water now, Isabelle opened her eyes against the sting of tears. Absently, she rubbed her aching thigh and swallowed. She had loved the president. She knew him—had met with him frequently—and was in the employ of the man charged with his safety. She would never be able to absolve herself of the feelings of guilt—that had she done her job better, he might still be alive.

It was her worst career failure in a career that had seen very few failures. She didn't miss details; she knew her work well. She approached each situation with confidence and an innate knowledge of people's basic human nature. The things she didn't know about those with whom she communicated and often spied upon, she ascertained after very little observation. Isabelle Webb was Pinkerton's most competent and accomplished private investigator, male or female.

And she had failed.

The price for that failure was one that an entire country would have to bear. It was almost a relief to be away from the United States. The South was in shambles, fires of hatred still ran high, and Sally had become Isabelle's focus. She had met Sally at the end of the war when Isabelle and her friends found Sally orphaned and attempting to care for her younger siblings. Isabelle had nursed Sally through a fever that nearly took her life, and if she had died, Isabelle most likely would have collapsed. She was honest enough with herself to acknowledge it. Isabelle helping to preserve Sally's life was, in some way, proof that she could still make a difference even though she had been unable to save Lincoln.

And it *was* important, Isabelle realized as she reached up and wiped a tear from her face. Sally's life was important, and Isabelle knew that her current stewardship over the young girl was as much a benefit to herself as Sally.

Isabelle was twenty-six years old and single. She worked in a man's profession and had absolutely no prospects for marriage, not that she'd spent much time looking. Her relationship with her younger sister was sadly nonexistent because of a long-ago conflict. Isabelle's new responsibility for Sally was a welcome diversion and provided a sense of purpose to a life that had begun seeking redefinition out of necessity.

The president was gone, and nothing she could do would ever bring him back. She had tried her best, but it hadn't been enough. She *had* been enough for Sally, though. Isabelle tried to tell herself these things over and over again, and often it seemed to work. There were days, however, when no amount of positive reflection would help, and her spirits plummeted. She missed Mr. Lincoln so much it hurt—she missed knowing he was at the helm, that things would survive under his stewardship. He had brought the country from the brink of disaster, and her faith in him hadn't wavered from the moment she met him when he had taken office. Now that he was gone, her view of the future was bleak.

Still, the war was over. For that she was truly grateful. It had been an ugly thing. As she looked into the dark water, Isabelle could almost see the images of the wounded, dead, and starved. She took a deep breath, inhaling the scents of the present, and allowed her mind to slowly turn toward other things, images of her friends at home whom she loved and who loved her. She walked slowly along the water, calming her thoughts and relishing the fact that she was still alive and healthy. She was here to smell, touch, and see life. So many in recent years had been denied those blessings.

Isabelle relaxed and so enjoyed the feel of the sea air against her skin that she lost track of time. Retrieving a small clock from within the folds of her skirts, she was surprised to realize she'd been gone from the inn for well over an hour. Sally would be beside herself if she didn't return soon. She turned slowly, leaning on her cane.

A noise to her left suggesting the beginnings of a night of revelry in the taverns along the wharf hastened her step; it really was foolish to be out alone in the dark of a strange city. And London or New York, taverns along the water all seemed much the same with their general aura of danger.

As she made her way back to the inn, she acknowledged to herself for what seemed the thousandth time that she must learn to let the past rest. If she couldn't manage to do that, she knew full well she would have no future.

Isabelle had very nearly reached the end of the wharf and was about to head toward the inn when the sound of footsteps behind her grew in volume. She turned to look back over her shoulder and caught sight of a man dressed in clothes that looked soiled and ill-kept, even in the ever deepening darkness.

"Ye're lookin' a mite out of place, lassie," the man said as he approached her. He wasn't overly tall but was stocky and larger than she was, at any rate. The weathered lines etched into his face showed evidence of his years at sea, and he walked with the gait of a sailor trying to find his land legs. "P'rhaps I can show you the way home," he said, his voice gravelly and deep.

Isabelle took a deep breath that came out as a resigned sigh. She had known better, and now she was going to have to defend herself on her aching leg. As the man loomed closer, she cautiously took a step back, trying not to noticeably recoil from the stench of his breath.

"A bit early in the evening to be so far advanced into your cups, is it not? Leave me alone," she told the man. "I won't hurt you if you turn around now."

His bark of laughter was incredulous, and she'd seen that same look on many a man before laying him low. "I've not had that much to drink, missy," he said, still chortling. "But I do enjoy a fight, I do—especially with a fetchin' one such as yerself."

Gripping her cane firmly, she took one more step back to prepare for the drunk's advance. The sound of rapidly approaching footsteps at her back had Isabelle glancing over her shoulder. James Ashby materialized from the shadows looking none too happy. "How fortunate that I decided to join you on your stroll, my dear," he said to Isabelle, still looking at her would-be attacker. He reached the man in a few quick strides and drew back his fist, punching the man full in the face. The man fell to the ground with a thud.

Isabelle stared for a moment at the prostrate form at her feet, finding herself torn between irritation and amusement. "Mr. Ashby, I thank you," she said. Before she could say another word, however, he turned his expression of anger on her with a heavy sigh.

"What could you possibly be thinking to venture outside alone on the *docks* at night?"

She felt herself go very still at the censure in his voice, all traces of good-natured humor fading quickly. "I beg your pardon, sir, but I do not recall requiring your permission," she said evenly. The poor man didn't know that Isabelle Webb never answered to anyone.

"And yet I find myself involved, as your young friend is back at the inn in utter hysterics."

"Sally sent you to find me?" Isabelle's eyes narrowed. She would have a talk with the girl.

"And apparently she had the right of it."

"Mr. Ashby," she said, straightening her shoulders, "I appreciate your protection, but I have no need of it. Had you not come along, I would have dispatched the man myself."

The expression on his face clearly showed his disbelief. He glanced down at the still form on the ground and then back up at her. He raised one brow and then shook his head slightly. "I will accompany you back to the inn now," he finally said.

She eyed him evenly for a long moment. She scarcely believed the man's authoritative tone—that he should take such with her, a virtual stranger, was beyond the pale. "I am returning to Pembroke Inn," she said flatly, "because I choose to and was on my way there when that man approached me."

"Miss Webb, it doesn't matter to me one whit why you return, just so that you do. I'm not moving an inch until you start walking."

"You wish to test my resolve? We may just stand here all night long, then. I don't know who you think you are, but I am not amused."

"Neither am I." Mr. Ashby's face still remained as hard as granite, angry and unyielding. "I was taken from my bed to find you, and I very much desire to return to it."

"And I apologize for that," Isabelle said, her voice raising a notch. "Sally should never have awoken you. That does not change the fact, however, that you are not my father, and I have no need of your guidance or protection. I take exception to the fact that you're now seeing yourself as my inconvenienced champion."

"Miss Webb," he said, grating the words between his teeth, "you may take whatever you please, but you will return to the inn. I'll not be awoken again in another hour by your dramatic young friend."

"That 'dramatic young friend' thought you charming," Isabelle muttered.

"She thought wrong. And unless you accompany me of your own free will, I'll haul you over my shoulder. I care little for convention at this time of night, and I'm tired."

Isabelle squinted her eyes at him. "I do believe you're no better than the man from which you've just 'saved' me."

"The supreme difference, dear lady," he said as he placed a firm hand under her forearm and urged her forward, "is that I seek to return you to the safety of your own bed. I suspect that man had other plans."

Isabelle jerked her arm free of his grasp and began walking back to the inn with as much speed and dignity as she could muster. It didn't help matters much that her leg was cramping and it was all she could do to refrain from groaning aloud.

When they reached the threshold of the inn and entered the common room, she turned on her rescuer. "Please, dear man, the next time my hysterical young friend knocks upon your door, don't answer." She turned and made her way up the stairs to the second floor.

2

Mayfair was teeming with people plying and buying wares. Sally watched the activity, fascination written clearly upon her features, and Isabelle smiled. "Are you feeling hungry yet?" she asked the younger woman.

"I am," Sally answered while keeping her attention riveted to a man selling meat pies from his cart. "I'm finding that my breakfast has deserted me rather quickly."

"We ate well over four hours ago," Isabelle said as she approached the man and purchased two meat pies that he wrapped in paper and handed to her. Smiling her thanks, Isabelle led Sally down the street a bit to a small park where she found a deserted bench.

They sat together and ate their food in relative silence, watching people as they passed. "I'm glad to see you eating well," Isabelle remarked to Sally as the young woman attempted to surreptitiously lick her fingers. "You became so thin when you were ill."

"I must take care that I do not outgrow my new clothes, however," Sally said, now wiping her fingers on a handkerchief Isabelle pulled from her reticule. "You've bought me so many lovely things, and I would hate to not fit into them anymore."

"We can always let the seams out," Isabelle said, enjoying the last of her luncheon. "You're still awfully thin."

"A fine thing, coming from you," Sally said, eyeing Isabelle's trim waist. "You would fatten me up while still staying fashionably shaped yourself."

Isabelle waved a hand at Sally's silliness and gestured toward one of the shops lining the street next to the park. "You were thinking of a new bonnet for your lavender day dress—shall we inquire at that bonnet shop?"

"Oh, yes, do you mind?" Sally's eyes danced.

"Not in the least."

The two spent considerable time looking over Madame Dubois's bonnet and hat collection. Sally found the perfect confection to match the lavender day dress, and Isabelle purchased a navy blue hat with a short mesh veil to complement an outfit of her own.

They next visited a bookshop where Isabelle purchased two books on the country of India and her history. She also bought a small, blank journal for Sally and one for herself. "We must write down everything," she said to her young charge as they left the shop and climbed into the hack that would return them to the inn, "or we will forget it all."

Sally reverently smoothed her gloved hand over her new journal. "I don't want to forget a moment," she murmured. She looked up at Isabelle suddenly, urgency in her voice. "Belle, let's never go home. Can't we travel forever?"

Isabelle sat back in her seat and accustomed herself to the sway of the carriage and said, "I wish we could. But truly, I believe we would eventually grow weary of it. There's something nice about going home at the end of a long travel."

"I have no home," Sally said, her voice curiously devoid of emotion.

"Yes, you do," Isabelle replied, her tone sharp. "You have a home, a rather large one at that, and brothers and a sister who will want to eventually see you again."

"What guarantees do I have that my home will still be mine when we return? My parents are dead, the Confederacy is dead as well—how do I know some Yank won't take the whole of it over?" Sally's eyes flashed a bit, and Isabelle was glad. She preferred the young woman's anger to her flatness.

"Some Yank *does* own your home now." At Sally's mutinous expression, Isabelle smiled. "I do. Because you're now my ward."

Sally sat back in her seat and rolled her eyes. She seemed almost relieved at Isabelle's reminder, but then her face clouded. "How do you know it will remain secure, even though you own it now?"

"Sally, I should have explained things better to you before we left. I spoke with some friends who are now instrumental in governing Richmond. They've agreed to look after the welfare of your home and holdings. All will be secure upon your return, and the house is yours— it's in my name only until you reach the age of majority or marry."

"Belle, it really is your house now. I consider it small enough payment for saving my life and taking me to India." Sally's expression softened, and Isabelle found herself hard-pressed to remember that there was once a time when the two of them had eyed each other with barely veiled mistrust and dislike. Isabelle had been a hated Yank, a symbol of all that had ruined Sally's life, and Sally had been attempting to refuse Union help to her own supreme detriment, a fact that had set Isabelle's teeth on edge.

"It's yours, Sally, and we'll not discuss that fact further. The pleasure in securing its safety for you is all mine." She paused for a moment and broached a subject she'd only just mentioned and which they never discussed. "Do you not miss your siblings?"

Sally's eyes misted for a moment, and she glanced out the carriage window. "I do. I wonder if they miss me, however."

"I'm certain they must."

"Yet my aunt sends no communication from them, nothing at all. And she turned over custody of me readily enough to you with no second thoughts."

"I didn't think you wanted to live with her."

Sally's face turned hard. "I don't. But that's beside the point."

Isabelle smiled. "It is beside the point, you're correct. Her loss is my gain. However, I think your siblings need to hear from you. You should write to them, and we can post your letters periodically. Think of how exciting it will be to receive mail from their sister in England or India."

Sally nodded reluctantly. "I do miss them so much," she murmured. "I try not to think about them."

"That's often the easiest approach. It doesn't mean they're not still there, though."

"Do you miss your sister?" Sally's question caught Isabelle off guard.

"I do," she said honestly. "We are two very stubborn creatures, however. I suspect it will involve an act of congress to see us on speaking terms again."

"That's silly," Sally said. "So much wasted time."

She was right, of course, but Isabelle chose not to comment on it. She was saved from having to answer her by the fact that they had arrived at the inn. They disembarked, paid the driver, and collected their packages.

As they entered the inn, Isabelle immediately registered the tension in the air at the main desk. Their hostess, the innkeeper's wife, was in a heated discussion with a rather large woman who stood in an aggressive stance, her face angry and nostrils flared.

Isabelle and Sally made their way to a corner where they took off their bonnets and hats, Isabelle motioning for Sally to keep quiet for a moment. "It is *imperative* that you tell me where he is!" the stranger was saying to the innkeeper's wife, Mrs. Hancock.

"And I'll say it again, I'll be tellin' you nothing! He was a paying patron whose privacy I respect."

"You saw me here speaking with him only just last week! I have information of great import I need to share with him. I must know, has he already gone on to India? This is all I'm asking of you!"

"If you don't leave this instant, Madam, I shall have my husband bodily remove you from this establishment! Ye'll not come into my inn and bark orders at me!"

The woman's outrage radiated from her body. Isabelle sneaked a glance at the confrontation while slowly stripping off her gloves. "*I* am the *wife* of a British officer!"

Mrs. Hancock's voice dropped a notch, probably in an attempt to quell the scene, but derision dripped on every word. "I don't care if ye're the wife of the Prince Regent himself! Ye'll leave this place at once, or I'll be callin' the constabulary."

Isabelle silently applauded the woman's pluck and her refusal to step aside in the face of class superiority. As the self-important Lady Something-or-other left the inn in a huff, Isabelle watched her go and wondered at the cause of the altercation.

* * *

James entered the parlor after dinner that night hoping to see Miss Webb. He wasn't disappointed as he looked around the room and noticed her young friend leaving to go upstairs to their room, saying something about wanting to write in her diary. Miss Webb told her that she would be up momentarily. He made eye contact with her then and wondered if she wasn't rethinking her decision to remain in the parlor as she gifted him with a tight smile that was, if anything, only slightly more friendly than an outright scowl.

"Miss Webb," he said, approaching her and motioning to the chair that Miss Rhodes had just vacated. "I wonder if I might join you for a moment."

"Certainly," she said after a moment's hesitation.

He sat and then regarded her frankly, meeting her open, golden-eyed gaze. "I have been told, on occasion," he said, "that I am often rather . . . heavy handed. I am accustomed to taking charge of a situation and, well, solving it."

Miss Webb folded her hands in her lap. "And you believe that I was in circumstances last night that were in need of solving."

"Miss Webb," he said, fighting to keep the exasperation out of his voice. After all, he had come to try and apologize. "You must agree that your assailant meant you harm."

"I do indeed agree to that."

"Then why would you be so, so offended at my timely arrival?"

"'Twas not your timely arrival that had me offended, Mr. Ashby. It was your attitude afterward and the fact that you refused to listen to me as I explained that I can care for myself."

James closed his eyes briefly. Yes, yes, it was his attitude that was the problem. It was for that very reason that he had sought her out.

But this continued nonsense about her defending herself? Against a man that easily outweighed her by twice? She was delusional.

"I apologize," he said rather stiffly, and even to his own ears he could hear how awkward it sounded coming out of his mouth. Apologizing wasn't something he did frequently. "My temper can be frightening, and—" Drat the woman, was she *laughing* at him? She was! She was genuinely amused.

"I wasn't frightened," she said. "Irritated, yes, but not frightened."

James wasn't sure he could determine why that fact seemed to matter to her, but apparently it did. She was very clear about the distinction.

"Well, at any rate, you have my apology." He placed his hands on the arms of the chair and moved to stand. She stopped him by placing a hand on his arm.

"Mr. Ashby, I thank you for seeing to my safety last night," Miss Webb said. "I am not a normal creature, and I hardly expect you to understand my sense of independence. I am sincerely grateful that you thought enough of my young friend to see after her wishes when you could very well have remained comfortably abed."

"Miss Webb, no man worth his salt would have ignored her pleas. From her tone, I rather expected to find you dead or already abducted."

"She does tend to get a bit emotional," Isabelle said, her lips lifting into a smile. "I have spoken to her about not bothering you in the future."

"And I should hope you'll make it a point to stay indoors after dark," James said, unable to help himself.

"I shall certainly take care. Have a good evening, Mr. Ashby." With that, she rose and left the room. It wasn't until she was gone that he realized how neatly she'd evaded his admonition.

* * *

The steamship had been en route to Bombay for two days when Sally took ill and closed herself off in the stateroom with a chamber pot and a cool cloth. The girl had eaten something that didn't agree with her stomach, and the movement of the ship upon the water only made matters worse.

Isabelle stood by the rail at the stern, watching the miles melt away with an unconscious grimace as she thought of her young charge below deck heaving up what little was left in her stomach. She was worried in the extreme. Sally had only recently regained her health, and Isabelle constantly feared a relapse. Sally insisted that her current malady was nothing like her prior illness and had finally ordered Isabelle from the room in no uncertain terms, stating that she wished to endure her humiliation privately.

"I'm sorry to hear that Miss Rhodes isn't feeling well." A masculine voice sounded at Isabelle's shoulder, and she turned her head toward the speaker. James Ashby's normally stern face expressed concern. "Is there anything I can do to help her?"

Isabelle hadn't seen much of the man since they'd left London. In truth, she had been spending her time in their stateroom watching Sally fall further under the weather.

"Unfortunately, I don't believe so. She won't even let me stay in the room." Isabelle shook her head with a small smile. "That girl is so stubborn. I thank you for your concern, however."

Mr. Ashby inclined his head. "Please tell me if I can be of service. I'm not much of a physician, but perhaps I can locate one for you when we reach port, should she still be ill."

"What is your profession, Mr. Ashby?" Isabelle asked him, her face upturned to look at his. The breeze off the water was gentle and blew a few stray strands of hair away from her face.

"I am a blacksmith by trade."

"Surely a useful profession when tromping off into the wilds of India. I imagine you would be quite handy."

His slight smile was accompanied by a shrug. "Handy. I suppose so. It would be nice to be adept at something—I'm not much of a seasoned traveler and find myself a bit out of my element."

Isabelle cast an appraising glance over the man; he always looked perfectly groomed and at ease, so much so that she would have found it hard to believe that he was a blacksmith if not for his large stature. She could well imagine him hefting tools and hammering away in his shop. "You needn't fear, Mr. Ashby." She leaned closer to him with a smile and a wink. "Your secret is safe with me. No one need know you prefer to be more of a homebody."

"I don't suppose that I prefer it, merely that it's all I've ever done. There hasn't been much time in my life for travel."

Isabelle nodded. "Well, if you have spent your time as a father for your younger brother, I can well imagine your time hasn't been your own."

Mr. Ashby squinted at her, tipping his head slightly to one side. "Forgive me, Miss Webb, but how in blazes did you ascertain *that?*"

"You've made no mention of a father, you admitted you're here looking for your brother at your mother's request—it's likely that if your father were still alive he would be here in your stead, or be with you, at least. Or you would have commented that your 'parents' wanted you to find your brother."

"Perhaps my father is a wastrel and I seek to cover for his behavior."

"In which case, you've still been acting as a father for your brother, then, have you not? I didn't necessarily say he was dead, although now I would venture to guess that such is the case."

Mr. Ashby studied her for a moment. "What is it that *you* do with your time, Miss Webb? Family money permits you to travel the world in search of adventure?"

Isabelle returned his frank gaze, trying to decide whether or not to be honest. He waited, his blue eyes holding hers with unnerving assessment. She finally heaved a sigh and turned her face more fully into the wind, closing her eyes for a moment. "Have you ever heard of Allan Pinkerton, Mr. Ashby?"

"The private investigator?"

Isabelle opened her eyes and looked at him. "Yes. I have been in his employ for several years."

"You are a private investigator?"

Isabelle nodded.

"Quite revolutionary for a woman to take on such a profession."

She looked at him, searching for signs of disgust or superiority. He leaned against the rail, his hands in the pockets of his trousers, regarding her with an expression that was openly curious and perhaps a bit skeptical.

"Pinkerton is indeed revolutionary in that regard. He employs women, and it has served him well. We have entry to places where he does not."

"And are you currently on assignment? Miss Rhodes's comments the night we met suggested you're taking a holiday of sorts."

"You have a good memory, Mr. Ashby."

"As do you, Miss Webb."

Isabelle smiled. "Sally and I are on holiday."

"Are you still in the employ of Mr. Pinkerton?"

Isabelle shook her head slightly in response. "At the moment, no. I'm not entirely certain what the future will hold, however."

"Pinkerton and his people had provided security and investigation for President Lincoln during the war these past few years, isn't that true?"

Isabelle's heart skipped a beat, and she felt a stab of frustration at herself. "Yes, that's true."

"I imagine you must have spent a good deal of time in Washington then."

Isabelle glanced at Mr. Ashby. When had he adopted her method of inquisition? She was uncomfortable with the turn of events. "I spent a good deal of time all over the country."

"Gathering information?"

She nodded a bit stiffly. "Among other things. So which is it? Is your father deceased or is he a wastrel?" Isabelle was sure that later, upon reflection, she would be aghast that she had been so tactless and abrupt with the man. It wasn't at all her usual style.

He smiled at her, and she knew that *he* knew she was flustered. "He's been dead for twenty years. My parents were crossing the plains to reach the Utah Territory, and my father was shot and killed by some anti-Mormons. I was a boy of thirteen, and my brother an infant."

Isabelle nodded, taking a deep breath of the clean ocean air and trying to regain her composure. "I, also, lost my parents at a young age. I can appreciate your experiences." There. If he had known her better, Mr. Ashby would realize that she had just given him a piece of information she never shared with people. It was an olive branch of sorts—an apology for being rude.

To her utter amazement, his expression softened a bit. "I'm sorry to hear that. How old were you?"

"Fifteen. My younger sister and I were left behind." Isabelle forced a smile. "You and I have more in common than we knew."

"Indeed. So, Miss Webb, what are your plans once you reach the shores of India?"

"I'm embarrassed to admit that we haven't any firm plans as yet. I had decided to reach Bombay and once there, determine our course. And you? Might I presume that your own course will be determined largely by what you discover about your brother?"

He nodded. This time, it was Mr. Ashby's turn to look out over the water in thought. "Phillip is a bit of a dreamer," he said. His tone was gruff, and he seemed rather embarrassed. "He was enticed by a legend about a jewel or some such thing . . ."

Isabelle waited for him to continue. When his pause stretched, she finally asked, "Is he traveling alone or with companions?"

"A companion. A man by the name of Thaddeus Sparks arrived in Salt Lake City from San Francisco nearly six months ago and introduced himself around town as a man who was going to head an expedition through India in search of a lost treasure." Mr. Ashby shook his head. "He was working his way eastward, looking for financial backing, and while most of those I spoke with regarding the matter dismissed him out of hand, he was apparently able to find someone willing to fund his venture.

"Somehow, he got into my brother's head and convinced him that he, Phillip, was key to this quest," Mr. Ashby continued. "Phillip left us a letter stating that he was going with Mr. Sparks and that we were not to worry over it."

"He is twenty years of age," Isabelle said gently. "Nearly the age of majority. When I was twenty years old, I found myself employed as a spy."

Mr. Ashby looked back at her with a quirked brow. "Miss Webb, if my brother possessed an ounce of your obvious courage, if not common sense, I wouldn't think twice about this adventure of his. I would wish him luck and hope that he might bring me something unique as a souvenir on his return." He shook his head. "Phillip has no sense whatsoever and is entirely too trusting for his own good."

Isabelle ignored his insult to her judgment. She doubted he even knew what he'd said. "Do you suppose that perhaps you misjudge your brother because he has always been the 'younger one'?"

Mr. Ashby snorted. "Hardly. No, Miss Webb, I'm afraid I have judged my brother all too accurately and have reason to be concerned for his health, if not his life. My mother is beside herself with worry, and it is not unfounded."

"Do you mistrust him or the company he keeps?"

"Without a doubt, the company he keeps. Phillip himself would never hurt a fly. Sparks, however, I don't trust at all. The man had a look about him I didn't like from the moment I first laid eyes on him."

Isabelle leaned both arms on the railing and looked out at the vast expanse. "What do you know of this Mr. Sparks's travel plans? Do you have an idea of where he was thinking to look for this treasure?"

Mr. Ashby shook his head. "Unfortunately, I know nothing of his plans. His ideas, indeed, his whole demeanor was so ridiculous that I lent him little mind. Had I realized Phillip was hanging on his every word I would have paid closer attention."

"So you have been tracking him mile by mile?"

"Yes. I reach one destination only to ask questions of those who might have seen them and then follow their trail bit by bit."

Isabelle nodded. "A rather time-consuming way to follow someone, but necessary. What do you know about this legend of which Mr. Sparks spoke?"

"Again, precious little. There is a stone—a valuable jewel—and some value or other for the one who possesses it."

"Value because of the stone itself or because of something the stone grants, I wonder," Isabelle mused aloud.

Mr. Ashby leaned forward and placed his elbows on the rail, mirroring Isabelle's stance. "Does it make a difference?" he asked, squinting a bit as spray from the ocean below glanced off the side of the steamer.

Isabelle nodded. "Perhaps. It could determine the level of intensity with which this Mr. Sparks searches for it. If he believes this jewel is worth a substantial amount of money, that may be one thing, but suppose the jewel grants untold riches, for example, and is the medium through which more and more are obtained. I would think that would be entirely different."

Mr. Ashby glanced at Isabelle. She felt his gaze and looked at him. "What is it?" she asked.

"You strike me as an intelligent sort, Miss Webb. Are you suggesting you might also believe in such a treasure?"

"Well, now, Mr. Ashby," Isabelle said with a wry smile, "it doesn't much matter what I believe. What matters is what Mr. Sparks believes."

"Fair enough. But do you?"

"Do I what? Believe in magical treasure?" Her smile remained. "Would you be disappointed?"

He considered the matter. "I suppose I might."

"Well, then, you can put your mind at ease. I have little patience for nonsense."

Mr. Ashby returned her smile, and Isabelle blinked a bit. She had seen little of such lighthearted emotion cross his features in the short time she had known him. It was a pity he couldn't, given his present worry, find excuses to display it more often.

"I am relieved, Miss Webb."

"Really, I shouldn't mind if you called me Isabelle."

"Then I give you leave to use my Christian name as well," he said, and she detected a hint of gentle mockery at such formal use of good manners. She could well imagine he preferred to spend time in his blacksmith shop over the parlor at teatime.

"James, isn't it?"

He nodded.

"Named for your father?"

"Again, you surmise my past correctly."

"You are the firstborn," she said. "Tisn't much of a leap of logic."

"I suppose. And your name? Is there family significance?"

"I am named for my maternal grandmother, who was from Spain. I was told my eyes and hair were a gift from her." Isabelle shivered a bit as the breeze off of the water cooled with the setting of the sun. Her skirts rustled against her legs, the fabric whipping around her and sounding much like sails.

"Would you care to go below deck?" James asked her.

"I am rather hungry. Would you like to join me for dinner?"

"I would be delighted."

"Sir, your manners are impeccable for a blacksmith." Isabelle smiled to take the sting from her words.

"My mother insisted." He offered her his arm, which was a vast improvement on the last time he had escorted her, and together they left the railing.

* * *

James, Isabelle, and Sally sat in a nicely appointed drawing room playing cards. The table was heavy and made of dark oak. It bore traces of those who had played games throughout many passages across various oceans.

Sally traced her finger along one of the scratches in the surface of the table. "I understand from listening to the crew that many shipping lines are looking to create luxury liners that will rival these current steamships."

Isabelle nodded and rearranged some of the cards in her hand. "Supposedly we'll soon be crossing the oceans in unimagined splendor."

James glanced around them at the well-cared-for, if slightly worn, accommodations. "This works well enough for me," he said and also moved some of the cards he held.

"I've certainly seen worse," Isabelle said.

Sally's brow wrinkled in a frown. "There was a day when I would have been aghast to be seated at a table that had seen any wear. That was before my mother and I were forced to sell our belongings so that we could eat." She forced a smile. "I suppose I'm better for it now."

"You have a better understanding about what matters most in life," Isabelle said. "You're not better because you lost so much."

"My, such unseemly talk I've instigated at the game table," Sally said, her face still pale from her recent illness. "We really should be discussing the fact that I just won this hand." She fanned her cards down before her. "Gin."

Isabelle smiled and made an inner note to herself. It seemed that Sally was as uncomfortable discussing painful details about her life as she herself was. They were an interesting pair. Sally, however, was young and didn't know how to cope with her traumatic past, and against her better judgment she kept bringing it into conversation.

"Sally," Isabelle said, tossing her cards on the table, "One of these days I will prove you for a cheat."

Sally fluttered her lashes. "Why, Miss Webb, all that I know I've learned from you."

James laughed and tossed his cards down as well. "Remind me I should be wary of both of you in the future. Are you certain you don't care for anything to eat, Miss Rhodes?"

Sally grimaced. "Thank you, no. It may be that I never eat another bite. And Belle, stop looking at me so. I'm not at death's door."

Isabelle held up a hand. "I wasn't thinking any such thing."

"Oh, yes you were. Now, why don't you go and speak to that porter over there—the one you said must be an Indian native. You can ask him your questions while Mr. Ashby tells me about his brother."

James's eyebrows shot skyward. "I beg your pardon?"

Isabelle shook her head as she rose from her seat. "Sally, sometime soon we must teach you the meaning of the word *finesse*."

"What is it that I should be telling her about my brother?" James asked Isabelle, rising from his chair as she stood.

Isabelle motioned for him to be seated and smiled. "I briefly mentioned to Sally the things you told me today on deck. I told her that it might be a good idea to question a native on board about the legend of this mysterious jewel. She, in turn, told me that she is very keen to learn more about your brother because she believes he must be a very interesting and brave person to pursue such a grand adventure."

James snorted. "I am fond enough of my brother, Miss Rhodes, but *interesting* and *brave* are not words I customarily use to describe him."

"Well, what words *would* you use, then?" Sally asked as Isabelle left the table.

"*Foolish* and *rash.*"

"Oh, Mr. Ashby, surely not," Isabelle heard Sally say as she moved out of earshot. She couldn't suppress a smile. Poor Mr. Ashby was up against a spirited Southern girl who had decided to become young Phillip Ashby's champion.

When she reached the porter on the other side of the room, she smiled and extended her hand. "Do you speak English?" she asked the young man. She knew for a fact that he did. She'd heard him speaking earlier that day in the cultured accents of a native raised in British-ruled India.

"I do," he replied and taking her fingers, bowed slightly over them.

"I have a rather curious question for you. Are you aware of an Indian legend involving a powerful jewel, supposedly of great worth? Enough that would cause people to hunt for it?"

"A jewel, you say?" The porter's expression remained blank enough, but his eyes flickered quickly, almost imperceptibly away from her gaze and then back again. He shifted his weight slightly away from her and shrugged. "I cannot say I know of such a thing."

Isabelle smiled and tilted her head a bit to the side. "Silly, isn't it? I heard someone back home mention a treasure, and I thought it a fun story. I wondered if there was any truth to it."

"I have never heard of it, Miss," the porter said to her in careful tones he tried to normalize with a smile. "India is full of treasures, to be certain. This jewel of which you speak does not exist, however."

"Thank you so much for your time, at any rate. I shall be sure to tell my friends that someone has told them a fanciful tale." Isabelle dipped her head in acknowledgement to the man as she turned and crossed the room.

"I think he sounds delightful," Sally was saying to poor James, who looked torn between amusement and frustration. "You must realize he has the heart of a poet, a soul meant to wander the earth in search for treasures and the meaning of life."

James muttered something unintelligible under his breath, and Isabelle fought a smile as she approached the table and took her seat.

"Oh! Well, that was fast," Sally said to Isabelle. "So is there a treasure or not?"

"There definitely is a treasure. My guess is there's also a curse attached."

3

"Of course there's a legend about the Jewel of Zeus; you ought to have asked me first," sniffed the woman to whom Isabelle sat next on the deck. "I've lived in India for over ten years now, lived through the Sepoy Rebellion and all of it. I would think I should know all there is to know about the place. In fact, I'm something of an expert on the subject. People have offered to pay me for my knowledge about it, if you can imagine something so vulgar."

"Of course, how silly of me not to have divined that immediately," Isabelle murmured to her companion. The woman was the very one whom Isabelle and Sally had witnessed arguing with Mrs. Hancock in London. When she had seen her aboard, Isabelle had nearly dropped her jaw in shock. The woman had drawn attention to herself by screaming at the porters for misplacing one of her trunks on a ship bound for Calcutta.

"My husband's military functions require me to entertain and regale our guests with stories of all aspects of Indian culture, you see. My husband is Colonel Bilbey, Lord Banbury naturally, as I am Hortence Bilbey, Lady Banbury."

"Naturally." The story would eventually be forthcoming, and Isabelle was good at being patient. To press the woman was pointless.

"I've been home visiting our sons who are studying at Eton. And my husband's ailing mother required my attention for a time. One does what one must, of course."

"Of course."

"My daughter lives in India with Lord Banbury and me, until next year when I'll take her home for her first London season! She'll be all the rage." Lady Banbury paused in her ramblings, and her eyes narrowed fractionally. "Tell me your name again."

"Isabelle Webb. Of Chicago."

"Chicago. What is it like there? I've never been."

"Windy."

"Windy?"

"The wind blows mightily off the river."

"Mmmm. And your family still resides in Chicago? I know of some Webbs in England—"

"My parents were second generation Americans, so it's been some time since we've had contact with relatives in the motherland," Isabelle replied. "Although I'm certain we tie into the family tree on a branch somewhere."

"Yes. Of course. I imagine the colonies are in a bit of a mess, as you've had all that nasty war business of late."

"Indeed, we have. Much like the Sepoy Rebellion, I would think. And you were living in the country at the time!"

"You wouldn't have believed it," Lady Banbury said, raising a hand to her mouth as though taking Isabelle into her confidence. "Imagine the soldiers rebelling and seeking independence after *we* spent all those years training and educating them! They slaughtered innocent men, women, and children!"

Isabelle nodded. "And were you ever in fear for your life? Your husband being an officer must have put you in a position of some danger."

It was the right thing to say. The woman's chest puffed out a bit and a superior expression crossed her features. "Of course one would suppose so, but our military was exceptional and crushed the rebellion on all fronts. It was then that the Crown took possession of the country from the East India Trading Company, you know. It really was for the best."

"I should certainly think you would know, having lived under both. And I imagine your wealth of information about the country is staggering."

"I don't like to boast, of course, but—yes, we were talking about the legend of the jewel! You wonder if there really is such a thing. Now, who told you it doesn't exist?"

"One of the porters. A native of India."

"Of course he would deny it. There is a curse, you see, and the natives are a superstitious people."

"What do you know of the legend?"

"There is a jewel that is said to glow in a beautiful royal purple. Its worth is immeasurable as it is the only stone like it in the world. It was cut from a rock said to have been touched by the hand of Zeus himself."

"I wonder why it would be of interest to the Indians specifically, then, if it stems from Greek mythology," Isabelle mused aloud.

"Precisely because it changed hands throughout the centuries. Every major religious leader has been in possession of it at one time or other. From what I've been able to gather, however, not only religious leaders have owned it. Ordinary folk have had their hands on it, too. Of course, one might assume they weren't ordinary for long, mightn't one? I can certainly imagine someone searching for it—its value today would be priceless."

Isabelle raised a brow. "Is the implication, then, that people in history who have risen to greatness might have been in possession of this stone?"

Lady Banbury shrugged. "One might believe that, yes."

"That's an incredible legend to have been kept secret for so long. Why is this not common knowledge?"

"I told you," Lady Banbury interrupted, irritated, "because of the curse." She took a deep breath. "Now, let's suppose I am in possession of the stone. I am allowed to own it and benefit from it only if I am one chosen by the stone to do so. I am sworn to protect it and never tell anyone else about it unless I feel so prompted by the stone. If I tell you against the wishes of the stone, within twenty-four hours, I will die a hideous death."

"Against the wishes of the stone," Isabelle repeated. *Lovely,* she mused. *The stone has a spirit.*

Lady Banbury's eyes gleamed as she warmed to her tale. "The natives of India have supposed the stone is in their country, and over time they have come to believe that it brings bad luck to but *talk* about the stone, even if one is not in possession of it. The legend itself has become more Indian in nature than Greek by now."

Isabelle smiled. "So now that you've told me about the stone, are you going to fall upon a piece of bad luck?"

"Posh. I've told this story countless times. I've yet to come to any harm. As I said, it's the natives who are superstitious. We've done well to teach them about how lacking in substance and refinement their own culture is."

Isabelle felt her lips tighten a bit and she made an effort to bite her tongue. She asked, "And what does the stone do for the one who is in possession of it?"

"Ah, therein lies the mystery."

Isabelle looked at her for a moment before posing another question. "Nobody knows what it does?"

Lady Banbury shrugged. "I'm sure somebody does, but I've been unable to ascertain it yet. Must grant some sort of power . . ." She lifted a finger and waggled it. "But I will, you know, discover the secret. I am like a dog with a bone."

"I believe you would be."

* * *

James listened to Isabelle as they sat together over dinner. Sally Rhodes seemed to be mending well—she managed to swallow a few bites of food. As annoyed as he'd been with the young lady upon their initial acquaintance, he found to his chagrin that her pallor and sickness on the voyage worried him against his will. It was becoming a comfortable routine, spending time with the women, and he felt a pang of regret as he realized their journey was nearing an end. Another thirty-six hours would see them in Bombay.

"I rather had the impression that she believes the legend herself," Isabelle was saying in reference to the indomitable Lady Banbury. "She certainly relayed it as though it were fact."

James mused over something Isabelle had mentioned before when she explained her position as a Pinkerton operative; she was allowed entrance to certain levels of society that most men were not. Here, indeed, was a prime example. He would never have found this information on his own, but Isabelle had sized the woman up and down and then approached her without a second thought. Isabelle had affected the exact manner necessary to extract information from Lady Banbury and had done it as naturally as breathing. He was impressed in spite of himself.

He now glanced at the woman in question who sat at the captain's table some distance away. "Shouldn't surprise me much to find that she believes many odd things," James murmured. "She seems very . . . impressionable."

Isabelle laughed softly. "You're certainly a master of diplomacy, Mr. Ashby. I would have said the woman is ignorance personified."

He inclined his head with a grimace. "That, too."

Sally was looking at the woman with a scowl on her face. "She's rather loud, is she not?"

Isabelle nodded. "Loud and ignorant. My least favorite combination." She took a sip of her drink and patted her mouth with the napkin she held in her lap.

James said a mental prayer of thanks for a mother who had taught him good manners. He could only imagine the level of discomfort he would feel had he not known how to comport himself in polite circles. As it was, he was beginning to feel a bit stifled and longed for the freedom of his cabin or the top deck. The only thing making his surroundings bearable was the company of his current companions.

"You know, Mr. Ashby," Sally said. "I really think Isabelle and I should join you in your search for your brother."

Isabelle glanced at the young woman, looking rather stunned. Seeking to relieve her distress and cover his own shock, James said, "No, truly. I wouldn't ask it of you." How on earth could he travel with two women? That kind of worry was the last thing he needed.

Isabelle cleared her throat and again touched her napkin to her mouth, swallowing her food. When she opened her mouth to speak, Sally interjected. "But you will need help, and Isabelle is the best there is! Besides, we don't have a firm itinerary. We're entirely at your disposal."

"Sally," Isabelle said firmly. She turned to James with a weak smile. "Truthfully, James, I was going to offer the same thing myself, but I wanted to speak to you about it at some length first, to see if you'd be interested in having some help."

"Oh, wonderful," Sally said with a clap of her hands. "There, you see? We're of a mind, Isabelle."

"However," Isabelle said with a quick glare at her young charge, "the decision must be Mr. Ashby's. This is his journey, not ours. And we wouldn't want him to feel as though we're more of a hindrance than a help."

It *was* what he'd been thinking, of course. He sat back in his chair and regarded the women, wondering how to extricate himself. In the end, Isabelle saved him.

"We'll not discuss it further," she said, a hand held up to ward off Sally's protests. "James, you know our offer stands. Should you decide we might be of assistance to you, if for no other reason than the company, please tell us by the time we reach Bombay."

They finished their dinner in relative and somewhat awkward silence. James rose from his chair as Isabelle and Sally left theirs and turned from the table to leave the dining room. He said his good-nights and resumed his seat, thinking.

A few moments later, Sally rushed back into the room by herself. "I must say one thing, Mr. Ashby," she said, breathless. She crouched down next to his chair, her pale yellow skirts billowing about her. "Forgive me, but you're a blacksmith. What do you know about tracking people—about private investigation?"

His lips twitched at her impulsiveness, while simultaneously he felt slightly offended. "I'm not entirely witless, Miss Rhodes. I've managed to track my brother thus far."

"I don't think you understand who Isabelle Webb *is*," the young woman insisted. "She broke her leg while attempting to save the president of the United States. She discovered the assassins' plans—very nearly saved the day! She—" James caught a flash of movement from the corner of his eye, and Sally turned toward the doorway.

"Sally." Isabelle grasped her firmly by the arm and hauled her upright. "My apologies, James," she said. "Good night."

* * *

A few hours passed, and James found himself restless and unable to stay in the confines of his cabin. Acknowledging that he should have followed his initial instinct to go up on deck, he shrugged into his coat and left the stateroom, walking the corridors until he found the stairway that led to the open air. A few deep breaths and he already felt himself relaxing a bit.

The sky was dark, but the moon and stars were out in spades, lighting the deck and the water below with an ethereal glow. He wished for just a moment that the drone of the ship's engines would be silenced so that he might enjoy the peace and quiet of the night.

He had been thinking, since dinner, about Sally's curious comments and her insistent offer that they join him. He knew the young girl most definitely wanted to meet Phillip. In her mind she seemed to have created a hero on whom she would most likely have romantic designs. He had to shake his head. She was impulsive and headstrong but somehow refreshing.

As for Isabelle, he hardly knew what to think. She had said she was going to offer their company for the duration of his "quest," but she'd seemed horribly embarrassed at Sally's outbursts. Perhaps she had said what she had only to cover for Sally's lack of polish.

They really wouldn't be a burden; he knew that instinctively, despite Isabelle's near abduction that night in London at the wharf. There was something about her that spoke of her self-sufficiency, and, as it was, they were traveling alone and managing just fine. If ever there was a woman equipped to handle the world on her own, he suspected it was Isabelle Webb. Sally's comments about Isabelle's activities in trying to save the president had piqued his interest, but he knew better than to ask Isabelle about it. Firstly, he wasn't certain they knew each other well enough to even be called friends, and secondly, it was something she'd already once shushed Sally over. The woman didn't want to talk about it, and he could respect that.

Something in the distance on the other side of the ship caught his eye, and to his surprise he recognized the familiar movement of skirts in the wind. It rarely failed; the many times he'd sought refuge in the fresh air, Isabelle had been there as well.

He wondered if he ought to join her or leave her to her privacy. His feet made his mind up for him, and he found himself walking to her side. "My apologies for disrupting your solitude, Miss Webb," he said as he joined her.

"'Miss Webb,' is it now, Mr. Ashby?" she asked with a smile as she turned to look at him with frank regard.

"Are we friends, Isabelle?" he asked her. "I don't know that we've been acquainted long enough to be considered such. And there was that time that I was rather . . . boorish."

"I believe we are friends despite your boorish behavior, for which I've already forgiven you," she said. Her smile turned a bit pained, and she closed her eyes for a moment. "I do, however, need to apologize for my impetuous young ward. She is . . . she is . . . ."

"She is very proud of you and your accomplishments."

"She exaggerates. She sees more than is there."

"The younger set often does," he replied.

"At any rate, I'm glad you're out tonight, because I was hoping for a chance to apologize but also to tell you that I was indeed going to offer some help in your search for your brother. Sally is correct—our itinerary is loose, at best. I confess I've become a bit curious about this mysterious jewel and your brother as well. So I repeat my earlier offer. We're at your disposal, should you decide. I worry, though, about the intrusion on your privacy. I would hate for you to feel as though we're stepping into family business that you would prefer remain just that."

"Isabelle, I hardly know what to think—I would very much enjoy your company but cannot help but feel that I should decline your offer simply for safety's sake. This man my brother is traveling with . . . I didn't like him when I first met him, and now I like him even less. I would hate for this journey to become dangerous only to have embroiled the two of you in it."

Isabelle nodded. "I do respect that, and I thank you. If your true reason for declining the offer is for our safety's sake, however, please set that aside as a worry. I've been in dangerous situations before and have extricated myself well enough, as you can see. Perhaps you are skeptical, but it's the truth." She held her hands aside with a smile. "If your reasons are other than this, however, and you'd rather not share them, I understand fully and will not invade your privacy further."

"Are you suggesting I've been looking for a reason to decline your offer and have settled upon possible danger as that reason?" he asked her with a smile.

"You wouldn't be the first person to cast about for false reasons to avoid something," she answered. "Wouldn't it be far easier to say you're worried about our safety than to say, oh, something along the lines of 'your company makes me insane, and I'd rather you didn't come along'?"

James laughed, and he realized it wasn't something he often did. "True enough," he said as he looked down at her smiling face, upturned and gently buffeted by the wind. "I imagine such a thing would be most awkward to have to say to someone." He sobered a bit. "I would very much enjoy your company. But I would worry for your safety."

She put a finger to her lower lip and tapped it in contemplation. "Well, mightn't one assume Sally and I would be even *safer* in the company of a strong blacksmith? A fellow American, raised on the wild frontier, no less?"

He snorted a bit at her theatrics. "Miss Webb, what of your claims that you don't need anyone for protection? Do you own a firearm?"

"I might."

"And you would undoubtedly be a crack shot with it, I would wager."

She smiled. "That would stand to reason."

"And you are trim and fit—I might presume from what you tell me that you would quickly outrun any assailant . . ."

Her smile faltered slightly. "There was a time when I would certainly have been able to outrun all but the fastest, even in cumbersome skirts and petticoats. Surely you've noticed I walk with a bit of a limp these days."

"I notice it mostly during the times when you employ the use of your cane," he said, motioning to the polished instrument she held in her left hand.

"Yes. It's become a rather hated necessity."

"I assume its use is because of an accident." James knew he was entering forbidden territory but found his curiosity getting the better of him.

Isabelle turned her face toward the water but not before he caught a tightening of her expression. She nodded once, curtly.

"We needn't speak of it further," he said.

She laughed, but he thought it sounded a bit forced. "It doesn't bother me to speak of it," she said, obviously lying. "I was on assignment and fell trying to climb out of a window." Shrugging, she added, "And that was that. I suppose I'm a wee bit upset that I can't use my leg to its fullest, as I'd become accustomed. I should be grateful though," she ended on a sigh. "The doctors told me I shouldn't expect to walk again. As it was, their first inclination was to amputate."

"I've seen a broken leg or two amputated in my time spent on the wild frontier," he said with a nod.

She glanced at him askance. "It's not really all that wild, is it?"

"Most of it not so much anymore," he said, shaking his head with a twitch of a smile.

"Well, wild frontier experience or no, I still say a blacksmith would be handy protection to have around. And you yourself have insisted that I require such."

He had to smile at her blatant manipulation. "Consider yourself protected then, Miss Webb. I should be honored to have your company on my 'quest,' as Miss Rhodes so charmingly calls it." And oddly enough, he found he was being honest. Where he usually felt put-upon and burdened by assuming responsibility for others, for the first time he felt only a glow of anticipation.

* * *

At the stern, a uniformed porter stood watch as a Greek native and two soldiers of the Crown carried a large trunk to the railing. The Greek was a handsome man, comfortable with and well aware of his own good looks. He was a man of some means who had fallen short on his gambling debts.

He was quite willing, therefore, to perform certain services for hire in order to replenish his waning coffers. When the occasion arose that his security might come into question, he meted out judgment upon his foes quickly and with little afterthought. It was for this purpose that he, with the aid of his three bribed associates, unceremoniously tossed the large trunk, containing one very dead Lady Banbury, overboard.

4

"It is the curse! I am telling you, I overheard the woman telling the American about the jewel. Now she is missing!"

Isabelle strained to hear around the corner of the corridor outside her stateroom. Lady Banbury had gone missing, and the whole ship was buzzing with the news. According to her maid, Lady Banbury had been absent since the night before.

Isabelle recognized the voice of the porter with whom she had spoken about, according to him, the nonexistent legend of the jewel. The voice answering him in return was British, cockney in its accent. "Ye're a bloody fool to be believin' such nonsense," it said. "Likely th' old bat imbibed too much 'n' got lost on 'er way back to 'er room. We'll find 'er in a corner sommer in an hour or so."

"We have combed every inch of this ship since midnight! She is not here."

The voices grew faint as they moved away, and Isabelle remained where she was for a moment, waiting in the shadows of the corridor and chewing on her lip. So the good porter was blaming the legend's curse. She couldn't suppress a shiver of apprehension. Isabelle was not a woman given to superstition or foolishness, but it bothered her in the extreme that they were out at sea and a person with whom she had recently communicated was now no longer to be found on board.

On impulse, she turned and walked a maze of hallways until she spotted a door with two porters stationed outside. "Excuse me," she said to them. "Might this be the Lady Banbury's suite of rooms?"

"Yes, ma'am. We're under orders to keep passengers out, however."

"Certainly. I wonder if you've seen her maid, by chance?"

"She's here in the maid's quarters, but I don't know that she'll see anyone."

Isabelle stepped forward and knocked on the door. After a short pause, it was opened by a small woman who looked frightened enough to jump out of her skin.

Isabelle introduced herself and asked if she might have a moment of her time. The other woman glanced over her shoulder. "I'm not Lady Banbury's main maid—Lucinda is."

"Might I speak with you both? It concerns your employer."

The woman reluctantly nodded and allowed Isabelle entrance. An older woman sat inside the small maid's quarters that housed two beds with a side table between them. Isabelle introduced herself to the woman, telling her she had some experience investigating and wondered if she might speak with them for a bit.

"I've seen you," the woman asked, wiping at her eyes. "You talked with Lady Banbury yesterday . . ."

"I did," Isabelle nodded. "May I?" She indicated toward the bed opposite the woman.

"What do you want?" Lucinda asked.

Isabelle took the comment for acquiescence and sat on the bed. "My sincerest condolences," she began. "I, too, am extremely uncomfortable with this turn of events. The Lady Banbury and I are not more than acquaintances; however, she was most helpful yesterday when I asked her some questions about India."

At this, the maid nodded. "Yes, she loved to talk about it."

"I'm sorry for your loss," Isabelle said.

The woman's eyes darted quickly up and then found Isabelle's face. "She just disappeared! She's gone without a trace, and I should know because I have been looking for her since last night! She was so upset and—" At this the woman pursed her lips together and placed her handkerchief to her streaming eyes.

If Isabelle had to hazard a guess, she would wager that the woman was more frightened than sad. "Did she say why she was upset?" Isabelle murmured.

Lucinda shook her head. "She was going to demand an audience with the captain."

"And did she find him?"

"He says she didn't. She was vexed, very agitated when she left to find him."

"Had she spoken with anyone before she went in search of the captain?"

The maid leaned forward and wiped at her nose. "I thought I heard her talking to a man before dinner last night in the passageway," she said to Isabelle. "I was gathering some clothing to be laundered, and when I left the cabin she was standing outside the door alone. I asked her who had been out there with her and she said nobody had."

"Did you hear what they said to each other?" Isabelle asked.

Lucinda's lips pressed together in a tight line. "I shouldn't be telling her business," she said. "I told the captain, but only because he is the captain."

Isabelle shrugged. "You certainly do not have to tell me. But I might be of some use."

After another brief hesitation, Lucinda said, "Lady Banbury told the man that he would get his money, that someone was going to pay her for information and that this person had loads of money from his financial guarantors. She was also very angry, though. She told the man that he hadn't done what she had instructed him to do."

"Did you notice anything unusual about the man, anything at all that might help you identify him?"

Lucinda shook her head. "I could barely hear him. I didn't hear what he said, but I know it was a man because of the deeper rumble of his voice."

"Is anything missing from her cabin?"

The maid's eyes widened, and she nodded fractionally then shook her head. "Not missing, precisely, but her trunks were rummaged through. It must have happened after she dismissed me for the night. I was in my cabin with Annie, playing bridge."

Annie, the smaller woman who sat as silent as a mouse, nodded her head. She was younger than Lucinda and pale. Her eyes were huge in her face, and she looked ready to bolt at a sudden sound. "Lady Banbury was upset quite a bit about her missing trunk," the young woman ventured.

"When did it go missing?" Isabelle asked.

"Oh, it never made it aboard. It was put on a ship bound for Calcutta."

"Ah, yes. I heard," Isabelle said. "Do you know what might have been in it?"

"I should say so," said the personal maid. "I helped her pack it. New clothing for Alice, some of the Lady's papers, and a few wrapped gifts for Alice and the colonel. He is being transferred to Calcutta so it's just as well that the trunk is going there. They will be moving in just two weeks' time, and many of their other belongings are already en route from Bombay to Calcutta. I don't know why she was so angry about it—I've never seen her so furious."

"And Alice is?"

"Lady Banbury's daughter."

Isabelle bid the ladies good-bye after again expressing her condolences. She slowly made her way to the ship's small library and reading den, where she'd agreed to meet James when they had parted the night before. He was to show her the documentation he'd gathered thus far on Phillip and his companion.

James stood as she entered the room and gestured toward a chair next to his at a small, round table. "Where is Miss Rhodes this morning? Given her enthusiasm for my errant brother, I'd rather assumed she'd be joining you."

"You really must start calling her Sally, or her feelings will be bruised. And I left her back in our room packing the remainder of her belongings. She is messy and disorganized in the extreme." Isabelle smiled and took her seat. "We disembark this evening. Are you glad?"

James nodded. "I look forward to continuing my search. All of this time at sea has me chomping at the bit."

"You worry about your brother," Isabelle said as she took James's map of India in her hands. "'Tis understandable."

James opened his mouth as if to argue and closed it again with a slight nod. "I do worry," he admitted and cleared his throat. "Once we reach Bombay," he said, pointing to the spot on India's west coast with his finger, "I plan to ask around at all of the obvious boarding houses as to whether or not they might have seen Phillip and Sparks."

"Do you happen to know if Sparks had any contacts in India? Anyone he might have known?"

James shook his head. "I don't believe he did, but I'm not certain."

"When you saw Mr. Sparks, was he . . . hmm." Isabelle paused. "Would you say he would blend well with British society, indeed with *any* polite society, or will he . . . offend?"

"Do you mean will he be able to pass himself off as a person of some quality?"

Isabelle nodded.

"I would say no. He seemed to think he was someone of some import, but the few times I met him I came away with the impression that not only was he incredibly thick-skulled, but also perhaps a bit . . . unhinged."

"Dangerous?"

"If not dangerous, then reckless. Impetuous. Full of a false sense of self-confidence that will only lead to trouble."

"And yet he was able to convince your brother that his cause was credible."

James shook his head, his expression suddenly weary. "Phillip is, as I've mentioned, gullible. Entirely too trusting and extremely naive."

Isabelle glanced at the notes James handed her and perused his scrawling handwriting. "Seems as though they stayed in consistent establishments along the way," she noted.

He nodded. "The most inexpensive available. With the exception of the Pembroke Inn, in London. On that, Sparks seems to have spared moderate expense. The innkeeper's wife told me that she saw Sparks and Phillip speaking with a person from London at some length during the first night of their stay. Meeting and talking with this man may have determined why Sparks chose to stay at an establishment that cost significantly more than his previous choices."

"Were you able to discover Sparks's friend's name? Anything about him at all?"

"No, unfortunately. She wouldn't tell me, said it was one thing for her to give me information about my brother but another altogether about a stranger."

"Did you bribe her?"

"Excessively."

Alarms suddenly sounded in Isabelle's head, and she caught her breath. "Suppose the person he spoke with wasn't a man?"

"I beg your pardon?"

Isabelle quickly told James about the exchange of words between Lady Banbury and Mrs. Hancock that she and Sally had witnessed in London. "She specifically wanted to know whether or not someone had already left for India, said she had spoken with him at the inn before. I wonder if it might have been this Sparks person. At any rate, Mrs. Hancock flatly refused to tell her anything."

James's brows drew together in thought. "Certainly possible, I suppose. But why would Lady Banbury meet someone at an inn? That seems rather beneath her station."

Isabelle took a few moments to tell James about the conversation she had had with Lady Banbury's maids. She then turned her thoughts again to James's brother. "What did Phillip take with him?" she asked.

"Minimal clothing, a few personal articles for grooming."

"Money?"

James shook his head. "I don't know how much he would have had at his disposal. Very little, if any. My mother said she didn't give him any. After all, he didn't tell her he was going."

Isabelle laid the papers on the table and sat back in her chair. "I overheard the Indian porter I spoke with telling another man that Lady Banbury has fallen abreast of the curse."

James's brow rose, and she smiled. "I know," she said, "but whatever the truth may be, the porter believes it. I find myself wondering who else believes it."

James leaned forward slightly and murmured, "You wouldn't have to believe in a curse to do away with someone else."

"But why?" She leaned in likewise, close to him. "Why would someone kill Lady Banbury?"

"Do we really know she's dead?"

Isabelle shrugged, her eyes wide. "She's not here, on the ship, that is. And if she is, she's not making any noise."

"Perhaps she's been abducted and is being held in one of the staterooms."

Isabelle shook her head. "They've searched all the cabins. Weren't you interrupted this morning?"

"I left my room quite early. If they searched my cabin, they did it while I was gone."

"Isn't it interesting, though?" Isabelle asked, still leaning in close to James. "I've found that there are very few coincidences in life. You're looking for your brother, who is in pursuit of a legendary jewel. I ask a woman in the know about said jewel, and she then disappears. This is the same woman who also happened to make an appearance at the very inn where Mr. Sparks was staying and was in communication with someone whose identity you were unable to ascertain."

James nodded slightly, concentration plain on his features. "I hate to jump to conclusions, however. She was not necessarily a pleasant woman and may have had more than her share of antagonized enemies. Were I a native of India, I would dislike her for her contempt of my country alone."

"Enough to kill her?"

"Miss Webb, are you suggesting that the curse killed Lady Banbury?"

"Not the curse itself, but perhaps someone who wants others to believe it."

James sat back in his chair, contemplative. "Well, she certainly seemed to owe someone money. That may have been curse enough for her."

"I don't know, exactly," Isabelle said, drumming her fingers absently on the tabletop. "I don't know, I don't know . . . Why kill her when she said she would soon have the money from another source?" She looked down at the map of India and wished it would give her some answers. She glanced up at James again. "But it's certainly obvious she has met with foul play."

James studied her for a moment. "If this is true," he whispered, "then I really cannot allow you and Sally to accompany me in my search for Phillip."

"It's too late," she murmured. "We're already committed. At this point, I'll simply trail you as you trail Phillip."

"You seem determined to make my life difficult, Miss Webb," James said without smiling.

"It has nothing to do with making your life difficult and everything to do with my curiosity, Mr. Ashby."

"I suspect our friend Miss Rhodes would suggest you seek to ease my burdens."

"Our friend Miss Rhodes thinks me nothing short of the Virgin Mary."

At that, he finally smiled. "It must be nice to inspire such devotion in someone."

She snorted and sat back again in her chair. "Speak for yourself."

* * *

James, Sally, and Isabelle stood at the railing and watched the city of Bombay approach on the horizon. As the land grew bigger and sounds of the city met the ship, Isabelle felt her heart thud in an anticipation that surprised her. The city positively bustled with humanity. People were finishing their work for the day, pulling in laundry baskets heaped with linens, and bartering for last-minute sales of wares, including food, clothing, and exotic jewelry. The whole scene showed people who were well dressed and those who wore rags and sat in doorways, begging.

It was some time later before the trio found their lodgings, James having decided to stay at the same establishment as Isabelle and Sally. The activity in the bustling streets slowed with the onset of evening, and by the time the bullock cart reached the collection of small cottages, it was one of the few still out and about.

The quaint buildings that comprised the English Tea Garden Cottages for Families, Respectable Ladies, and Gentlemen were situated around beautifully landscaped lawns and gardens. The properties were nestled in a quiet area of Bombay, sheltered from businesses and slums alike by a natural fencing of trees that hung with lush vegetation.

A young Indian porter dressed in crisp, white linen pants and a long shirt deposited the women's trunks and baggage in their cottage, while another young man similarly dressed did the same with James's belongings in the adjacent cottage.

Isabelle tipped the young man, at which point he bowed and thanked her, his white teeth flashing in a smile.

"I'm Isabelle Webb," she said, extending her hand to the young man.

"And I am Hatmas," he answered, taking her hand in some surprise as she gripped it in a gentleman's handshake. "Please, you will tell me if you are in need of my service," he said.

"I will."

He bowed and left them to stare at the small building in wonder. "This is simply stunning," Sally exclaimed in awe.

Isabelle had to agree with her. The cottage consisted of a sitting room, a small kitchen, and a bedroom that housed two narrow beds. It was open and airy, the windows adorned with diaphanous white curtains, the furnishings in deep wood tones. The decor about the room was an interesting blend of Indian and British.

Sally turned to Isabelle, a troubled expression on her face. "Those people, lining the streets . . ."

Isabelle nodded but stayed silent, allowing Sally to formulate her own thoughts.

"They live there, don't they? In doorways and behind piles of garbage."

"Yes, they do. I probably didn't prepare you enough for the sight."

"When you told me we would see many poor people, I had no idea . . ." Sally put a hand to her midsection and drew in a breath. "I have felt the pain of hunger, but I always had a roof over my head."

Isabelle nodded. "People at home who are knowledgeable about this country told me that we would see the richest of the rich and the poorest of the poor."

"It rather makes me feel guilty that we have such a nice place to sleep tonight."

Isabelle nodded and walked toward the mantelpiece. A carved wooden statue sat in proud splendor, exquisite in its detail.

"What is that?" Sally asked her.

"The God Vishnu. See the many arms?"

Sally walked around the room, trailing a finger along the smooth wooden surfaces of the furniture. She turned to Isabelle suddenly, her eyes shining. "Belle, we're in India!"

Isabelle smiled, her eyes misting as Sally rushed toward her and threw her arms about Isabelle's own small frame. "We're really here," Sally whispered to her. "I can hardly believe it. Thank you so very, very much. This means the world to me."

Sally pulled back, and Isabelle's emotion intensified as she looked with affection on the young girl who had lost so much in the war. "It's my pleasure, sweet girl," Isabelle murmured, uncomfortable with the lump in her throat. She briefly laid a hand alongside Sally's cheek and cleared her throat. "I believe I shall see how our neighbor fares."

Sally smiled. "He's most handsome, Belle. I do wish you would give him more than your cursory glance."

Isabelle rolled her eyes and headed for the door. If Sally only knew how often Belle had given the man more than her "cursory glance," she would have clapped her hands in unabashed glee.

* * *

James stepped from the doorway of his small, temporary home and inhaled the fresh, fragrant aroma of the beautiful flowers edging the paths that connected the cottages. He moved farther into the yard, taking in the trees and vegetation that surrounded the beautiful little oasis in abundance.

"Quite incredible, wouldn't you agree?" a voice asked him as he surveyed his surroundings.

"Absolutely," he said, turning his attention to Isabelle, who joined him in his appreciative perusal.

"There are so many colors—my eye hardly knows where to fall." She took a deep breath and released it on a sigh.

"The smells here are different enough from the docks, to be sure," he noted, placing his hands comfortably in his trouser pockets and matching her slow stroll as she began moving down the path.

"Sally mentioned feeling a bit guilty that we are here in such a beautiful place while others are outside suffering." Isabelle paused. "I have to agree with her. I'm not quite certain how to reconcile my appreciation for this," she said, indicating to their environs, "with my pity for them."

"I confess, I've never seen such poverty," James admitted. His life, while filled with its own share of pain, had known nothing on the scale of the beggar children and old women living in the streets of Bombay. He'd felt a flickering of overwhelming pity that coincided with his philosophy, long since set, that life was hard and that it was meant to be.

Isabelle motioned to a bench alongside the path overlooking a small pond. He joined her on it, watching as the water moved with small fish that darted to the surface for their evening meal of insects.

Isabelle placed her hands in her lap, twisting her fingers a bit. "I was very hungry not long ago," she murmured, watching the fish. James remained quiet while she appeared to search for words.

"It was in Vicksburg, Mississippi."

"During the siege?" He couldn't help his exclamation of surprise. She had lived through Grant's siege of Vicksburg? How on earth had she found herself on the wrong side of the lines? "How? Why?"

"I followed a woman who had . . . tricked me into believing she was no longer a Confederate spy. When I learned that she had fooled me, I was angry, and Pinkerton gave me permission to track her and try to learn what secrets she might be passing along."

"So this woman went to Vicksburg?"

Isabelle nodded. "To be with her sister. I arrived in the city, and by the time I found her, the whole place was under siege, and I was eating rats with the rest of the citizens. We lived in holes dug into the hillsides. Everything else was bombed out."

"Were you incognito at the time?" James asked.

"No, I had abandoned all pretenses by then."

"Then why not approach the lines and identify yourself? Surely the guards would have allowed you to leave."

Isabelle shrugged, a half smile playing on her mouth. "By then I'd befriended the woman. Didn't seem right to leave her behind."

"Funny she and the others didn't kill you."

"Oh, I think they probably wanted to. But they must have figured I was suffering more alive than dead."

He felt a surge of something he couldn't quite define, but it was akin to anger. Perhaps it was her calm assessment of the situation that set his teeth on edge. "Miss Webb, why would you stay behind and risk starvation for someone who had played you for a fool?"

She glanced at him, one brow raised. "Miss Webb again? I'm detecting a pattern, Mr. Ashby. When you make assertions about my character, things that you feel only an appropriately close associate would know, you resort to the excruciatingly formal."

"And I'm detecting a pattern, Miss Webb. When I ask you questions you find yourself unwilling to answer, you instead analyze me."

"Very well," she said, inclining her head. "Given my character, I admit that it was unusual for me to subject myself to certain death in Vicksburg rather than flee to the safety of the Union lines."

He said nothing, merely prompting her confession with his own quirk of a brow.

She held his gaze for a moment and then turned her face back to the fish darting about in the pond. "I felt guilty."

"Guilty? Guilty for what?"

"My entire career. Indeed, most of my life had been spent on lies and subterfuge. The only reason I even knew this particular woman was because I'd lied to obtain access to her social circle. And then I grew to trust her, to be her friend, only to realize she'd been lying to *me*. Once I tracked her down, I had to admit to myself that I was no better."

James shook his head. "So you thought to offer your health, maybe even your life, for what—absolution? You didn't need to do that. Someone else already has."

Isabelle laughed. "Do you find me to be the religious sort, James? I've not had much use for it."

"A shame. You might have found a measure of peace."

"Do you feel peace? You seem angry to me." She waved an impatient hand at him as he stared at her. "Don't bother to answer that. As for me, it's not in my destiny to be truly at peace. My life is proof enough of that. I grow weary of this conversation."

"Of course you do," James murmured, his eyes locking with the golden intensity of hers.

She looked at him for some time before drawing a breath. "Mr. Ashby, I do believe I'll go and see to my charge. She does become a bit fretful if I'm away from her for too long."

James suspected the matter was also true in the reverse but said nothing. "I'm feeling rather weary myself. I believe I'll turn in for the night. Would you like to meet with me in the morning for breakfast, and we can discuss the day? Provided I'm not too angry, of course." He worked hard to keep the edge from his voice.

"Have you taken offense, then?"

"How can I be offended by a misconception?"

Isabelle laughed. "It's no misconception, and I suspect you well know it. However, if you insist, we shall pretend otherwise."

"Very well," he said, the thread of extreme irritation that had begun to spin itself somewhere in the back recesses of his brain making its way to the fore. "Why would you assume I am an angry person?"

"Your expression is very often fierce."

"I'm concerned for my brother's welfare."

"You're angry about your brother's welfare."

James's nostrils flared of their own volition. "I beg your pardon, but I most certainly am concerned for my brother!"

"Understandably. It would be even more convincing if you could speak of him without a hint of annoyance in your voice."

"I am not annoyed with him." James clamped his mouth shut at Isabelle's skeptical expression. "Very well, I suppose I am often annoyed with him. But certainly not angry."

"I see."

"No, you don't! You're being deliberately provoking." He took a deep breath.

"Why are you so well spoken, Mr. Ashby?"

She caught him completely off guard, and he answered her honestly. "My mother made me read."

"What did you read?"

"Everything. She insisted while Phillip was going to school that I should learn everything he brought home as well."

"And you enjoy learning?"

He nodded. "Very much so."

Isabelle tipped her head to one side. "So why a blacksmith?"

Old hurts, anger, and resentment rose to the surface at an alarming rate. He'd sworn to himself to never again revisit that particular flood of emotion. "You assume blacksmiths do not enjoy learning?" His voice sounded cold, even to his own ears.

"I think you know what I mean. Why not become a scholar, a newspaper man, something of the like?"

James looked away from her. The last person who had posed those questions to him had left him at the altar. In the end, his profession hadn't been good enough for her, and she'd found someone better. "Our neighbor and friend was a good blacksmith. When I was fifteen, I apprenticed with him as a way of supporting my mother and brother. When the time came for him to retire, I took the responsibilities of his shop." He looked at her, feeling defensive and mentally daring her to belittle him. If she did and he gave his anger full rein, he was likely to verbally tear her in two. "It seemed the natural course of things."

"'Tis a noble profession," Isabelle said, her tone gentle as though she knew she'd pried too openly. "A credit to your character that you cared so well for your family."

"Yet you question me about it as though it were lacking." He was chagrined to find himself feeling slightly winded.

"No, not lacking. Merely a . . . unique choice for someone who might have enjoyed scholarly pursuits."

"My mother is often ill—someone had to care for her and Phillip. And besides, there wasn't time or money enough," he admitted quietly, leaning forward to rest his arms on his knees. He examined his hands, work-worn and calloused. Once said, he wished he could swallow the words back into his throat. Why was he exposing himself so thoroughly? He had made a point throughout his life of hiding his shame from the bullies in the schoolyard to the politicians on Main Street. Now words that would betray his innermost thoughts seemed to fall from his lips of their own free will. He winced.

Isabelle sighed. "There rarely is. Time or money." She shook her head. "Never enough. Shall we turn in for the evening?"

He nodded, relieved and somehow grateful that she understood, that she didn't try to lay blame somewhere—either on him or his mother. He rose with her, and they began the short walk back to their cottages. "Breakfast sounds fine," she said. "Sally and I are looking forward to exploring the city a bit."

He inclined his head slightly as she bid him good night and entered her cottage, closing the door softly behind her.

5

James's frustration was at its peak. He could hear Phillip calling for him in frantic tones but couldn't find him. Just when he thought he would reach his panic-stricken brother, Sparks appeared before him, laughing. By the time he finally awoke at early dawn, James felt as though he hadn't slept a wink.

As he went about his morning routine, he tried to rid himself of the notion that Phillip was in mortal peril. Sparks was harmless enough, surely, and Phillip could more than defend himself physically. He didn't trust Sparks's motives, but what would be served by harming Phillip? A vague sense of unease prickled at the back of his neck, however, and when the breakfast hour finally approached, he was grateful to escape his own solitary company.

Breakfast was served outdoors under a small white canopy between his cottage and the ladies'. He noted that both women seemed to be in good health and spirits and wondered if his restless night showed itself on his features. His concern was validated when Isabelle, after seating herself in her chair and placing her napkin on her lap, scrutinized him with narrowed eyes.

"You've not slept well," she accused.

"The first night in a strange country," he said.

"Ha! I slept like the dead," Sally exclaimed, cracking her soft-boiled egg with a fair amount of gusto.

"That you did," Isabelle agreed, "except that the dead do not typically snore."

Sally's spoon clattered against her plate. "I beg your humble pardon, Isabelle Webb, but I most certainly do not snore!"

"I'm sorry," Isabelle said with a chuckle. "It must have been James making such a racket, then."

"I confess, I did sleep with my window open, so it may very well have been me," James said.

"Well," Sally said with a sniff, "you, sir, at least have the decency to shoulder the blame. *Some* people I know have the most lamentable habit of discussing *entirely* inappropriate things in polite company!"

"Again, my apologies," Isabelle said, still smiling as she spooned a piece of fresh fruit into her mouth. "Now then, James, where are we going first?"

James was distracted from her question by taking a good look at the spread before them on the table. "Seems rather like being in England again," he said.

Sally nodded. "India is subject to the British Crown, you know. I've been reading on the subject. Belle brought books along."

"I suspect we'll see an interesting blend of ancient India and modern England," Isabelle added.

James turned his attention to her earlier question. "I need to return to the docks and ask if anyone remembers seeing my brother and Sparks and where they might have gone. If that should prove fruitless, I had hoped to visit some of the local temples, if only to see if perhaps they might have tried them in their search for the treasure."

Isabelle nodded. "I had wondered the same thing. As the legend is largely religious in its origins, perhaps they began their quest there." She paused for a moment and noted James's half-hearted attempts to eat his breakfast. "Are you not feeling well this morning, James?"

He sat back in his chair and rubbed his eye with the heel of his hand. "My sleep was a bit . . . restless." He remembered his dreams with vivid clarity and felt his heart skip a beat.

"Are you concerned about something other than your brother?" Isabelle asked, setting her fork down.

"No, no. Only a bit more concerned altogether, I suppose." He felt foolish that a few bad dreams would have him so unsettled. "It's nothing, really. Perhaps I'm beginning to doubt the possibilities of finding him."

"We'll find him," Isabelle said with a nod. "You mustn't fret on that score."

"I don't fret."

Isabelle smiled. "Of course you don't. Men never do." She winked at him, and he somehow felt that he and all men everywhere were the brunt of her own private jest.

"I'm sure some do," he said, fighting defensiveness. "I'm merely stating that I do not."

Her eyes widened in what he recognized as feigned innocence. "I understand," she said.

"I don't fret," he repeated.

"Clearly."

"Oh, for heaven's sake. Daylight is wasting as we sit here," Sally interrupted. "Finish your breakfast, the two of you. I'm going to retrieve my parasol from inside. It promises to be a warm day today."

* * *

James returned to the women with a frustrated backward glance at the dock worker with whom he'd just spoken. "He said he wouldn't remember if he'd seen Phillip unless I paid him something. Then, of course, he admitted he'd never seen him."

Isabelle's lips twitched as she looked at the young man, who really, upon closer inspection, was probably little more than a boy. "Very clever of him," she said. "He received a tip either way."

James shook his head and surveyed the area they'd traversed, looking for someone who might have knowledge of Phillip and Mr. Sparks. The enterprising young man was the last of the line. "I suppose we now move on to the temples," he said, removing his gentleman's top hat and running a hand through his hair. "I'm half tempted to rid myself of this suit coat and roll up my shirt sleeves," he muttered.

"Such a scandal you would cause," Isabelle said and twirled her parasol. Her hair beneath her bonnet was damp, and she winced at their collective discomfort. "Perhaps you may be able to pass yourself off as a native," she said as they made their way into the city from the water's edge. "Then you would at least be able to wear light linen."

"Oh, Belle," Sally said beside her as she caught sight of a group of young women who worked a market stall. They were dressed in light cotton fabric that had been dyed in intensely vibrant colors: beautiful, deep shades of reds, golds, and blues. "Do you suppose *we* might pass ourselves off as natives?"

Isabelle laughed as she considered the lily-white condition of Sally's skin. "Most likely not, but perhaps we can inquire as to whether or not we would offend if we were to dress likewise," she said. "If it would be appropriate, I'll purchase something like that for us."

"That would be most divine," Sally said, her eyes still glued to the women and their clothing.

Isabelle glanced to her other side, where James walked with an expression on his face that suggested he was miles away from their conversation. She felt a stab of pity for him. He was a bright man who otherwise would most likely have enjoyed the opportunity to relish his time spent in a foreign country. Instead, his energies were focused on an errant brother for whom he had cared all his life.

"Most likely, I will not be able to go into the temples," she said to him.

He looked at her with a blank expression. "Why?"

"I'm a woman."

James shook his head slightly and she smiled. "Why Mr. Ashby, are you a supporter of rights for women?"

"I don't understand the segregation. In my church, we have temples and women are full participants. And when we vote in our meetings, women do so as well."

This information gave Isabelle pause. For all the oddity surrounding the Mormons and their practice of polygamy, the fact that women voted and were not barred from temple ceremonies was a cause for admiration.

"I find that impressive," she said. "I'm glad to know you hold women in high regard."

His answering nod was curt, almost as though he was embarrassed by her praise. She did not press the matter further.

They approached the temple and stopped, taking in the detail. The front roofline rose to a peak, and below it red and gold décor adorned the pillars and a small, decorative balcony. The doorway was outlined in a gold, onion-shaped archway, and there were windows on either side of the door that mirrored it. The stone on the building itself was a pale blue.

James looked at the structure with a slight frown. "I'm not even certain what I should ask once inside," he said.

"Perhaps just inquire as to whether or not two men meeting Sparks's and your brother's description might have poked around the place in the last week or so," Isabelle said. "Show them the photograph of Phillip that you showed me. We'll wait out here."

He retrieved the daguerreotype from his inner coat pocket and walked up the steps. Isabelle and Sally stepped back a few paces and looked over some of the wares being sold at the outdoor market.

People thronged the city streets. The city bustled with an industry that would have surprised Isabelle, had she not done some research on the region before leaving home. Bombay's business district had grown exponentially as a direct result of the American Civil War; when the northern states had blockaded the southern ports, restricting the cotton trade, Great Britain had turned to India to provide cotton and textiles.

Isabelle glanced at Sally and decided not to mention that fact to her. The young Southerner wouldn't take the news well. It wasn't long before they saw James at the front door of the temple. "I know that man," Sally whispered to Isabelle and gestured toward a man standing near the temple as James exitited and began his descent down the stairs.

"Which one?"

"The Greek."

Isabelle glanced askance at her. "How do you know he's Greek?"

"He told me. He was one of the passengers on our voyage here from London. I had a conversation with him once in the dining room over breakfast while I was waiting for you."

Upon closer inspection, Isabelle realized that there was indeed something familiar about the man. When he turned his face toward them, she recognized his features. He was a pleasant enough sort. He was handsome and had always exchanged smiles with her on board the ship.

He hadn't appeared to notice them, and Isabelle tipped her parasol slightly to better shield her face as she watched him. And as she watched him, she realized *he* was watching James. She'd done enough surveillance in her life to know it when she saw it.

"Is this the first you've seen him today?" Isabelle asked Sally.

"Yes."

"What was your conversation like? Aboard the ship?"

Still keeping her gaze focused on the Greek, Isabelle caught the motion of Sally's shrug out of the corner of her eye. "Our voyage, the purpose for our visit to India. He asked about James and his brother. Mostly he just paid attention to Lady Banbury."

Isabelle turned her attention with curiosity to Sally. "He did? How did I not see that?"

Sally flushed. "I only noticed because I thought him handsome and couldn't understand why he would be so interested in that loud old woman."

Isabelle glanced back at the man in question with narrowed eyes. Why, indeed? It was a crude thought, but might Lady Banbury have been paying the young man for his attention? "What did you observe them doing or speaking about?" she asked Sally.

"Mostly he said flattering things, and she giggled like an idiot schoolgirl."

Isabelle struggled to hide a smile at the venom in Sally's voice. "How many times did you see them together?"

"Only a few. Two or three, perhaps."

"I wonder if they knew each other before boarding the ship," Isabelle murmured as she watched the man approach James and catch his attention. She began moving forward and motioned Sally along.

Isabelle again tipped her parasol slightly to hide her face and glanced over at Sally. "Say hello," she whispered and gestured toward the man with her head.

As if on perfect cue, Sally smiled and quickened her stride. She extended her hand when she reached the pair and said, "Why Mr. Kilronomos, what a pleasant surprise!"

The handsome young Greek took Sally's fingers and bowed over them, placing a kiss on her gloved knuckles. "Indeed!" the young man exclaimed. "When I noticed Mr. Ashby leaving the temple, I could scarcely contain my surprise!"

"I don't believe we've been formally introduced," Isabelle said, extending her hand as well. "I am Isabelle Webb."

Mr. Kilronomos lavished the same ardent attention on Isabelle's hand. When he raised his head and released her fingers, he looked at James with a broad smile. "How fortunate for you, my good man, that you travel in the company of such exquisiteness. I must know your secret!"

"Desperation," James said flatly and without an answering smile.

"Ah, yes. The search for your brother. Miss Rhodes told me about him."

James and Isabelle looked at Sally, who blushed scarlet. "Oh, dear," Mr. Kilronomos said, noting her reaction. "Was it to be kept secret?"

When James made no move to answer, Isabelle spoke for the group. "Not at all. The more people who know about Phillip's predicament the better. Many hands make light work. Isn't that so, Mr. Ashby?"

"Quite," he answered her finally, a twitch in his jaw belying his irritation.

"In fact, we're going about the city inquiring as to whether or not Phillip and his companion might have been seen in the last few days," Isabelle continued, placing her hand in the crook of James's elbow. He drew his arm up in reflex as if he'd accompanied many a woman on a stroll. The arm beneath her fingertips was as hard as oak. Rather like the expression currently playing across his face.

"It grows near the lunch hour," Isabelle said as she began to walk, James having no choice but to follow. "I was just thinking we should take a moment for something to eat. There's an establishment just down this way with the loveliest scents wafting from its doors. See?"

She motioned with the hand that held her parasol tilted to one side. "And there's a shingle out front—I daresay it's a restaurant."

"Lovely," Sally said. "I'm rather looking forward to a refreshing drink. It's so very warm."

Mr. Kilronomos offered her his arm, and she took it with a smile. "Oh, good," Sally said. "You'll join us for lunch, then?"

"I should be most delighted."

They crossed the street, dodging a bullock cart, a jumping monkey, several pedestrians, and an elephant to reach the restaurant.

* * *

James's head was beginning to pound. Perhaps it was the spiciness of the food or the oppressive heat that was barely lifted by the aid of restaurant employees who stood in the corners of the room fanning the patrons with large fronds. Whatever the cause, he begrudged Isabelle her ability to eat with relish and look as comely as ever. She engaged their Greek companion in charming conversation, and he found himself growing surlier with every passing moment.

Why, exactly, he was so irritated over the fact that Sally had shared his private information with Mr. Kilronomos, he was uncertain. It wasn't as though his purposes for the visit were secret. In fact, Isabelle had the right of it. The more who knew, the better. Something about this particular man, however, set his teeth on edge.

He picked at a piece of the curry-laden fowl on his plate and reviewed the events of the day. They had visited the temple as well as the docks, and nobody had seen Phillip or Sparks. It was an intensely huge city, this much was painfully true. He could spend days, perhaps weeks, before being able to honestly claim that he had combed every inch of it. He fought a momentary stab of dejection.

"And what brings you to India?" Isabelle was asking Mr. Kilronomos.

"Ah, I have visited twice already, and I find myself unable to stay away."

"Mr. Kilronomos makes his home in London for six months of the year, and Greece the other six," Sally said.

"Your memory is impeccable, Miss Rhodes," the man said with a flash of his brilliant smile at the impressionable young girl who basked in the light of it. James did his best not to snort in derision. He was irritated with Sally, but he didn't want to see her fall victim to a philanderer.

Mr. Kilronomos turned to James and said, "Mr. Ashby, I understand your brother is keeping the company of a man who is searching for the legendary Jewel of Zeus."

James gave up on the food and sat back in his chair, wiping his fingers on a white linen napkin. "You know of this thing?"

"I should say so! The legend dates back centuries, you know."

Isabelle smiled and leaned forward a bit in her chair, her body language suggesting eagerness and interest. "What do you know of the legend, Mr. Kilronomos?" she asked. If he hadn't spent so much time in her presence over the past two weeks, he might not have recognized the act for what it was. She was allowing their Greek friend to see her as rather giddy and easily entertained. He was beginning to witness firsthand how she'd been so effective as one of Pinkerton's operatives.

"I can tell you a very interesting story," Mr. Kilronomos said. "Many, many years ago, a student of Greek philosophy left Greece to study in India—he wanted to learn of Buddha. He came here and met with a wise man who taught him many things. He had spent nearly three years here when, one evening, the wise old man told him a secret."

At this point, Mr. Kilronomos paused for effect and looked at Sally, who was hanging on his every word. James resisted the urge to roll his eyes and closed them instead, massaging the bridge of his nose with his thumb and forefinger.

"The secret was this: the wise man had, in his possession, a jewel. The rarest jewel in all the world! It was a jewel so beautiful that it rivaled the sun in its glory. The old man showed the jewel to the philosopher. The jewel was filled with power that transferred itself to the bearer of it."

"What sort of power?" Sally asked, the food in her hand poised midair.

"Knowledge."

"Knowledge?" The disappointment in Sally's voice was palpable, and James fought back a laugh despite his agitation with the situation as a whole.

"Ultimate knowledge. Complete knowledge! Imagine, Miss Rhodes, with such knowledge, one would know how to conquer the world, how to turn mere rocks into gold!" Mr. Kilronomos smiled at the girl, his eyes glowing with the tale.

"Oh, I see," Sally said.

"Indeed! Who would not want to be in possession of such a thing? One would be a god!"

"So what happened to the young philosopher?" Isabelle asked.

"Well," Mr. Kilronomos continued. "Associated with the jewel is a curse. The person in possession of it must not speak of it unless he is supposed to, or he will die before the earth completes its next journey around the sun."

"That might have been a bit troublesome in the days of geocentrism," Isabelle murmured.

Mr. Kilronomos blinked. "I beg your pardon?"

"When people believed the universe, including the sun, revolved around the earth."

James watched Isabelle as she toyed with the man, much like a cat pawing a mouse, and his lips twitched in reluctant admiration. "Oh, but I'm being silly," she said, reverting to her playful, former manner. It was as though she had allowed herself to step out of character for a moment to deliver an intellectual jab at the man. "Please, continue." She gave Mr. Kilronomos a wink and a smile, and the Greek was instantly mollified. James scowled.

"You'll hardly believe what happened then," he continued. "When our young philosopher awoke the next morning, the wise old man was dead, and the jewel was missing!"

"How did the old man die?" Sally asked.

Mr. Kilronomos shrugged. "Nobody knows."

"And the jewel?" Isabelle asked.

"Ah," Mr. Kilronomos said. "There are those who believe it was taken by native Indians and that it still remains in this country. And then, there are those who believe the young philosopher found it and returned with it to his former master."

Again, Mr. Kilronomos paused for effect, and Isabelle played along. "And who was this master?" she asked.

"A man by the name of Socrates."

"Oh, for the love of all things holy," James muttered and pushed his chair back. "You'll excuse me," he said a bit louder and looked at Isabelle, who was biting the insides of her cheeks. "I find myself in need of some fresh air."

* * *

The day had spent itself by the time Isabelle, James, and Sally made it back to their lodgings, accompanied by a most insistent Mr. Kilronomos. "I've noticed the three of you using each other's given names—you must do the same with me. I am Ari."

Isabelle wanted to tell him that such was all well and good but that he did not have leave to use her given name, or Sally's, but she squashed the impulse. She'd played with the man enough already. Glancing at James, she took in the set of his dark and thunderous features. He had become progressively more irritated and angry as the day wore on, no doubt due to his frustration over the lack of success in finding information about Phillip and the company of the overeager Greek who insisted he see them safely to their lodgings.

He wants to see where we're staying, Isabelle mused as she watched Ari ply Sally with compliments and flattering attention. She hadn't forgotten that when they had come upon the young man outside the temple, he had definitely been watching James's movements. She only wished she had noticed him earlier and wondered if he'd been following them all day.

They entered gardens near the cottages, and Isabelle breathed a sigh of relief. She turned to James, prepared to ask if he'd like to join them for dinner and found him already standing very close to her.

"Get rid of him before I kill him," he muttered to her between clenched teeth.

"My pleasure, but then I must speak with you," she murmured with a smile and stepped to the side as James made his way toward his cottage. She wasn't sure why she found his irritable mood over the Greek so amusing.

"Mr. Kilronomos," she began and approached him and Sally where they stood near the gates of the establishment.

"Ari," he corrected her.

"Ari, Sally and I are most weary and must retire for the evening. I cannot thank you enough for accompanying us here. One just never knows if one big, strong man will be enough protection."

Sally shot Isabelle an irritated look that suggested she heard well the tones of sarcasm in Isabelle's statement. *Oh dear*, Isabelle thought. *She's falling for his charm*. Sally opened her mouth to say something and then looked beyond Isabelle's shoulder. Her brow wrinkled in a frown and Isabelle turned, following her gaze.

James stood at the door to his cottage, surrounded by a man in British military uniform, a young woman in beautiful, billowing skirts, and three of the establishment's management who were speaking rapidly and gesturing at the military man and the woman. As for James, he appeared ready to throw the whole lot of them into the pond down the pathway.

Isabelle squinted and moved in their direction, forgetting for the moment the handsome Greek and her besotted young charge. The conversation at James's front door became clearer as she approached.

"Humblest apologies, Mr. Ashby—I tell them they must ask first if you would like to receive guests . . ."

"We have been waiting for well over an hour," the young woman snapped. She appeared to be no older than Sally, Isabelle noted as she drew near. "We've come to ask this man questions about my mother!"

James held up his hand and spoke over the din. "Thank you for your concern over my privacy," he said to the manager of the establishment, an Indian man of middle age. "I do appreciate it, but I believe I shall be fine."

The manager and his two employees bowed and retreated back to the offices, and Isabelle turned her attention to the man who was introducing himself as Colonel Bilbey, Lord Banbury.

Ah. So much explained in the one introduction. They had most likely come seeking answers, although why they chose James was a mystery. He hadn't even had a conversation with Lady Banbury.

"I wonder if we might have a seat somewhere. I am looking for some information and in return have some you may find of interest." The colonel was rather tall and thin, his British uniform impeccably crisp and pressed. He had a high forehead on a face that openly showed signs of worry and concern.

To Isabelle's relief, staff had begun to lay dishes for their dinner on the table under the white canopy where they had eaten breakfast. White mosquito netting billowed in a gentle breeze and framed the canopy with transparent walls, the entire picture serene and lovely. She glanced at James and gestured toward the table. He followed the direction of her thoughts and said, "Perhaps you'll join us—we were just about to dine."

"Thank you," the colonel said and motioned for his daughter to precede him to the canopy. "Oh, forgive me," he said, his hand on her back, "this is my daughter, Alice."

"A pleasure to meet you," James said with an incline of his head. "And allow me to introduce to you my friend, Miss Isabelle Webb."

Alice Bilbey looked Isabelle up and down as one would examine horseflesh. Apparently, she found her lacking, because she instead turned her attention back to James with a flare of interest sparking in her eyes.

"Miss Webb," the colonel said with a slight bow.

"The pleasure is mine," Isabelle said. "And might I add that we're so sorry about the loss of your wife."

Alice's eyes jumped back to Isabelle's face. "What do you know of it? Why do you say *loss* as though she's passed on?" Her voice reached a shrill peak, and her father gently but firmly guided her toward the canopy.

"We'll speak of it over dinner, Alice," Colonel Bilbey said to her quietly.

Isabelle motioned to one of the employees who was adding plates to the table. "How many more will be joining you, memsahib?"

Isabelle glanced over her shoulder to see Sally approaching with Ari Kilronomos, who was looking most interested in the proceedings. She sighed. "It appears that there will be six, total."

"Very good."

Dinner was eventually served, and all the guests were seated, Isabelle at James's right in response to his request that she sit by him with a jerk of his head. Her amusement with him grew, which surprised her. Had anyone else on the planet gestured to her so curtly a command for her presence, she would have smirked and then sat wherever she pleased.

"You need to remember your ultimate goal and that you will not attract flies with vinegar," she whispered to him as she placed her napkin on her lap.

"I don't want to attract flies," he hissed back.

Her lips twitched, and she caught his gaze, holding it. His eyes smoldered, and she felt a stab of compassion for him. He looked bone weary and frustrated. "Well, like it or not, they've gathered," she murmured. "Use them."

"*I* am not accustomed to using people," he said in quiet undertones that nobody else heard as they began choosing their food from various dishes.

His comment stung, and she bit her lip. She averted her gaze, her fingers clenched in her napkin.

He must have realized the rudeness of his comment and her uncomfortable response to it. "My apologies," he mumbled. "I did not mean to insinuate anything insulting."

Isabelle forced her fingers to relax and waved her hand at him in dismissal. It was only fair, really. She'd accused him to his face of being an angry person. His observations of her own character were nothing less than she should expect.

Isabelle glanced up at the rest of the diners. Thankfully, Sally had commandeered the conversation. "It's so very good to get off my feet!" she was saying. "This weather is most warm and humid, and we've been about in it all day. Of course, it does tend to get warm back home, as well, so I suppose I should be accustomed to it." Sally glanced at Isabelle as though determining whether or not she had finished her private conversation with James.

Isabelle smiled at her and the others. "One never grows accustomed to this kind of heat, I suppose," she said.

Alice Bilbey glanced at her father in irritation. "Enough about the weather, Papa. Honestly, ask them why his brother," she said, stabbing her finger toward James, "was poking about, asking questions about Mama!"

6

James's spoon clattered to his plate and he stiffened. "I beg your pardon? You've seen my brother?"

Colonel Bilbey nodded and straightened a bit in his chair as well. "Mr. Ashby, nearly a week ago, a man named Thaddeus Sparks, accompanied by a younger man, Phillip Ashby, inquired of me the whereabouts of my wife. Truthfully, I had expected her to arrive earlier, but she sent word saying that she had been delayed."

Isabelle forgot the food sitting on her plate. All day, they had been searching for information about Phillip, and now it was laid out before them.

"Colonel, what is it you would like to know? I'm afraid I cannot tell you why my brother and his companion asked after your wife. As it happens, I'm searching for my brother," James told him.

The colonel nodded. "One of my men told me that you were down at the docks, asking about the young Mr. Ashby and Mr. Sparks. I have people scouring the area, searching for them as well, for they are the last who spoke of my wife, and now she has gone missing. I had hoped to find them, to see what they might be able to tell me. You have no idea of where they are going, then?"

"I only wish I did."

"Colonel, if I may ask a question," Isabelle said to the tired older man, "will you tell us exactly what Mr. Sparks and Mr. Ashby said to you?"

He nodded. "Mr. Sparks told me that he had corresponded with Lady Banbury by mail approximately eight weeks ago and that they had met in London as well. According to him, she had information she would give him when they reached India, but he was under the impression that she would have arrived here before they did."

At this, Alice sniffed. "Information indeed, as though she were some common merchant, trading with those two," she said. "I'm certain they must have been mistaken, now that I think on it."

Sally glared at the young woman. "Kindly remember, Miss Bilbey, that you speak of Mr. Ashby's brother. As you are a guest at this table, I might suggest you not cast a slur upon his name."

"And I might suggest that you keep to your own affairs," Alice told Sally, "because this certainly doesn't concern you. It's not *your* mother who has gone missing!"

"*My* mother is dead, thank you," Sally shot back.

"Ladies." James's firm voice halted the argument and had both young women staring at him. "Miss Bilbey, Miss Rhodes is a friend of mine, and my affairs concern her." Sally flushed with pleasure and shot a look of triumph at Alice, who ignored her. "And Miss Rhodes," James said, "we must understand that Miss Bilbey is anxious about the welfare of her mother."

When the young women remained silent, James turned to the colonel. "Sir, I wonder if you recall any other statements Mr. Sparks may have made. Also, did my brother say anything?"

Colonel Bilbey shook his head. "Mr. Sparks's only question was whether or not I knew when my wife would arrive. He stated that she had some information for him that was of the utmost importance. Your brother did not speak at all. In fact . . . " The colonel paused. "I'm sorry to tell you that your brother seemed most anxious. Almost . . ."

James waited expectantly, eyebrows raised.

"Afraid."

James nodded absently, as though confirming something to himself. Isabelle glanced at him, her appetite growing less urgent with each passing moment. It was as though James had suspected all along that Phillip may be in danger.

She cleared her throat. "Colonel, I wonder if we might be able to answer any questions you might have."

The colonel placed his utensils at the side of his plate and regarded her with tired eyes. "Please, any information you have might be helpful. Did you come to know her on the voyage? Speak with her about anything?"

"I did introduce myself to her, and I asked if she knew anything about this legendary jewel that Sparks and Phillip are after," Isabelle said, stopping when the man's mouth dropped open.

Bilbey looked at James. "Your brother and Sparks are looking for the Jewel of Zeus?"

"Yes, that's my understanding from the note my brother left behind," James said.

"I wasn't aware of that . . . it explains some things." The colonel's face had gone pale.

"What things?" Isabelle asked him gently.

He shook his head slightly, his face pained. "My wife considered . . . considers herself an expert on the subject. She's known among British military circles as one who is rather . . . obsessed with it."

"That dratted jewel," Alice said under her breath. "Such an embarrassment when she goes on about it."

"At any rate," Bilbey continued, "it would explain Mr. Sparks's interest in my wife. He was hoping she could tell him of its whereabouts, I'm sure."

"Did she know of its whereabouts?" Isabelle asked him.

He shook his head. It was a simple enough denial, and heaven only knew the man's pain seemed real, but something wasn't quite right. It might have been a flicker in his eyes that lasted but a fraction of a second, or perhaps the set of his shoulders and hands. She would have to think on it later, but of one thing Isabelle was certain—Colonel Bilbey believed his wife thought she knew where the Jewel of Zeus was located.

The small dinner party finished their meal in relative silence, and when the Bilbeys and Ari Kilronomos stood to leave, Isabelle, Sally, and James followed them to the front gates of the small, darkened compound. Light shone from gas street lamps, throwing shadows over the beautiful flowers whose colors had deepened with the setting of the sun.

"What are your plans, if I may ask?" Colonel Bilbey asked James as the two exchanged an awkward handshake.

James shrugged and ran a tired hand through his hair. "I suppose I'll continue to search the city for any who may have seen my brother. Tomorrow it would make sense to check at various boarding houses or hostels—*chawls,* I understand they're called."

"I wonder if you would allow me to accompany you? I'm most anxious to find this Sparks fellow, and at any rate, I can gain admittance where you may not be so fortunate."

"Sir," Isabelle touched his arm. "There's a detail I had forgotten to share with you," she said and told him of the encounter she and Sally had witnessed at Pembroke Inn concerning Lady Banbury and the innkeeper's wife. "I'm assuming that Lady Banbury may have been asking after Sparks for the reason of sharing whatever information he wanted from her."

Bilbey nodded, his face grim. "That stands to reason," he said.

"My *mother* would never have set foot in a common inn for the purpose of speaking with that person!" Alice's face was flushed and angry, visible even in the dim light of the lanterns.

"Perhaps I was mistaken," Isabelle said, meeting Alice's gaze directly and holding it until Alice averted her eyes.

"My daughter is overwrought," the colonel said.

"Understandably," Isabelle replied with a small nod at Bilbey. "Tempers often flare when one is worried for the safety of a loved one." Although she would have wagered all the money in her possession that Alice Bilbey's temper flared on a regular basis, worry or no.

"I just want to find my mother," Alice whimpered, her lips pouting in a very pretty manner that had probably taken her considerable time before a looking glass to master. She looked first at James, then at Ari, her lashes dampening with tears.

"But of course," Ari said to her, nodding. Sally looked as though she wanted to strangle her pretty competition. Ari, outwardly oblivious to the silent war being waged between the two young women, said to the colonel, "Sir, I would be most honored to help you with your quest. I know India intimately and speak quite respectable Hindi."

"We would hate to impose on your free time," James said to the man flatly. "Surely you have a full itinerary."

"Nonsense," Kilronomos said. "I can think of no better use of my time than to help locate your brother and the Lady Banbury."

Colonel Bilbey inclined his head. "I thank you for your offer, Mr. Kilronomos. Any and all help will be greatly appreciated."

James bid the uninvited guests farewell and accompanied Sally and Isabelle back to the front door of their cottage. Pleading extreme fatigue, Sally climbed the few front steps and entered, softly closing the door behind her.

He turned reluctantly to Isabelle, who looked down the path, her moonlit profile to him. "You said earlier you wished to speak with me," he said, uncertain about the degree to which he'd hurt her feelings with his comment at dinner.

She nodded and finally turned to look at him. "I merely wanted to tell you that when I saw Kilronomos at the temple, he was definitely lying in wait for you. I wanted to warn you that he's most likely not to be trusted, that he probably has his own ends to meet, but you've already ascertained that."

Her tone was cool and distant. He'd most assuredly hurt her feelings. "Isabelle," he said, "it was unkind of me to imply that you thoughtlessly use people. I apologize."

"Yet it's true," she said. "It's what I do for a living. I use people."

"If that's so, and you're so very blasé about it, then why were you offended by what I said?" His repentance was quickly turning to defensiveness—how dare she become distant when *she* was usually the one to make unflattering comments about his character?

She closed her eyes briefly. "Because I have so few friends," she admitted quietly, her words tight. "And I am not using *you*."

He felt a slight ache in his chest. "Again, my apologies," he murmured, his words sounding as stiff as hers. "And I thank you for your help today. Shall we dine again in the morning at the same time?"

She nodded. "James," she said as she climbed the steps to her door, "you may want to try for a few minutes of stolen conversation with the lovely Miss Bilbey."

He felt his face contort in displeasure. "Why?"

"Perhaps there was something she heard Sparks say, something she noticed about their arrival, departure, their method of transportation . . . or perhaps she noticed nothing at all. But I've a feeling she would welcome attention from you. Of course, you would be using her for your own ends. You might ask your conscience if it can bear the strain."

With that, she turned and went inside. He briefly closed his eyes and conceded her the point, vowing to make an effort to keep from offending her in the future. He found he much preferred her smiles and laughter to her distance.

* * *

When James and Colonel Bilbey joined Sally, Isabelle, Alice, and Ari for lunch, James realized it would probably be wise to follow Isabelle's advice to question Alice Bilbey. Her father had confirmed that she had been with him when Phillip and Sparks had paid them their visit and that Alice left the building at the same time to take the carriage into town.

He looked at her now, sitting on one side of Ari. Alice was watching the Greek with a petulant expression as Ari paid his attention not to Sally this time but to Isabelle. She was speaking, and he watched her as though she were the most fascinating thing on earth.

James ground his teeth together. He did not like the man. If forced to explain why, he knew he wouldn't be able to, but there was something about him that James distrusted.

Under the direction of the colonel, the group found an establishment with seating outdoors and, after a very short wait, found themselves served *ambot-tik,* described to them by their server as "a tangy fish curry with tamarind." Once again, he ate the food with very little relish as it was not to his liking, but Isabelle, he noted, ate with the love of a native. Of course, living in a besieged, war-torn city with nothing but rats for dinner might give a person an appreciation for good food, whatever the kind.

Isabelle had been her usual self that morning at breakfast, taking but a moment to warm up to her customary degree. He was glad she didn't hold a grudge, and he asked himself now for what seemed the fiftieth time why he had been so curt with her the night before at dinner. He had been angry and on edge and had taken it out on her. What was it about her that made him blurt out every thought that was on his mind, and why did he care whether or not she used people? That she had all but admitted later on that night that she considered him a friend had put his mind at ease for reasons he didn't care to contemplate.

James had carefully maneuvered the seating arrangement at the table so that he was situated next to Alice Bilbey. When the conversation around the table had reached a comfortable hum, he turned to her and attempted a warm smile, knowing full well she might see him as little more than an old man.

"Miss Bilbey," he said, "I'm wondering if you might be able to help me with a matter."

Her eyes lit up and he felt pity for the girl. She was barely more than a child who longed to be an adult. And judging by the look on her face, she didn't think him too old. He wanted to thrash Isabelle for putting the idea of speaking to Alice in his head in the first place.

"Certainly, Mr. Ashby. How might I assist you?"

"Well, as you know, I'm searching for my brother. Your father tells me that on the day my brother and his companion visited your father, you exited the building at the same time to take a carriage into town. Do you remember this?"

She nodded. "Of course."

"Do you remember any conversation at all between the two men that you might have overheard as you were leaving? Anything at all?"

Alice frowned. "I remember thinking the older man was angry. The only thing I heard him say was something about the Sepoy Rebellion, which struck me as odd, because it's the one topic other than that dreaded Jewel of Zeus that my mother seems to enjoy talking about."

"The Sepoy Rebellion? Of '57?"

Alice nodded. "I would assume that is the one he meant. I know of no other in recent history. And if he was looking for information on it, he would definitely have come to the right place had my mother only been here."

"I see." James paused. "Miss Bilbey, I'm terribly sorry about your mother's disappearance. It's my hope for you that she is found safe."

Alice shrugged a shoulder with the slightest of movements. "She really is most annoying. Still, I am rather fond of her." Her face clouded in what was probably the first genuine, unselfish expression he'd seen on the young girl. "All in all, I've spent more time with my governess, but she is my mother, you know?"

He nodded, suddenly feeling quite awkward. What to say? When his father had died, it was as though his whole world had collapsed. No words of kindness from anyone had made the least bit of difference. He had been a bit younger, though, than this young woman and hadn't had a governess or anyone to help fill the loss, other than his mother, who had been bearing her own grief.

"I'm to have my first season next summer, you know," Alice said, brightening. "Mama says I will be all the rage in London. I so look forward to returning. My brothers are already there in school, but we must remain here with my father." She leaned closer to him. "I do hate it sometimes," she whispered fiercely. "All the heat and the natives with their castes and religions! It's enough to make a body very frustrated!"

James wished the ground would open and swallow him whole. He had never been good at participating in conversation with young girls—it had caused him no small amount of panic as a young man, and now that he was a man of thirty-three years, he found himself distinctly uncomfortable. He placed a finger under his collar and pulled it a bit, wondering what to say as Alice continued to prattle on about what seemed to him very inconsequential things. As her ramblings continued, he came to realize that she didn't require him to say anything at all, merely to occupy his seat and nod at her.

He glanced across the table at Isabelle in some desperation to find her trying valiantly not to laugh. He narrowed his eyes, annoyed that she would make light of his pain, until he finally saw the humor in the situation and allowed himself a wry smile. He shrugged a bit and she winked at him, turning her attention to Ari, who was seated on her left and asking her a question.

His smile evaporated as he saw the way the younger man addressed her, leaning in close and attempting to work his charm on her. She answered whatever he had asked her with a ready smile and a playful slap to his forearm. Her answering comment had him blinking for a fraction of a second in apparent confusion, but he recovered well enough with an uncertain laugh.

James felt his smile return as he watched Isabelle. She could definitely care for herself in nearly any setting. He had yet to see her fail at commanding her surroundings, unless he counted that night on the docks in London. And if he were truthful, he wasn't so certain she hadn't been in command there as well. He almost wished he had hesitated for just a moment in the shadows to see how she would have handled the situation.

At his side, he heard Alice clear her throat, and he quickly glanced at her, feeling guilty for looking elsewhere while she was so ardently spilling her heart about everything she hated in India. He nodded and then shook his head when he realized she'd asked him a question.

"Well, which is it?" she asked him, impatience stamped clearly on her features.

"I'm sorry, which is what?"

"I said, Mr. Ashby, that I thought your brother most handsome, and if you'll forgive the forward nature of my question, I wonder if he is married or affianced?"

"No. Neither."

"Splendid! Well, then, Mr. Ashby. When we find your brother, I should dearly love an introduction."

"Didn't he introduce himself to you and your father?"

"No. The other man, Mr. Sparks, hardly let anyone get a word in edgewise. Your brother mostly stood behind him, looking a bit worried."

James recognized the unsettled feeling that had come to him of late when he thought of Phillip traveling with Sparks. Phillip's manners were impeccable. And he was a gregarious young man. There was hardly a shy bone in his body. He was often considered a must-have in certain social circles in Salt Lake City because of his ability to entertain people and make them laugh. The thought of Phillip being in the same room as a British military officer and a lovely young woman without introducing himself was so out of character that James wondered what it was Sparks was using to control him.

As the meal finished and the diners busied themselves in gathering their personal items, Sally, who was seated on James's other side, clutched his arm. He looked at her in some surprise. "I have claims on the first introduction to your brother," she muttered quietly between clenched teeth. "I don't care how sad she is right now—her dead mother does not supersede my rights!"

James choked back a horrified laugh and coughed instead. He wondered if Sally had had such an obvious edge to her personality before the war. Losing everything had a tendency to make people a bit jaded. He leaned down and whispered, "We don't know she's dead, Sally."

Sally looked at him with an expression that called him a fool. "Really, James," she hissed. "Where could she have gone? She was nowhere on board! And if you ask me, *that girl* doesn't even look very sad!"

James took Sally's elbow and ushered her ahead of the others as she continued in her quiet fury.

"When I lost my mother . . . I . . ." She cut herself off and looked into the distance as they entered the street.

James looked down at her with consternation. The gods must have been laughing themselves silly at his expense. Two overwrought young women in the same hour were enough to have his head pounding in pain. As he watched Sally struggle with her emotions and valiantly keep her tears from falling, he saw in his memories himself grieving over his own father.

He patted her shoulder awkwardly. "I understand," he said to her quietly. "I do understand."

Mercifully, Isabelle had caught them by this time and swept Sally along in her stride, catching her about the shoulders and steering her toward a vendor. "We passed this stall earlier, my dear, and I believe we are in need of this woman's wares," she said, placing a quick kiss on Sally's cheek.

"What is it?" Sally asked, clearing her throat. James matched their pace, turning to see the others following behind.

"The most beautiful fabrics this world has ever seen," Isabelle said. "And many of them already sewn into clothing."

"Oh, Belle, truly? And we can wear them?"

"Yes, we can. I've asked the colonel. He assures me it will be fine."

James slowed his step and allowed the women to approach the stall together. Ari soon caught him, as did the Bilbeys. Alice wrinkled her nose in distaste when she saw the object of Isabelle's and Sally's quest. "Are they thinking to *wear* those?"

"Alice." Colonel Bilbey's voice was soft but firm, brooking no further argument. "Mr. Ashby," Bilbey said, turning to James. "I'm returning to my office to finish some correspondence to London that cannot wait. I should very much like to join you later this afternoon, toward evening, to discuss further inquiries about your brother. I'm sorry that our activities this afternoon have yielded nothing."

"I appreciate your efforts, sir. And forgive me, but have you spoken with the captain of our steamship regarding the onboard investigation of your wife?"

He nodded. "Unfortunately, he could tell me nothing. The ship was searched, and she wasn't on board." He hesitated, glancing at his daughter who was still eyeing Isabelle and Sally with superior disgust. "Her belongings had been thoroughly ransacked, however," he added in an undertone.

James nodded. "Was anything taken?"

Bilbey shook his head. "I received word this morning, however, that one of her trunks did not make it on board when she left London. It should be nearing Calcutta as we speak." His shoulders sagged and he stepped away from his daughter. James walked with him a short distance away.

"Mr. Ashby, it pains me to admit this, but I have no idea what my wife was about. What could she have been thinking?" Bilbey's hands clenched into fists. "Her actions of late—this meeting with Sparks in London, whatever it was she promised him—have been most confusing. It does not cast a good light upon my family, however, and if nothing else she was always conscious of appearances. And I understand from my wife's maid and the captain that she had a conversation with an unseen man about money. Of course, the investigation on board turned up nothing and the captain wonders if the maid imagined the conversation as my wife never did tell her the nature of it." He glanced at his daughter, his face grim.

James didn't know what to say to the man. Nothing he thought of seemed to be any more than meaningless platitudes. Bilbey turned his gaze from his daughter to James. "Do you suppose there's a chance she might be alive?"

James stared at him for a moment. The man was seasoned military—he had to know that his wife was most likely at the bottom of the ocean. "Sir, I don't . . . I suppose anything's possible." He paused. "Did the captain tell you the entire ship had been searched?"

Bilbey nodded.

"Do you have any reason to suppose he wasn't telling the truth? Do you know of the man's past or history as a captain?"

The colonel sighed. "Unfortunately for the sake of my optimism, the captain has an impeccable record. I have no reason to expect that he wasn't speaking the truth. I was just hoping for some false . . . hope, I suppose."

James nodded. "I understand."

"While I must eventually face the fact that my wife is most likely dead," he paused, swallowing, "I should very much like to help you find your brother if you're willing. I am most anxious to learn some answers to all of this."

James was torn between gratitude and frustration. His circle of acquaintances in this odd journey was growing, and he was very much a man who liked to maintain control. The more elements introduced, the less control he would have. The colonel had access to places he wouldn't, however. That much was plainly clear.

"I would be most grateful for that," he told Bilbey and was gratified by the look of relief that crossed the man's features. James could hardly deny Bilbey what he sought in the face of having just lost his wife to such suspicious circumstances. "Incidentally," he added, "did Mr. Sparks happen to mention anything at all to you about the Sepoy Rebellion?"

The look on Colonel Bilbey's face was genuinely confused. "No, no he didn't. Did you expect that he would?"

James shook his head. "Not necessarily, I'm just trying to understand what he is looking for." James glanced at Alice, who was watching Isabelle and Sally complete their purchases. He would have to ask Isabelle what she knew about the Rebellion as soon as he could get her alone.

7

"As it happens, I came prepared." Isabelle glanced up at James, who sat next to her on their favorite bench beside the pond near the cottages.

"Of course you did," he said. "I would never have thought otherwise."

Isabelle raised a brow as she flipped pages in her book. "Do you mock me, Mr. Ashby?"

"Never, Miss Webb."

"Ah, here it is. The Sepoy Rebellion of 1857. I read parts of this on our passage from England. And you know, I do remember when it happened. I was living in Chicago—it was quite the item in the news for a while. It seems that roughly eight years ago, the British developed a rifle that was rumored to require the use of animal fat to grease the ball's passage through the barrel. Pig fat is abhorrent to Muslims and cow fat is sacred to the Hindus."

Isabelle ran her finger down the page until she found the paragraph for which she searched. "'A sepoy named Mangal Pandey of the 34th Bengal Native Infantry fired upon his senior officer. This act served as the spark lighting the inferno that became the Rebellion. Indian soldiers in cities and towns throughout central India slaughtered British men, women, and children in a frenzied and animalistic mayhem that was eventually squelched by the superior forces and intellect of the British officers and soldiers.'"

Isabelle stopped reading. "Many British innocents died, it's true," she murmured with a glance over her shoulder, "but the aftermath that followed the mutiny was every bit as harsh and unjust."

James frowned, his voice equally hushed. "How do you know?"

"Pinkerton made reference not long ago to a friend of his who was a British statesman, a moderate of sorts. Now that I can place it in the proper context, I see that it was this rebellion to which he made reference. This statesman pleaded before parliament for cooler heads to prevail, but the entire body, it seemed, cried out for blood. It was merciless. And the looting—he said that many a British fortune was made during the taming of the rebellion."

James leaned forward and rested his forearms on his knees, his fingers steepled as he stared into the pond. "Eye for an eye, I suppose."

"But how can you?" Isabelle's voice was urgent, and she clutched the book, leaning forward and closer to James. "How can you march into a town and slaughter all of their women and children just because your own were killed? That doesn't make it right! How could you look into the face of an innocent mother and child and run them through with a sword? Or slit their throats? Or fire point blank with a musket as they sit in their homes?"

"I wouldn't." James scowled at her. "You act as though it was all my idea."

Isabelle huffed out a sigh. "I'm not saying *you,* per se. I don't understand it. It just isn't right."

"This couldn't all have begun from a controversial weapon. There must have been discontent in the first place."

"Perhaps." Isabelle lowered her voice again. "It's clear from this passage that the British believed the Indians to be morally and intellectually inferior. Is it possible that the populace at large, and the sepoys specifically, tired of this?"

James's lips twitched in a smile. "Wouldn't be the first time someone rebelled against the Brits."

Isabelle laughed softly. "No, it wouldn't. But all of this, interesting as it is, has *what* to do with your brother?"

James sat up with a sigh and leaned back against the bench, propping one ankle on the other knee. "I don't know." He rubbed his eyes. "Why would Sparks have been talking to Phillip about this rebellion?"

"What, exactly, did Alice say to you?"

"Only that Sparks said something to Phillip about the Sepoy Rebellion as they were leaving and that it was a shame her mother wasn't there—the rebellion was another of her favorite topics of discussion." James shrugged. "It makes no sense to me."

Isabelle absently tapped her forefinger against the open book. "What would the rebellion have to do with the jewel?" she murmured.

"I don't know." James rubbed the back of his neck. "This is beginning to feel like looking for a needle in a haystack. I'm starting to wonder—"

Isabelle glanced at him sharply. "Starting to wonder what? If you'll ever find him?"

James nodded, a muscle in his jaw betraying his clenched teeth, but he said nothing.

"Well, I, for one, believe it is possible to find a needle in a haystack. We just have to be very methodical about it."

"We have no idea where to go from here. This country is massive." James's voice was flat. She had the impression that his admissions were not easily given. He wasn't a man used to failure, and the stakes were exceptionally high.

"You're forgetting a valuable resource."

"You?"

Isabelle rolled her eyes. "Well, of course, me, but I was thinking of Colonel Bilbey. He has access to places we do not. And he also has a vested interest in finding Sparks."

James remained silent and looked at her in the darkening shadows. She smiled. "Don't despair," she whispered. "We won't stop until we find him." Isabelle patted his knee with her hand and rose, closing the book. "Let me look at this some more and then ponder it in my sleep. I'll find the connection between the rebellion and the jewel."

"Isabelle," James said and grabbed her hand, his thumb tracing a path across her knuckles. "I . . ." He paused, seemingly at a loss for words. "Thank you," he finished, his voice hoarse and hushed.

Isabelle felt foolish at the thump of her heart against her ribs. She fought the urge to snatch her hand back and prove to herself that the jolt she felt at the simple physical contact was nothing significant. She tilted her head and tried for a smile that didn't materialize. "You're welcome." Finally, calling herself a coward, she broke contact with his gaze and pulled her fingers free, walking to her cottage without looking back.

* * *

James's sleep was fitful at best. He dreamed he was in his blacksmith shop, hammering away until he finally pulled himself into a semiconscious state. The pounding hadn't originated in his dream; it was coming from the front door of his cottage.

He rose from the bed and left the small bedroom, pulling a robe about his shoulders as he entered the front room. He thrust his arms at the sleeves several times before finally succeeding in pulling them on. Opening the door a crack, he squinted in the moonlight at the woman who stood with her fist raised, ready to thump again.

"You must sleep like the dead," Isabelle hissed. "Let me in!"

"What on earth . . ." James moved aside as Isabelle entered the cottage and closed the door firmly behind her.

"Much longer out there pounding on your door and someone would have seen me. Rumors would have been flying by morning," she said in a huff.

"So why are you here?" he asked, bewildered.

Isabelle moved to the curtains, drawing back the heavier fabric to reveal a shaft of moonlight that sliced through the window and bathed the room in a subdued, silver light. She crossed a short distance to one of the chairs in the seating area. "I know what Sparks is doing," she said.

James slowly crossed the room and sat in a chair opposite hers. It creaked under his weight, the silence in the room amplifying the noise. He tilted his head slightly to one side and gazed at her, still trying to shake off the dregs of sleep. "I beg your pardon?" He reached absently for his pocket watch, which, of course, he wasn't wearing.

"It's half past three," she informed him, glancing at his searching hand. "I read some more before going to bed, and once asleep I must have heard a noise or something, because I awoke, and it struck me as clearly as day!"

"What did?" he gritted out.

"Sparks is following the trail of the Sepoy Rebellion!"

James studied her in silence. She looked as fresh as a daisy and rather glowed like one as well. Her nightgown was a long, white cotton affair with sleeves that reached her wrists. The matching robe was sleeveless and wrapped atop the gown; so much white material illuminated in the moonlight had her resembling an angel. There was something else that was different about her, though, and he realized as he pulled himself more fully awake that her hair was unbound and hung down her back and around her shoulders in dark silken strands that curled slightly at the ends.

Absently, she tucked her hair behind her ear and pulled her small book from within her robe. "Consider this," she said as though trying her case before a jury. Rapidly flipping through the book, she finally settled on a page and trailed her finger along a passage, holding it up to the light. "It says the British were outnumbered by tens of thousands of sepoys. The odds were against them, yet in the course of a year they managed to subdue the rebellion and restake their claim on the country."

"There may have been several reasons for that," James said.

"I'm certain there were, but what matters is what Sparks believes. Don't you see? Sparks thinks the Brits had the jewel."

Her pronouncement hung between them, thick and heavy. Isabelle's breathing was slightly labored, as though she'd been running a fair distance. Eventually, James slowly nodded. "It makes sense," he admitted. "It's really the only logical tie. Unless he mentioned it to Phillip in passing that day as they left Bilbey's offices."

Isabelle snorted. "You think Sparks was just making interesting conversation about Indian history?"

James shrugged. "I suppose not."

"It's possible," Isabelle sighed, "but highly unlikely. I know it. I can feel it."

He nodded once, conclusively, after studying the resolute set to her expression. "We'll tell the colonel about this first thing in the morning."

"I wonder," she said, tapping a finger against her lips, "might I borrow your map of India? The one on which you've been making your notes?"

"Now?"

"I couldn't sleep if I tried. I want to chronologically mark the places on the map where the events during the mutiny occurred."

James nodded and retrieved the map for her from amongst his papers in the bedroom. When he returned, she was standing near the door. "Leaving so soon?" he asked. "The night is young. Or the morning is fresh. Or some such."

"I know," she said. She ducked her head in a rare display of self-consciousness. "I apologize . . . I could hardly contain my excitement when I realized . . . I just wanted you to know as soon as possible."

"And you wore your bedclothes out into the night," he said, rather enjoying the upper hand. He reasoned he might as well. He wasn't sure when he'd have it again.

Her head came up defensively. "I wore my robe," she said.

At that he laughed. True, she was covered from neck to toe, but there was something strangely intimate about her apparel that had him feeling uncomfortable in spite of himself. "Yes, you did," he said. "Your robe that is as thin as the nightgown itself."

"This is highly improper," she said, her hand on the doorknob. "A gentleman doesn't discuss a lady's bedclothing."

"Then the lady probably ought not to wear it outside her lodgings."

Isabelle floundered for a moment, undoubtedly looking for something biting to say. Instead, she bit the inside of her cheeks as though to keep from smiling, turned the knob, and left.

* * *

"But Father, I insist I be allowed to go along! You absolutely cannot leave me here with the servants."

Isabelle glanced at James. The two were sitting in Colonel Bilbey's office and were privy to the conversation transpiring outside the door.

"Alice, I have no way of knowing how long we'll be. Besides, you hate to travel." Colonel Bilbey's weary voice was substantially lower in volume than his daughter's.

"But with Mama missing," Alice said and sniffled, "I can't bear the thought of being apart from you."

Isabelle closed her eyes briefly. James's frown was fierce enough to scare away all but the bravest of creatures. "She's not coming!" he mouthed to Isabelle. He leaned on the arm of his chair and whispered in Isabelle's ear, "I'll not have this become a traveling circus!"

"We may not have much of a choice if Bilbey decides to allow it," Isabelle whispered in return.

"Then we'll go without him."

Isabelle pulled back a bit and looked at his determined face. "James," she whispered, "we need him."

His frustration evident, James sat back in his chair and shook his head.

"I was supposed to have my season already! And now that Mama's gone, I don't know when I'll have it! She was supposed to take me home to England in just a few weeks." Alice's pouty performance was reaching new levels.

"Alice, I didn't want to have to tell you this—indeed I had hoped there might be another way—but there isn't going to be enough money for a season anyway. Not this year. As it is, I'm going to have to retrieve your brothers from Eton."

Isabelle looked at James, her eyes wide, unsure she'd overheard that last statement correctly. "Oh, my," she whispered. Transferring her gaze to Bilbey's cluttered desk and the richly appointed office, she felt a few more pieces of a curious puzzle take shape in her head and attempt to fit themselves together. Slowly, she nodded to herself. The Lady Banbury had been in need of money.

James leaned forward in his chair and rested his arms on his knees, a pose that was becoming familiar to Isabelle. "We shouldn't be hearing this," he said to her. He tapped his fingers together, looking for all the world as though he wished he could disappear.

"Don't you see?" Isabelle said to James. "I would wager my last dollar that Lady Banbury was hoping to extract money from Sparks in exchange for her information about the jewel. Or perhaps she thought she knew where it was or was planning to sell him an imitation . . ."

James glanced at her, his expression speculative.

"And so I said, 'Sally, I just don't think that shade of green is at all good for your complexion.' And you would have thought I told her she had a wart on her nose!" Isabelle said to him, her face animated.

James slowly sat up straight and looked at her as though she'd taken leave of her senses when he heard Bilbey's footsteps in the office behind his back. "Well, then, you must be certain to speak more gently with her from now on," he answered, sounding ridiculously awkward.

"I suppose I shall," Isabelle said, her hands spread wide. "I'd no idea she would be so affected."

By this time the colonel had resumed his seat behind his desk and smoothed a hand over his hair. "I apologize for the interruption," he said. "We were discussing . . . yes. I do believe, to answer your question, Mr. Ashby, that we should exhaust all efforts around the city here before leaving for Barrackpore. No sense in heading out of town if Sparks and your brother are still here."

James nodded. "I confess, sir, I'm at a bit of a loss. I'm not certain how to narrow the search. They could have stayed anywhere."

"I agree. In fact, I've been thinking that another trip to the railway station wouldn't be amiss. Our inquiry there was cursory at best. I'm certain that someone can be persuaded to remember *something*."

* * *

The Victoria Terminus Railway Station was an incredible work of architectural beauty. Entirely gothic in appearance, it was lavish and large, sculpted with detail that represented both India and England. A huge central dome boasted a thirteen-foot statue atop and water spouts shaped like animal heads at the base. It was as impressive as any palace or cathedral.

Isabelle, James, and Colonel Bilbey were preparing to leave the train station after questioning a young Indian porter. Isabelle glanced back at the young man whom the colonel had been unable to crack. It may well have been that the porter truly knew nothing about two American men traveling by rail in the past week or two, but there had been something in his eyes that had given her pause.

That they had come across this particular man was a stroke of luck. Or Providence, if one believed in such things. On a whim, Isabelle, James, and the colonel had stopped by a shabby chawl that housed entire Indian families near the rail station. The matron of the place confirmed that yes, two Americans matching Sparks's and Phillip's descriptions had indeed rented a room for just over a week. Further coaxing revealed the date and time the pair had left the sanctuary of her humble lodgings. They had been gone for just over two days.

The porter now in question was identified by the rail master as one working on the day Sparks and Phillip Ashby checked out of their room. The porter had been less than forthcoming, to say the least, and had eyed Bilbey with a flat expression that gave little away. They were left to assume that the man was either lying, that another porter would have to be questioned, or that Sparks and Phillip hadn't left town by rail.

"Let me have the photograph, and then keep going," Isabelle said to James as the three of them made their way to the colonel's carriage. "Wait for me out of sight."

Without comment, James handed her a photographic likeness of his brother, and Isabelle turned around and approached the young Indian porter. Bilbey had talked, cajoled, probably even threatened, but to no avail. Isabelle and James had stood some distance away at Bilbey's request; all she knew of the exchange was that the porter spoke English. She resisted the impulse to grind her teeth together in impatience. True, they needed the colonel. But really, why send an amateur to do professional work?

"Sir," she said and touched the porter lightly on the arm. "I wonder if I might speak with you for a moment?"

The young man nodded, his eyes wary. "Certainly, memsahib."

"I'm not certain what Colonel Bilbey asked of you, but I wonder if I might ask you a question. My friend and I are looking for his brother, whom we believe is being held against his will by his traveling companion." Isabelle produced the same small portrait of Phillip that Bilbey had just shown the man. "Are you certain you don't remember seeing this person?"

The porter's eyes glanced at the picture, flickered away almost imperceptibly, and then found Isabelle's direct gaze. He matched it with one of his own. "I tell you the same thing I told the officer. There are many people going through here in the course of a day. I cannot remember particular faces."

"I do understand," Isabelle said, opening her reticule and withdrawing a change purse. "How much money did this man's traveling companion pay you to keep quiet?" Isabelle gestured to the photograph.

The porter frowned slightly. "I don't understand."

"This much?" Isabelle pulled a large coin from her change purse. "This much?" she pulled another coin forward, doubling the original amount. She then tripled the amount, looking up at the man's face.

His lips pursed slightly. He cleared his throat, lowering his voice. "It wasn't only the money, memsahib. He was most . . . persuasive."

"Did he tell you he was in possession of the Jewel of Zeus?"

The porter's eyes widened in shock. "Mem . . . memsahib mustn't . . . He said . . ."

"He's a liar. He doesn't have it, nor will he." Isabelle handed him the coins. "Where did they go?"

The porter bit down on his lower lip and took the proffered money. "Barrackpore," he said, pocketing the cash.

"Thank you," Isabelle said, placing the picture of Phillip back in her reticule.

"He has a bad karma about him," the porter said as Isabelle turned to go. She looked at him with a smile and a casual dismissal that died on her lips as she noted the intensity in the young man's eyes. "He walks with the devil."

Isabelle nodded. "I'll tread with care."

8

Isabelle swayed slightly with the movement of the train as she walked the deserted, narrow corridor. The rail lines were new, as was the car itself. For those with full pocketbooks, the transportation was fairly comfortable. Isabelle shared a compartment with Sally and Alice; it contained four bunk-style beds that certainly provided more rest than some of the train's passengers were bound to receive in their uncomfortable seats in the coach compartments. She felt fortunate. Having survived Vicksburg during the war, she didn't take luxury for granted.

When Ari had learned of the group's plans, he had, of course, insisted he come along as he had no better plans for the moment, and Alice had, of course, worn her father's will down to the point of exhaustion, thus ensuring her accompaniment. James's frustration with the situation was palpable.

Isabelle had gone so far as to pull Ari aside before they boarded the train and suggested that perhaps fewer people on the hunt for Phillip might ultimately prove more effective. Ari had responded with his usual drama that he wouldn't dream of leaving his newfound friends to face the wilds of India without his company. When she had drawn his attention to the fact that Colonel Bilbey not only knew India but was an officer of the Crown, Ari had merely sniffed in disdain and muttered something clearly unflattering under his breath in Greek.

"You do not wish me to accompany you?" he had asked her, one dark brow quirked.

"Certainly I do, certainly," she had replied, hastening to take his arm and pat it with one hand as she lightly threaded the other through to rest in the crook of his elbow. "It is only that poor Mr. Ashby worries about the safety of innocent friends as we go about searching for his brother in . . . uncertain circumstances."

"But what nonsense," Ari said, subtly pulling Isabelle closer to his side. "There is safety in numbers, no?"

She nodded her agreement and on impulse added, "Ari, I understand you conversed with Colonel Bilbey's wife several times when we were aboard the ship."

He tensed, or perhaps she had imagined it. "I did. Delightful woman."

"And so odd, her disappearance, wouldn't you agree?"

"Indeed it was. Very sobering, the way she was never found."

Isabelle considered his words and wondered why she had pushed him, albeit gently. Her warning instincts deepened with each conversation she had with the man, and now she had tipped her hand.

"But as I said," he had continued with a smile, "there is safety in numbers."

As if to underscore his comment, the entourage found themselves in cabins that lined the majority of one train car. Isabelle shared a compartment with Alice and Sally. The compartment adjoining Isabelle's housed Colonel Bilbey, Ari, and one extremely grumpy James Ashby. The compartment on the other side of the men held three additional men, the Sergeants Lyle, Linford, and Weber; they were assistants to Colonel Bilbey, sent to guarantee the safety of the group. It was three days into the journey but still too soon to determine one way or the other whether or not their company would be beneficial or bothersome. They had kept mostly to themselves. They were young and healthy and had already caught the ever-vigilant eyes of Alice and Sally, who wasted little time in bickering about them when they were alone in their compartment.

And so there they were, an unlikely bunch pulled together by a common cause, each bearing a separate agenda. Isabelle smiled to herself and shook her head in slight bemusement as she exited the car at the back and stood outside on the small balcony-like platform. The night air was warm and smelled of things exotic. She was a long,

long way from home and, oddly enough, was enjoying herself immensely.

Wrapping her hands around the rough metal railing that stood waist high, she leaned slightly out and closed her eyes, letting the night air whip through her hair and across her face. *I could travel forever,* she thought, and the notion brought forth a stab of joy she hadn't felt for a long time. *I could circle the world, and then again.* Her savings wouldn't hold out forever; she would eventually have to return to some sort of employment, but she shoved the thought aside resolutely for the moment and lost herself in the balmy Indian air.

The violent shove that caught her from behind had her tumbling over the side of the railing. The only thing keeping her from an untimely end beneath the wheels of the train was a terrific surge of adrenaline that lent strength to her arms. She pulled herself up on the railing, embracing the top with her arms and desperately seeking for purchase with her feet that kept slipping and sliding off of the shiny metal.

She pushed desperately with her feet, only to have them repeatedly snagging in her skirts and glancing off the side of the metal enclosure. As she hung on in panic, she glimpsed a dark flash of clothing behind the closing door that led to the small platform. Since she couldn't identify any specifics about the person who had shoved her over the side, it could have been anyone.

She finally gained a foothold, and with a last, desperate heave, flung one leg over the side and pulled the rest of her body up and over. Isabelle fell to the floor of the platform, her heart beating frantically, her breath coming in gasps. She felt the sting of tears, a mixture of fear and utter fury. Perhaps the worst part of the whole assault had been the fact that a personal moment to herself had been violated.

Isabelle grabbed the doorknob and pulled herself to her feet. She wrenched the door open with enough force to tear it from its hinges, although it remained remarkably intact. Making her way into the interior of the car, she moved with determined strides, ignoring the blossoming pain in both her weary arms and hands and her injured leg. She walked from one end of the car and back again, finding nobody out in the hallway. Theirs were not the only compartments in the car; there were faces she hadn't recognized as they all began settling in for the night. She went so far as to enter the adjoining car, a dining salon, to see who might be there. It was empty of all but a few servers dressed in white linen. It seemed everyone was abed for the night.

Knowing that sleep would elude her if she tried, she opted instead to stay in the deserted dining car. Seated at a table alone, she stared out the darkened window at her reflection that swayed with the gentle, rhythmic motion of the train.

* * *

Something woke James from his sleep with a violent start. He felt as though he were falling through space while the train sped by. Sitting bolt upright, he smacked his head against the ceiling of his sleeping bunk, after which he let fly a string of curses guaranteed to call forth the dead.

"I say!" Lord Banbury sat up groggily in his bunk and fumbled for his spectacles, which he promptly put on his face upside down. "What could possibly warrant . . ."

"My apologies," James muttered to Bilbey and Ari, who had also arisen and propped himself on one elbow. James waved a hand at them, a quick, irritated motion meant to assure them all was well. His attempt clearly fell short of the mark, as evidenced by Ari's narrowed eyes.

"But what is it that has you so upset, my friend?" the Greek asked him. "You worry about traveling by rail, perhaps? It can be rather alarming, to be sure. Such high speeds."

James threw a scathing look in Ari's direction as he jumped down from his bed and fumbled in the dark for his clothes. "I am not afraid of traveling by train," he said as he thrust his leg into his trousers. He didn't bother with a jacket but left the confines of the small room in his trousers and shirtsleeves alone. He absently registered the fact that he hadn't bothered with cuff links. His mother would be mortified to find him in public so shoddily dressed.

James made his way down the corridor toward the dining car, not really knowing where he was headed. He ran a trembling hand through his disheveled hair and tried to clear his mind of troublesome thoughts. Not even thoughts, really . . . thoughts he would be able to dispel with logic. It was more of an extremely unsettling *feeling* that he was unable to shake. Something had awoken him from a fairly sound slumber, and that something had rattled his nerves.

He reached the door of the dining car and peered absently through the glass after running a tired hand over his face. A movement within the car caught his eye, and he squinted at the woman seated at one of the dining tables. Perhaps it was his unsettled state of mind, but the sight of her in there at such an odd hour shot a surge of angry energy through his blood.

"Are you insane?" he growled at Isabelle after yanking the door open and stalking up to her. "What on earth are you thinking to be up at such an hour? And alone!"

"Thank you for coming to my rescue, although we will have to work a bit on your timing, I suspect." Isabelle's face was as white as a sheet, and it wasn't until he looked closely that he noticed her hands clutched tightly together on the table in front of her.

"What are you talking about?" James sat opposite Isabelle and glanced again at her hands. The side of one fingertip was smeared red with blood. He grabbed her hands and began to lift them from the table. When she pulled back in resistance, he tightened his grip on her wrist until she released her fingers. He turned her hands palm up and examined the scratches and light bruising that marred them. "What in blazes have you done to yourself?" he asked gruffly, pulling a white handkerchief from his pocket. He placed it against the biggest of the cuts on one hand and watched as the crimson color soaked into the snowy white of the fabric.

When she didn't answer him immediately, he glanced up at her face. Something in her eyes gave him pause. "Isabelle, what happened?" he asked, his tone dropping a level.

"I was just sitting here thinking that nobody has ever attacked Isabelle Webb before," she murmured. She looked out the dark window, staring. "Emma Greene, now *she* was a target. But never Isabelle."

Her conversation sent a fissure of alarm racing down his spine. She wasn't making any sense. "I don't understand," he said quietly.

Isabelle finally looked back at him. "For a good part of the past four years, I was incognito as a Southern woman named Emma Greene. People made several attempts on my life when they thought I was Emma. And I was also a woman named Bridgette Moyet. Someone tried to kill her once, too. Nobody has ever tried to kill Isabelle."

James looked at Isabelle's haunted eyes for several moments, feeling his heart thud in his chest. "Are you telling me someone just tried to kill you?"

"I believe that was the intent, yes."

His grip on her hand tightened, and he forced himself to loosen it when she involuntarily winced. "When? Where?" His tone was flat.

Isabelle inclined her head toward the car behind him. "Outside, on the back of the sleeping car. Ten minutes ago, roughly."

"Isabelle, why were you outside?"

"That's not really the point, now, is it? I should be able to go outside without fear of being pushed from the train. I went out for some fresh air and someone opened the door, very hard, and shoved me with his hands over the rail." She frowned a bit. "He must not have seen that I didn't fall. Of course, I was hanging down far enough for my feet to scrape against the ground."

James made a strangled sound in the back of his throat and leaned across the table, unconsciously gripping her hands again. "No more of this nonsense! I am sending you home!"

Isabelle laughed, and it caught him by surprise. "You're sending *me* home? I'm not yours to send home, James. And besides, to whom would you send me?" Her voice caught, and she fell silent.

"Isabelle, please. You must understand, I cannot bear your death on my conscience. This search for my brother has flown completely out of control! If something were to happen to you on my account I simply could not forgive myself."

"James, this has become very personal to me. Someone traveling on this train has just tried to get rid of me, and I am now *very* angry. I will discover who this person is, and he will live to regret it. I am not leaving."

He sighed. "Please . . ."

She cut him off with a raise of her brow and a slight tilt to her head. Her gaze was focused and unblinking, her normally golden brown eyes now nearly black. In that moment, she looked absolutely formidable, and he fell silent.

"I will not be caught unaware again," she murmured.

James eyed her for a long time before finally nodding once in assent. "Very well," he said. "For my peace of mind, however, I would like you to agree to some conditions."

Her expression turned wary. "What sort of conditions?"

"Should you feel the need to wander the train at all hours of the night, you won't do it alone. And since we don't know who might or might not be trustworthy, your likely companion will be me."

"I don't relish the thought of awakening you at midnight for a stroll."

"Then might I suggest you try to sleep?"

"What about you, kind sir? Why are *you* wandering the train at such an hour?"

James sat back in his chair, unconsciously trying to distance himself from her question. He released her hand, and she pulled it close to her body, holding the handkerchief to her palm. "I was dreaming . . . I suppose."

She nodded. "And rather than toss and turn in your bed, you felt the need to walk around a bit. That sounds familiar."

He glared at her. "*I* walking the train at night and *you* walking the train at night are two different situations entirely."

"What were you dreaming of?"

"I thought I was . . ." He stared at her face for a split second then shook his head slightly.

"Thought you were . . . ?"

"Falling from the train," he finished.

Isabelle looked at him for the space of several seconds before responding. "Odd."

"Hmm." He nodded absently and stared into the black night. All he could see was their reflections in the window. He looked back at her face and thought he could detect a smudge of dirt on her cheek that looked to have a tear track running through it. "Are you certain you are well?" he asked, his voice gruff.

She drew a shaky breath, one of the few signs she had shown as evidence of her rattled nerves. "Well enough. I believe I'm more angry than anything, which is fine, really. Anger has its uses, after all."

* * *

James sat in the darkened interior of the dining car long after escorting Isabelle back to her berth. All of the lights but one had been snuffed, and he was able to catch fleeting glimpses of the moonlit countryside as the train rolled along. He never in a million years would have dreamed he'd one day be traveling across India by rail.

He also never would have believed he'd feel a stirring of emotion and attraction toward another woman ever again. He'd been engaged once, and when it had ended badly, he had steeled himself against all but the shallowest of attachments to women in general. He trusted his own mother and few others, yet he now felt himself feeling extremely protective and more than a little territorial about one Isabelle Webb. Ironic, he mused, that he would be attracted to the one woman on earth who probably didn't need a man.

She did, though, he realized as he massaged his weary and burning eyes with his fingers. At her core she was dreadfully alone, and it twisted his stomach into knots to think of her putting a brave face on for the entire world, even for herself, and to know that she hurt internally. He wished he could claim his growing feelings for her were little more than pity. He knew his life would be much simpler if he could truthfully say he merely felt sorry for her and leave it at that. He had only to examine his instinctive reaction every time Ari wandered a bit too close to her, though, or leered at her with that wolfish smile, to know that it wouldn't be long before he found himself bowing and scraping to her every whim and assaulting any man who so much as said hello to her.

Pity, indeed. He shook his head and even smiled a bit. If he so much as thought to offer her pity, she'd likely hurl it back in his face—undoubtedly with a sarcastic, double-layered comment that would take some time to decipher.

His smile faded as he thought of the attempt on her life. It didn't make sense. Who would want her dead, or would benefit from it? Were enemies from her former life as a spy dogging her footsteps? Perhaps someone was trying to get at him by harming her. Whatever the reason, the whole experience left a bitter taste in his mouth, and he dared the fool to try it again. From that point forward, Isabelle wasn't going to leave his side.

* * *

"So I said to my parents, 'I simply must take this holiday in India.' They could hardly refuse, after all. I am a grown man, no?" Ari was talking to the women at the breakfast table as though he were the center of the universe. James choked down some curry-laden food, swallowing it with a swig of something warm from his teacup. The Greek man's arrogance knew no bounds, and James was tired of his theatrics.

As for Isabelle, she looked pale. Amazingly enough, however, if he hadn't known better, he'd think she was feeling perfectly normal, as though an attempt on her life hadn't been made a mere seven hours earlier. She appeared to be hanging on Ari's every word, and James might have believed she *was* if he didn't notice her hand clenched tightly in her lap. It was the hand that had sustained the most cuts during her "mishap," and he wanted to take it and smooth her fingers open, forcing her to relax.

Isabelle laughed lightly at something Ari said, something James was sure was idiotic and inane, and she made a comment meant to flatter in return. It worked, for Ari beamed at her. James wanted to shove him right out of the dining car. He envisioned hauling the man up by his lapels and hurling him out the door and into the adjoining car. It brought a fleeting moment of satisfaction that had him smirking.

"Ah, so you agree with me then, my American friend?" Ari was asking him.

"I don't presume to know what you're talking about," James answered.

"But you haven't been listening to this jovial conversation?"

"I confess, I find myself distracted."

"Indeed. Such loveliness at this table. It does rather dull the senses." Ari glanced at the women seated around him and smiled with his large, white teeth.

Alice and Sally smiled back at the man and truly batted their eyelashes, a gimmick James had thought was in reality little more than a parlor trick. Women really did this?

Isabelle looked at him, her head turning away from the others. Her expression was neutral, nearly unreadable except for the slight flare of her nostrils that told him she was irritated. The knowledge sent a warm glow spiraling down through the pit of his stomach, and he smiled at her in genuine camaraderie.

He leaned forward and lightly tapped her arm, which rested on the arm of her chair. "Unclench your fist," he murmured.

She glanced down at her lap in some surprise and slowly released her fingers, wincing slightly. The cuts and bruises on her palm were ugly and decidedly darker than they'd been hours before. "Didn't realize I was doing that," she whispered.

"It surely did not feel good."

"Kept me focused, most likely," she said, glancing at him in some apparent chagrin at having been caught being less than perfect. He shook his head and opened his mouth to reply when Ari leaned toward them.

"I was just asking the young ladies if they are packed and ready to disembark. We arrive at Barrackpore in less than an hour," Ari said.

James reluctantly turned his attention to the Greek. "And are they packed? Or perhaps you require that I ask them?"

"Mercy," Isabelle muttered under her breath.

"Why no, sir," Ari said, his tone darkening a shade. "I try to draw you into our conversation, this is all."

"I was speaking with Miss Webb."

"Ah, but sir," Ari laughed, "at a table full of other diners, such is impolite."

"Not when she is seated directly by my side."

"But I am bereft for even a moment without her attention," Ari said, again turning his brilliant smile to its best advantage on Isabelle.

"I've known Isabelle for some time," James said, feeling his anger smolder.

"Indeed? I was under the impression that—"

"I don't much care which impressions you found yourself under, Mr. Kilronomos. I will speak with Isabelle privately whenever I wish to do so. Doesn't much matter to me if we're in a crowd or alone."

Ari stiffened perceptibly. "I wouldn't expect a tradesman to be concerned with a woman's reputation," he said. "Speaking to women unchaperoned is grossly inappropriate."

"She's not a child."

"Enough," Isabelle said, rising from the table. The men rose abruptly with her. "Gentlemen, I need to pack. And Ari, as you correctly ascertained, so do the young ladies." Isabelle made a quick motion with her hand that had Alice and Sally jumping to their feet and moving toward the door. "Mr. Ashby, a word."

He nodded and threw his napkin onto the table, following her from the dining car. He barely resisted the impulse to turn and shoot Ari a look of triumph. Isabelle was irritated, yes, but who was leaving the dining car with her?

"Don't say it," he muttered as he walked beside Isabelle and placed a hand under her elbow. "I understand what you're trying to accomplish, but frankly I wouldn't be surprised to find he was the one who pushed you overboard last night."

"Shh," she said quickly and cast a quick glance at the girls who walked in front of them.

"You haven't told Sally?" he murmured.

Isabelle shook her head. "I don't want her to worry."

His lips pressed into a thin line. "I don't know that it's wise to leave her in the dark. She needs to be on her guard."

Isabelle slowed their pace and waved the girls forward when they glanced back. "James," she said, pausing, "she's had so much worry lately . . ."

James increased the pressure on her elbow slightly and stopped their progress. His fingers trailed their way from her elbow to her wrist, finally capturing her fingers in a light grasp. He turned her palm over and traced a fingertip along a particularly nasty scrape. "Didn't you once tell me that the reason the two of you were so adversarial when you first met was because you were harsh with her about the necessity of caring well for herself?"

Her breath caught, and when he glanced at her face, he felt a surge of male satisfaction at the glazed look in her eyes. His lips twitched when she attempted to formulate a response. She wasn't a woman who responded to empty flattery or charm. The knowledge that he'd given her pause was heady, and for a moment he forgot his brother, Sally, and the situation as a whole.

Isabelle blinked once, and her fingers curled. She tried to pull her hand free, but he merely smiled and tightened his grip on her wrist. With utmost care, he slowly lowered his lips to her palm and gently placed a feather-light kiss on the ugly scratch.

"What did you say to me?" Isabelle asked him when he lifted his head. She was no longer fighting to free her hand.

He smiled. "Tell Sally to be careful."

* * *

Isabelle scowled as she threw a few things into her trunk. "Tell Sally to be careful indeed," she muttered. Be careful of men who are entirely too handsome for their own good. She was hard-pressed to remember the last time she'd felt such a stirring for any one man in particular. This one was different, though. He had substance, and she admired his work ethic and fortitude.

She also particularly enjoyed the way his well-muscled physique filled the lines of his suitcoat.

"Honestly!" Isabelle scowled at the book in her hand as one rough corner caught the edge of one of her cuts. It oozed a fresh drop of blood, and she tossed the book into her traveling case with a curse. Placing her hand to her mouth, she sucked on the drop of blood and turned to find Sally watching her with one brow cocked.

"Paper cut?" Sally asked.

Isabelle shook her head and pulled her hand from her mouth, examining the cut. "I slipped this morning on the platform outside the sleeping car," she said. "Caught myself on those iron rails."

Sally marched over to Isabelle's side and held out one hand, palm flat. "Let me see."

"No, it's fine."

"Let me see."

Isabelle sighed and placed her hand in Sally's. Sally's eyes widened, and she let out a squeak. "Belle! What on earth were you doing to slip enough that your hands are such a mess?"

"I lost my footing. Those metal platforms are rather slick."

Sally's eyes found Isabelle's and began to narrow fractionally. "You're lying to me."

"I beg your pardon. I most certainly am not."

"Isabelle Webb, that you can look me in the face and lie like this is an absolute disgrace."

"Sally, why would I lie to you?"

"Oh! Look at you! All innocence, not even a blink of the eye! Well, I have news for you, Miss Webb, you may have fooled the Confederacy, but you don't fool me."

"For goodness' sake." Isabelle snatched her hand back and continued tossing things into her trunk.

"You see?" Sally moved around to the other side of the trunk, which stood open on the floor. "One needn't have known you for long to realize how meticulous you are. You're flustered! You're just throwing things into that trunk all pell-mell, no rhyme nor reason. Isabelle, you did *not* slip!"

"I most certainly did slip!" Isabelle slammed the lid of the trunk closed. "Sally, I swear to you on my life that this happened out on the platform while I was grabbing the railing."

"You don't slip!" Sally's voice rose substantially. Isabelle was sure that by now half the train could hear them.

"I am recovering from a broken femur!"

"Oh, there you go, trying to disguise the truth with crudity!" Sally's eyes, though angry and defiant, clouded with tears. She sucked in a shuddering breath. "Belle, for the love of heaven, *what happened?*"

Isabelle sank down on the bed, knowing she could not continue to blur the truth without breaking stride, at least not any more than she already had by becoming agitated. Darn the girl, Sally knew her too well. It was true that Isabelle would never have packed sloppily had she not been distracted.

She had been completely truthful and honest with so few people in her life that to give everything away, even small, inconsequential things, left her feeling vulnerable. It was true enough—she didn't want Sally to worry. It was also true, however, that Isabelle had become a solitary creature out of necessity. She never shared much and rarely depended on anyone but herself.

Isabelle sighed and shrugged her shoulders. "I was on the platform early this morning and someone pushed me over the side of the railing," she said.

Sally stared at her, speechless.

"So I pulled myself back up and over the side. The railing is rough underneath—I cut myself a bit." Isabelle shrugged again. "I didn't want you to worry about this."

Sally moved around the trunk and sat next to Isabelle on the bed. She didn't say a word but put both of her arms around Isabelle's shoulders and pulled her close. Isabelle was too stunned to react. She had expected more yelling, perhaps something a bit more theatrical.

I am tired, Isabelle admitted and allowed herself the small luxury of placing her head on Sally's shoulder. *I am very tired.*

"Who is the enemy, then?" Sally whispered as she held Isabelle.

"I'm not certain yet." Isabelle closed her eyes.

"This is most vexing."

"Yes, it is." Isabelle eventually lifted her head and pulled back to look at Sally's face. Sally dropped her arms and instead reached for Isabelle's hands. "I don't want you to be afraid," Isabelle told her. "We can continue on our own way, if you wish. This holiday was supposed to be a joyful thing for you."

Sally looked at her with eyes that were equally weary. For such a young woman, she had seen too much suffering for her soul not to have aged. "I was enjoying every moment until now. Nothing is worth risking your safety, Belle."

"I'm not worried about my safety."

"I think you should be."

Isabelle shook her head. "Might have been an accident. One never can be sure about such things."

"It doesn't seem like much of an accident to shove someone from a speeding train. Do you want to leave James and continue alone, Belle?"

The thought of leaving James made Isabelle wince, and Sally held up her hand. "Say no more. We stay."

"I didn't say anything at all," Isabelle said.

"Yes, my friend, you did."

9

"They definitely stayed here, sir," Sergeant Linford said to Lord Banbury. "They poked around our officers' headquarters asking questions about the rebellion, and the landlady here confirmed it. She said they also visited the temple across the way. Went into it at least three times."

Isabelle scrutinized the chawl in which Phillip and Sparks had apparently stayed. It was small, nondescript, and seemed clean from the outside. They were in eastern India, and the countryside was laden with dense swamps, reportedly home to Royal Bengal tigers. The vegetation was thick, lush, and beautiful—the result of extreme humidity and clement temperatures.

Sally employed the use of a paper fan purchased from a vendor and tugged a bit at her bodice. "Feels rather like the deep South," she murmured to Isabelle, "only more so."

"Absolutely *beastly* is what it feels like," Alice said. "It's as though we're underwater!"

"Much as I hate to," Sally said in her light drawl, "I must agree." The girls eyed each other for a moment in an uneasy truce.

Isabelle fought a smile, flipping open her own fan and straining to overhear Sergeant Linford's comments to Bilbey and James. The sergeant had lowered his voice and his face flushed beet red as he glanced at the women. Her curiosity climbing, she watched as Colonel Bilbey's mouth dropped open in apparent shock and James's eyebrows shot skyward. Bilbey looked at James in discomfort, and Isabelle heard him say, "Might just be easier to tell them they aren't allowed to come in at all."

James shook his head slightly and made eye contact with Isabelle. He walked toward the women, looking decidedly grim. He motioned his head to one side, and Isabelle moved away from Sally and Alice. "What is it?" she asked him.

He scratched his head, wincing. "There, ah, is apparently a rule about women entering the temple."

"We're not allowed? I told you such might be the case."

"Weeeeeell," James said, "you are allowed, but not at certain times."

"Certain times of day?" Isabelle watched him in bemusement, wondering why he wouldn't look her in the eye. He stared off into the distance, chewing on his lip.

"More like certain times of the month, I would say."

Isabelle's mouth fell open, and then she laughed, soon bending over double. "Oh, you poor men," she choked out and glanced over at Bilbey and his sergeants, who were looking all the more conspicuous in their attempts at inconspicuousness. She grabbed James's arm to steady herself and finally stopped laughing.

"Well, I am glad you find our discomfort so amusing!" James ground the words out from between clenched teeth. "And you might control yourself a bit."

"Are you chastening me about propriety?" Isabelle began laughing again. "Ah, yes, I forget. Your mama raised a gentleman."

"My mama certainly never tutored me on how to broach a subject such as this," he hissed. "Isabelle, really!"

"Oh, James, my apologies. I'm probably the only person on the face of the earth gauche enough to find amusement in this. No, I forgot about my friend Anne. She would definitely be amused. I shall have to write her immediately."

"You do that, Isabelle. And in the meantime, *hush!*"

"Anne disguised herself as a man so she could enlist in the war and have a reporter's firsthand story. I never did ask her how she handled her own awkward moments . . ."

James muttered something that sounded suspiciously like a curse and pulled Isabelle farther down the dusty road. "I can see you need lessons in decorum."

Isabelle placed a hand on her midsection and drew a breath. She had tamed her laughter for the moment. "Oh, I know all I need to about decorum," she said. "I've dined in America's finest homes and danced in her finest ballrooms. James," she said, and laid a hand alongside his cheek, "I am so very sorry for embarrassing you."

His lips twitched a fraction, and he closed his eyes, shaking his head. "Then why are you still smiling?"

"Because I find this very funny. A group of big, strong men who could probably each hold his own in a good brawl . . ." she paused, looking at Ari. "*Probably*, I said, and each of you reduced to stammering school boys at the thought of discussing such a matter." She sighed. "And yes, it's true—most women would be discreet enough to blush. But I, unfortunately, am not most women."

"Understated," James muttered.

Isabelle reached up on tiptoe and placed a kiss on James's cheek. "Bless you for being a gentleman," she said. "The world has too few."

When Isabelle and James returned to the group and proceeded toward the temple, the men studiously avoided looking at her and spoke earnestly to each other instead. Isabelle pulled the two young women back as they reached the arches and motioned the men ahead. They appeared all too happy to oblige.

"What is happening?" Alice asked. "Why all the laughing and blushing?"

"Because, ladies, we are apparently unwelcome in this temple if any of us happens to be experiencing her monthlies."

Their mouths dropped open in perfect unison, but Sally recovered first, reacting much as Isabelle had, her laughter a bit more horrified. "He had to *tell* you that?"

Alice narrowed her eyes, blushing herself, and scowled at the temple. "Why on earth would they care? Are we going to defile it or some such?"

Isabelle shook her head and shrugged. "I don't know. I suppose we would be considered unclean. The status of women in this country isn't exactly . . ." Isabelle trailed off. "I daresay you've experienced some of it," she said to Alice.

Alice shook her head. "Not so much. I associate only with the British civilians and military."

"Well, ladies, are we to proceed?"

Both girls nodded. "I'll not defile their temple this week," Sally said.

"Nor shall I," Alice added. "Although I admit I'd like to."

Isabelle glanced at the girl with a smile as she guided them through the front arches. Alice possessed pluck that could be channeled in the right direction by a mentor, had someone a mind to do so. Isabelle's satisfaction deepened as Sally agreed with the Alice, and they seemed to form a tenuous companionship over the issue as they moved, still muttering, into the beauty of the Indian temple. "Be respectful," she whispered to the young women, who merely glowered at her in return. "To others it's sacred."

* * *

James walked around the perimeter of the room, taking in the stunning detail in color and symbolism. The outside of the temple was square in foundation, its walls terra-cotta and ornately decorated. Arches adorned the exterior walls, and passing through them led to outer corridors and inner arches that fed into the main body of the temple. There were four large, square-based spires that rose from each roof corner and one large dome in the center. Everywhere the eye fell, it saw carvings of foliage, flowers, and scenes from the Lord Krishna's daily life.

A young Indian native stood across the room, speaking to a small group of Europeans. He was a Brahmin. Because of his high caste, he was allowed into the temple while older men who were of a lower caste were not. Colonel Bilbey explained as much to James while they waited for the young man to join them and answer some questions.

"Supposedly, this man has been here at the temple for the last several days. If anyone will remember your brother and his companion, I suspect it will be him," Bilbey told James.

James watched the man, who moved and spoke with an easy grace. He seemed completely comfortable conversing with the visitors. When James mentioned as much to Bilbey, the colonel nodded.

"A definite product of British influence," the man said, his tone neutral.

"You must be proud," James said, watching Bilbey's reaction.

Bilbey glanced at James and paused before responding. "Not exactly. You see, Governor Lord Canning is a personal friend of mine, if you understand my meaning."

"I'm sorry. I'm not familiar with the man."

Bilbey sighed. "It's just as well. He does not speak for the majority." When James remained silent, Bilbey continued. "After the Sepoy Rebellion, retribution was swift and brutal. Most considered it just. After all, innocent British civilians, including women and children, had been slaughtered. But it became more . . ." Bilbey shook his head. "The retribution was . . . excessive. I was here. I saw it happen, and as a commander of my own troops, well . . . I should just say that I'm fortunate to still hold my command. I began ignoring orders."

"Orders of restraint?"

Bilbey laughed. "Orders of restraint would have been a welcome thing. No, on the contrary. And I wrote home, suggesting we reign in the madness. Canning agreed with me, and he was openly derided. 'Clemency Canning' they called him."

James looked again at the well-spoken man across the room. "So you feel the British presence here is inappropriate?"

"I don't feel the need to obliterate their culture by supplanting our own. We are killing what they are in so many ways . . ."

James looked at Bilbey, at the rise in the man's color and the odd intensity in his eyes. He looked again at the young Indian man and back at Bilbey. The Indian didn't seem any worse for the wear, and James said as much to Bilbey.

Bilbey nodded. "Yes, it's true, he converses well with the Western world; he knows Western history and is cultured and educated by our standards. But he has also studied from British-produced books that teach him that his own culture has little merit to it, that it is substandard, and that his history shows a lack of intelligence of his people as a whole."

"And I presume that you do not subscribe to this theory."

"Indeed, I do not. Mine is not the popular opinion, however." Bilbey's jaw clenched, and he was silent for a moment. "I had a friend, a dear friend and her child . . ." He closed his mouth as the young Indian finally made his way toward them.

"Dear sir, I am sorry to have kept you waiting," the man said, extending his hand to Lord Banbury.

"Not at all," Bilbey said. "Allow me to introduce my companion, Mr. James Ashby."

James shook the man's hand and returned the affable smile. The man's name was Mohandas. They exchanged pleasantries, and James commented on the beauty of the temple. Eventually, Bilbey broached their reason for seeking the man out.

Mohandas's smile slipped a bit. "I do indeed remember them," he said. "They seemed on the trail of something extremely outlandish."

"Is it something of which you have never heard, then?" James asked. "This Jewel of Zeus?"

Mohandas's eyes widened substantially, and he laughed, placing a hand on either man's arm and guiding them from the room. "Perhaps we should discuss such things outside," he said, quickening his pace.

"I meant no offense," James said, catching Isabelle's surprised glance as they passed her on the way out. "I fear I've said something inappropriate."

"No, no, my friend," Mohandas said and stopped walking as they reached the outer corridor. "I take no offense." He drew a deep breath and smiled again. "This pair of which you speak—they were looking for something, this Jewel of . . . of . . ."

"Zeus?" James supplied.

Mohandas's smile slipped yet again. "You think me foolish. 'Tis only that . . . you must understand . . ."

"We do understand," Bilbey said quietly. "Things that have brought about unhappiness are not to be trifled with, even in casual conversation."

Mohandas's face held a measure of surprise before he slowly nodded. "People have died asking for this thing. People who possess it die . . . At least, this is what I have heard."

"Why is that, do you suppose?" James asked in an undertone, glancing up as people passed by them on their way into the temple.

Mohandas pulled them farther into the shadows of the corridor. "Greed," he whispered. "Greed will kill everything if it is allowed."

"You don't believe a . . . mystical, unexplainable force is at work?" James asked.

"It doesn't much matter, does it? Dead is dead."

"I suppose I just . . ." James raked a hand through his sweat-dampened hair in frustration. "I want to know what we're fighting."

"I believe people want the jewel, and they are often willing to kill to obtain it," Mohandas whispered. "Greed is the mystical force of which you speak. Often it motivates where little else will."

"But the jewel itself! What does owning it do for a person?"

Mohandas shrugged. "I suppose only the owner would be able to answer that." He pursed his lips for a moment as if torn in thought. "There seems to be a common thread among the owners of the jewel," he said. "A marking that they all possess but of which few are aware."

"What kind of marking?" James asked.

"A mark from birth. On the lower back, to the left of the spine. A mark in the shape of a five pointed star." Mohandas regained his smile. "I only tell you these things to be of service, you understand. To help you find your brother. Only an extremely superstitious person would believe such nonsense."

James leaned up against the wall of the temple and tried to catch his breath. He vaguely registered Bilbey thanking Mohandas for his time and bidding him farewell. As he followed the colonel around the corridor and under the archway that led to the outside sky, he could think only of the birthmark that adorned his brother's lower back, to the left of his spine.

* * *

Isabelle examined the interior of the carved and intricately detailed walls of the temple, wondering what in the world would have induced Sparks to visit the place three times. While she wasn't well versed in the Indian carvings, she was relatively certain that none of them included scenes from Greek mythology.

"Perhaps you have some questions I can answer?"

Isabelle turned to see the young Indian native who had escorted James and Bilbey from the temple as she had entered. She smiled at him. "I am absolutely in awe of this building," she said. "It is an incredible work of art."

The young man inclined his head slightly. "I am pleased you find it so."

Isabelle paused. "I do have a rather . . . delicate question, I suppose."

He nodded for her to continue.

"Nearly ten years ago, when your country experienced her trouble with the British . . ." She paused again, genuinely worrying about offending him. "I've heard . . . that is . . . I've read . . . I understand that many places of value to the Indian people were taken over, ransacked, even."

The young man's face remained neutral, and he nodded. "It is true," he said. "It was an ugly time."

"And this one? Was it left largely unscathed?"

He glanced over his shoulder then looked back at her with a smile. "I do not like to criticize. And forgive me, but you travel with an officer of the Crown."

"Oh, no," Isabelle said, chagrined. "I am not probing or asking questions for the colonel." She took a breath and lowered her voice. "Forgive me, but we are looking for my friend's brother, and they spent considerable time in this temple. I believe they are visiting scenes where the rebellion was the most prevalent, and I'm wondering if he was looking for something he might have thought had been hidden here."

"And this thing for which they search—why would it be in here?"

"I don't know," Isabelle admitted. "I'm trying to understand their actions with very little information at my disposal."

The man looked at her for the space of several heartbeats before responding. "There was considerable British activity here during the rebellion," he said. "There were things taken from the temple that were never returned, and during the space of several months, soldiers 'visited' this and other temples on a regular basis. So this man you seek—it may well be that he assumed someone left the object of his quest at a temple such as this."

"And was it ever here? The object of his quest? As a place of safe-keeping perhaps?"

He took her arm and guided her toward the outer corridor, much as she had seen him do with James and Bilbey. Once out of the inner rooms, he turned to her. "I was but a child at the time. And of course there were rumors, but I certainly cannot say whether or not it was here."

"But it's not here now."

"No. It is not here now."

Isabelle locked her gaze onto his deeply brown eyes. "Do you know where it is?"

"No. And if I did, I would go to my grave denying it. I do not believe the curse is in speaking of it. I believe the curse is in the possessing of it."

"Why? What does it do?"

"It brings to the surface the worst parts of a person's soul."

Isabelle squinted at him. "Then why . . ."

"Isabelle, there you are!" Sally and Alice approached the pair in a huff. "You should have told us you were ready to leave."

The young man backed away from Isabelle with a light bow. "Thank you for your visit," he said with his bright smile, and he disappeared back under the inner arches.

10

Isabelle and James walked along the road in silence. The vegetation was thick around them in the jungle. She carried a parasol, which would be largely ineffectual should the rains descend again, and James walked with his hands thrust deeply into his pockets. An even deeper frown was etched into his face, and while Isabelle was curious, she didn't press.

"The rain leaves the world smelling fresh," she commented, deeply inhaling. "And I do believe this humidity has my hair curling." She glanced at him, noted his distracted nod, and put her hand through the crook of his elbow.

James looked at her in apology. "I'm sorry. I'm hardly fit company—I shouldn't have suggested I come along and ruin your excursion."

"Nonsense. You're not ruining anything." The woman at the European-styled boarding house where the group was staying suggested they visit the tea gardens down the road if they were looking for something beautiful to experience before leaving Barrackpore. The extreme humidity, a prior downpour sent from celestial buckets, and general fatigue had most of the group resting in their beds. When Isabelle mentioned she wanted to see the gardens, James had offered to join her. In truth, she was glad for the time alone with him.

Isabelle glanced skyward. "With any luck, it won't rain again until we return. Oh, look, there's the bungalow." To the right, set back a bit from the main road sat a tea planter's bungalow, very European in style. It was one of several tea estates in eastern India, established roughly fifteen years earlier in an effort by the British to provide tea for the British market.

"According to our housekeeper, the bungalow houses the tea planter and his family, and the estates themselves become small communities. This one has its own shops and schools for the people who work here." Isabelle hailed a young woman who was standing out in front of the home and asked permission to wander the grounds. The woman nodded, and Isabelle and James proceeded around the back.

The thick jungle vegetation had been cleared to allow for rows upon rows of tea plants. It was late in the afternoon, and much of the picking had already been done for the day, but women were still visible, working in the waning light. The aroma was rich and flavorful—a combination of herbs, earth, and the recent rainfall had Isabelle closing her eyes in appreciation.

"What a heavenly place," Isabelle murmured as they began walking along the edges of the planting field. "Now, isn't this a perfect setting for unburdening one's soul?"

James sighed. He pulled his hand from his pocket and slipped it into hers, linking their fingers. Her thrill at his touch was eclipsed as he closed his eyes briefly and she caught genuine signs of worry on his face. She'd grown accustomed to the anger; his concern was somehow more alarming.

"James, what is it?"

"It's worse than I believed. Sparks is a fanatic."

"We suspected as much."

James looked at her. He stopped walking and glanced around, seeming unsure. Isabelle pulled him away from the gardens and into the thick undergrowth edging the field. There were unsettling noises as small creatures scuttled about, and Isabelle chose to ignore the prospect of snakes. James seemed so unlike himself suddenly that she wanted to shut away the whole world.

"There's nobody else here," she said, restlessly shaking his hand. "What has you so worried?"

"Mohandas told me that the previous owners of this bloody jewel have all borne a peculiar birthmark on their lower backs. My brother has one that matches the description. I don't know how Sparks discovered it, but it's obvious to me that he thinks Phillip is the key to his quest." He ran an agitated hand across the back of his neck. "I've tried to shrug off the superstition, but it just keeps mounting. Everyone we talk to about this is afraid, and I'm beginning to believe there might be sound reason for it."

"James, the jewel will not kill your brother."

"No, but people who want it will. Isabelle, I grow more uncomfortable by the day. Someone has already tried to kill you. This is not mere child's play, and I worry about what will happen next. I'm considering telling Bilbey about the attempt on your life."

"No. We don't know who we can trust. I daresay it wasn't Bilbey, but we don't know his men well. As much as I've tried, I cannot get a proper feel for them. Besides, I'm relatively certain I know who is behind all of this chaos. Other than Sparks, that is."

"Ari?"

She nodded. "I don't know what he stands to gain, but I haven't trusted him from the moment I saw him watching you in Bombay."

"But why would he want you dead? And why are you not more afraid?"

Isabelle smiled. "I'm always afraid. It keeps me aware." She sighed a bit. "Just before we left Bombay, I all but accused him of having something to do with Lady Banbury's disappearance. My guess is that I was hitting perhaps too close to the mark for his comfort. My one consolation is that should anything ever happen to me, Pinkerton would use his resources to hunt down the man responsible and set up the gallows himself."

James shook his head with a slight roll of the eyes, and the familiar anger crossed his features. Oddly enough, it was comforting. "Forgive me, Isabelle, but I find that small consolation. Pinkerton should have kept you at home where you were safe."

At that, Isabelle laughed out loud, and James's mouth turned up in a reluctant smile. "I'm safer here," she said. "And I'd rather be traveling with my enemy than wondering where he might turn up next."

James sobered. "If you leave now, he'll have no reason to turn up again. You're in danger because of me."

"We've had this conversation before. I'm not going away." Isabelle paused. "Do you want me to? Leave?"

The light continued to fade from the countryside. His dark hair, dampened by sweat, combined with the emotion that lined his face made him look formidable. The piercing blue of his eyes stood out from the tanned skin of his face and the darkening green of the foliage around them. "No," he admitted, his voice barely audible. "And in that I disappoint myself."

She moved a step closer, thinking to embrace him, when a sound to her left had the hair on her neck standing up in warning. "We should go," she said. "This is tiger country." She nearly expected to hear a growl and see a flash of white fangs emerge from the dim light, but all was still, so they slowly made their way back to the edge of the undergrowth and the tea fields.

* * *

The rooms in which the group stayed were simply furnished, and Isabelle had little trouble finding Ari's personal belongings later that night while Ari himself was sitting on a verandah to the back of the establishment in the courtyard area having tea with Bilbey and the other officers. The fact that she had broken into Ari's room without his knowledge bothered her conscience little. She knew he was up to no good; the problem lay in proving it to be true.

She picked the lock on his trunk without leaving a telltale scratch. The trunk held his clothing, toiletries, perfumed tonics of which there were plenty, and a small, leather-bound book. She grasped the book and gently lowered the lid of the trunk, making her way to the window and the light of the moon.

Upon closer inspection, she found that the book contained notes, addresses, lists of travel items, and miscellaneous comments, some in

Greek and many in English. A good portion of the book had been used, and she looked to the most recent entries hoping to find something that might give her a clue as to his doings.

Ari had listed an address in Bombay, along with a name: Siri Hinshaska. Further perusal had her heart increasing its rhythm, for a few pages later showed a listing for an inn in London. The establishment wasn't named, but she knew it anyway by its address. It was the Pembroke. She looked closer to be certain she wasn't mistaken. The light was dim and the writing hastily scrawled, but there was no mistaking the address.

Had he been following her from London? Or was it James he had been pursuing? Another page showed the name of the steamship that had borne them from London to Bombay, with their exact departure date and the number of a stateroom, presumably Ari's. Isabelle flipped back to the address in Bombay and did her best to commit as many of his notes as possible to memory. She wished for the luxury of time and a pen and paper to copy the information but had to be satisfied with the fact that she'd gained access to his room.

Spoke too soon, she mused as she heard footsteps in the hall. Ari was just outside the door, talking with someone in an undertone. She quickly dashed back across the room and placed the book exactly where she'd found it in the trunk. She then closed the trunk again and locked it.

The room was on the second floor. Just outside the window was a sloped overhang that shaded the rooms below, and she'd checked the specifics carefully before entering. James's room was below Ari's, and she hadn't told him of her plans. She was nearly as anxious to avoid him as she was the Greek.

Isabelle had chosen her clothing well. Wearing the dark blue, lightweight cotton Indian clothing she had purchased in Bombay gave her much more freedom of movement. Making her way back to the window, she noiselessly slid it open and put one leg out on the ledge.

She was about to hoist herself through the window when she heard the person speaking to Ari raise his voice. Ari shushed the man and continued in a low undertone. Balancing the need to overhear the conversation with her need to escape the room, Isabelle hovered for a moment in the window, straining her ears.

"I have no choice," Ari was saying. "She has powerful allies . . . can't risk it . . . "

"So now ye're thinking to go through with that insane alternate plan?" his companion said in return. "I'm taking all the risks by doing your every whim!"

"The risk to you is minimal. I have a contact in Egypt who will pay handsomely. He deals in special . . . trade."

Isabelle focused intently on the other voice, trying to place it. It eluded her, and she wished the window were closer to the door.

"Besides," Ari continued, "the Crown is beginning to find her conscience about what happened in '57."

"So now it's to be blackmail, is it?"

"Your choice." Ari rattled his key in the lock, and Isabelle slipped through the window, closing it quietly behind her. She braced herself carefully against the wall and held her breath, waiting for what seemed an eternity before the lamp Ari lit upon entering was finally extinguished.

Isabelle winced as she cautiously shifted her weight and prepared to quietly slide to the edge of the overhang. Once there, she planned to lower herself over the side and drop the remaining five feet or so to the ground. She didn't relish the prospect of landing wrong on her healing leg, but the mental specters she faced were far worse than the physical pain was bound to be.

As if on cue, her wounded thigh screamed in protest at the movement after holding itself so long in such an awkward position. She bit her lip to keep from groaning aloud and clutched her leg with her hand. Without warning, her foot slid out from beneath her, and she tumbled down the overhang and over the side, only just stopping her fall by grabbing the ledge with one hand.

Stunned and swinging from the ledge by sheer will and her fingertips, she found herself facing an equally stunned James, who had his hand pulled back and was ready to punch his intruder. Stopping his fist midpunch, he stumbled forward a bit and instead reached up and grabbed her about the waist just as Ari's window opened above.

Isabelle put a frantic finger to her lips, her eyes huge in agitation as she clutched James's shoulders. She motioned toward the door that led to his room, and he took her there, closing the door quietly behind them after setting her unceremoniously on the floor.

"What in *blazes* are you doing?" he growled at her.

"Shhhh," she said, closing her eyes briefly. "Please!" She pointed up at Ari's room with a shake of her head. She began to pace, limping. "This stupid leg!" she said, still whispering. "Honestly, I'd be better off with a wooden one."

"Isabelle, I'm trying very hard to understand, but I find myself at a total loss," James said to her in low undertones. "What were you doing on the roof?"

"I was in Ari's room," she admitted. "He was drinking tea with the colonel, so I took a moment to go through his things."

James stared at her.

"It wasn't a total loss, despite the fact that he now probably knows I was in there. Wretched, wretched leg!" That she was comfortable enough around James to be so crude as to make reference to a leg spoke volumes about the level to which their relationship had progressed. Were she relaxed and feeling fairly contemplative, she would have considered it from every possible angle. As it was, all she could do was wish for a reversal in time. How could she have fallen from the roof?!

"Isabelle! What—" James broke his statement at the sound of a firm knock on his door.

Looking around the room for a place to hide, Isabelle ran to stand behind a changing screen in the corner.

Isabelle tried to still her breathing behind the screen and calm the pounding of her heart. She was absolutely furious with herself. Her mental litany was harsh: *Mistakes like these will find you dead . . . Mistakes like these will find your president dead . . .* She choked on the bile that suddenly rose in her throat, putting a hand over her mouth to still the noise.

It was Ari at the door. Isabelle's nostrils flared in distaste at the sound of his voice. "I know something just fell from the roof above your verandah," he was saying to James. "It was just outside my bedroom window. I heard something slide down."

"I don't know what it would have been," James answered him. "You know this place is full of animals. Perhaps something scuttled down—"

"And then jumped to the ground?"

"Mr. Kilronomos, do you see anything out there? Look out the window. I certainly don't see anything. If you're nervous, we can go outside together and look."

"I am not nervous!" The offense in Ari's voice was clear. "Mr. Ashby, I believe you were up on the roof!"

"Why would I be on the roof?" There was a deadly calm to James's voice that Isabelle had come to recognize. Ari was a foolish man.

"To look into my room, perhaps?"

"Are you mad, man? Why on earth would I want to look in your room? You are wasting my time, and I wish to retire for the evening. Don't bother me with this again."

Isabelle heard the door slam and put a hand to her midsection, trying to calm her nausea. Her eyes closed, and she felt the hated sting of tears that never did her any good. She rarely cried, and much to her dismay, she couldn't seem to stem the flow.

James approached her from the other side of the screen, and she felt him watching her for a moment before his arms gathered her close to his chest. It was her undoing, and she quietly released her frustration and fear. "Twice, now, I've fallen. I cannot afford such mistakes," she whispered against his shirt front.

"Isabelle, why did you do it?"

"We need information. It's what I do, what I *did*. It's all I am," she quietly cried. "If I can't do this, what will I do?"

"Isabelle, I don't believe your body is entirely healed. You're asking the impossible of yourself. And you're tying me in knots. How could you go into that man's room, believing he tried to kill you?"

"I knew he wasn't there and probably wouldn't be for some time." Isabelle took the handkerchief James reached into his pocket to hand her. Wiping her nose and eyes, she willed the tears to stop falling and failed. "I knew what to look for and knew how to get out quickly. You don't understand, James. I am not inept. This is unacceptable for me."

"Isabelle, you're a bright woman," James said quietly, placing his hands on her shoulders and forcing her to look at his eyes. "You're asking too much of a wound that hasn't properly healed. Besides which, you're allowed to make mistakes. No one on this earth is perfect."

"People die when I make mistakes," she said, her throat burning. The need to lose her dinner was overwhelming, and she was afraid she might disgrace herself in front of James. He led her to a settee and motioned for her to sit. Taking another handkerchief from his traveling case, he dipped it in a basin of cool water and wrung it out. He then approached her again and squatted down next to her, washing her face with the cloth and then folding it and placing it on the back of her neck.

The show of compassion made her tears flow afresh, and Isabelle muttered a curse. James shushed her gently and brushed a stray curl away from her face. "You take too much responsibility on yourself, Belle," he said, using the familiar version of her name that only her dearest friends used. Hearing it on his lips felt comfortable, right. "The world is not yours to carry. Lives will be lived and lost, and it is not for you to own."

"James," she whispered, "I don't know what to do other than my work. Do you understand? *I don't know what to do.* I've never done anything else."

"You are a woman of enormous talent and intellect. Aside from sneaking into and out of gentlemen's quarters, I would say there are no limits to what you can do, should you but decide. You are going to have to be brave enough to choose something else."

"I don't know anything but intelligence work."

"There's no reason you cannot still do some form of it. But antics requiring you to leap from tall places may well have to come to a halt." James smiled. "Or perhaps you're a coward and cannot accept new challenges."

She knew what he was trying to do, and she appreciated it. She nodded and wiped her eyes and nose with a deep, shuddering breath.

"Incidentally, I should tell you that your escape was absolutely spectacular, tumble and all. I know of no women and few men who would have managed to hold on to the edge of the roof. You're very fortunate on two counts, however."

"And those would be?"

"One, that I happened to be out for a breath of fresh air."

"And two?"

"That I didn't hit you in the face."

* * *

It was uncanny, really, James thought, as he studied Isabelle's sleeping form, which was curled up on his settee. He had felt absolutely compelled to step outside on his verandah mere moments before she had fallen from the roof. Had she landed wrong on her injured leg— well, it didn't bear contemplation. And now, looking over the notes of Ari's diary she'd written from memory, he had to wonder how he was going to survive the anxiety of trying to keep pace with her.

Her eye for detail was impeccable, her memory exceptional. He had no doubt that had they looked in Ari's diary, her notes would match his to the letter. Isabelle had written everything she'd seen without hesitation as soon as she'd calmed herself and wiped her tears. And she had definitely been right about the fact that they'd needed the information she'd found. Ari was most definitely up to no good.

He turned the facts over in his head repeatedly. Was the Greek after him or Isabelle? Was he following them in an effort to find Sparks? Perhaps he, too, was on the trail of the dreaded jewel.

The hour struck one and then two. Still Isabelle slept, and still he stewed. He was loathe to awaken her when she slept so soundly but would have to do so soon so that she could return to her room before Sally and Alice realized she was gone. They would be scandalized. It was his last thought as he lay down on his own bed and stared at the ceiling, his hands under his head.

11

Isabelle awoke with a start. She sat, groaning softly and rubbing her sore neck. How long had she slept on James's settee? Mercy, Sally was going to have an absolute fit. Justifiably so. Rash and irreverent as Isabelle was, she was not one to spend entire evenings in gentlemen's rooms.

"What time is it?" she mumbled sleepily to James, who was turning over on his bed. He was still fully clothed, thank heavens.

James looked at a pocket watch on the bedside table. He sat up with a groan and said, "Six o'clock. You must go."

Muttering under her breath and still trying to pry open eyes that were swollen from intense crying, she shoved her feet into her shoes and quickly made her way out of James's room and to her own, which was two doors down the hall. Opening her own door with equal stealth, she slipped inside and held her breath, hoping Sally and Alice were still abed and hadn't noticed her long absence.

She looked around the room, only to find the girls absent. The beds were rumpled, nightclothes strewn on the floor, trunks wide open. Isabelle shook her head. The girls were as sloppy as could be, and she tired of it. They must already have left the room for an early breakfast. They had made a habit of early rising—Sally didn't want to miss a moment of her adventure and begrudged the time she had to sleep.

Isabelle changed and washed herself with cold water from the washbasin that chilled her skin. Instead of dressing in her customary clothing, she donned a second outfit purchased in Bombay, this one a combination of oranges and yellows. The material felt light and unobtrusive, and she wondered if she would ever again find the wherewithal to shove herself into a corset.

She plaited and pinned her hair into place and examined herself in the looking glass above the washbasin. Her eyes were still a bit swollen, as were her lips, and her face was decidedly pale. She pinched her cheeks for a bit of color and finally shrugged. It was the best she could do.

Isabelle made her way out of the room and down the hallway to the dining salon, expecting to see the girls and more than ready to deliver them a lecture on tidiness. Puzzled, she spied two servants setting breakfast out on the sideboards but no Alice or Sally.

"Odd," she said.

She looked outside in the courtyard, finding nobody about. Returning to the dining room, she asked one of the workers if she had seen the girls and was informed that the girls had not been down that way all morning.

Isabelle ventured into the front yard, stepping as far as the road and looking either way down the tree-lined street. Returning to the inn, she quickened her step and made her way to the second floor. Knocking firmly on Colonel Bilbey's door, she wasted no time in speaking when he opened it. "Have you seen the girls yet this morning?" she asked him.

His look of surprise answered her question, and she stifled a groan of dismay. Turning from him, she made her way to Ari's door, telling Bilbey as she walked, "I can't find them." Isabelle knocked on Ari's door to no avail. She knocked again and louder. Finally, she turned the knob and looked inside. The sight caused her heart to increase its rhythm. The room was completely bare.

Bilbey looked in behind her. "Where did he go?" he asked, bewildered. "Our train doesn't leave until noon."

"No, the train *we* decided to take doesn't leave until noon. The first train to Lucknow left an hour ago." Isabelle bit her lip and tried to quell her rising panic. "I think Ari took the girls."

"By himself?"

"No, he had help. Are your men still here?"

Bilbey frowned and turned to the next door. Banging on it, he rousted a sleepy Sergeant Linford. "Are you all accounted for?" Bilbey asked without preamble.

Linford looked back into the room, rubbing his eyes. "Yes, sir, of course. No, wait . . . Weber, where is Lyle?"

Isabelle gritted her teeth and ran back down the stairs to James's room. "They're gone," she said, bursting in without knocking to find him in the process of buttoning a clean shirt.

"Isabelle, do you mind?" He looked mildly abashed, and had Isabelle not been so frantic, she would have been amused.

"Sally and Alice. Ari has them."

* * *

Isabelle paced the length of the train station platform, fighting to not wring her hands. Ari had left a note, of course, and she hadn't seen it earlier on Sally's pillow. As long as they didn't try to follow him or call the authorities, the girls would be returned to them in Delhi. Isabelle was to be at a certain place in one week's time to await instructions on where to find them.

She should have realized he was going to take them. The conversation she overheard the night before made sense, now that she thought it through, but she'd been too wrapped up in her own angst at the time to realize it. Ari obviously considered it too much of a personal risk to harm Isabelle further, so he moved on to the girls instead, using them as the insurance he needed to be left alone. She could only speculate as to what kind of arrangement he had going with a contact in Egypt.

He must have overheard her speaking with James at the tea gardens the day before; it was the only thing that made sense. Ari was the reason her senses had gone on alert. He heard her tell James that she had a powerful ally in Pinkerton. Or perhaps she had an overinflated sense of her own self-worth, and he wasn't referring to her at all when he spoke of risk.

She rubbed her forehead with her hand, thinking that surely by now she should be used to the intense humidity brought on not only by the region itself, but also by the fact that they were at the end of monsoon season. She looked around and wondered what she'd dragged Sally into. There was little time for recriminations; that could come later. She needed to focus her energy on thinking like the enemy.

"He knows of our plans," she said to James, who moved to pace beside her. "He knows our itinerary, knows exactly where we are going and who we're looking for. So now it's probably safe to assume he's not after you or me, but Sparks or Phillip."

"And you believe he is going to follow that same plan? Might he not just go straight to Delhi? That's where he said the girls would be."

Isabelle folded her arms, her fingers tapping restlessly. "Well, we know they were all at the train station this morning and were headed for Lucknow. Whether or not he stays there once they arrive would be anyone's guess, I suppose. But notice he gives himself a week before instructing me to meet him in Delhi to retrieve the girls. I believe he still plans to search Lucknow for Sparks, just as we'd planned all along. Obviously he'll hide the girls somewhere there, search for Sparks, and if it's as we believe it might be, the trail will lead to Delhi."

"We could go directly to Delhi."

Isabelle shrugged a bit. "But suppose your brother and Sparks are still in Lucknow."

James shook his head. "Isabelle, I'm very sorry."

"It's my fault. I should have returned directly to my room. Instead, I carried on like an infant and fell asleep."

"You can't blame yourself. It would be pointless."

"Then you mustn't blame yourself, either. You've given me ample opportunity to take Sally and go somewhere else. I've stayed for my own selfish reasons."

"As much as I would enjoy details about those selfish reasons, I feel compelled to comment that Sally didn't want to leave either."

"No," Isabelle conceded. "She was having the time of her life. If Ari hurts her, I will tear out his throat myself."

"I believe you just might. We'll find them both unscathed. If there's one thing Ari isn't, it's stupid. He's dealing not only with your ward but with the daughter of a British officer."

"But why? Why take them merely to insure that we let him go ahead? What does he have to gain by finding Sparks first?" Isabelle fell silent, willing her mind to find any shadow, no matter how small, she may have overlooked.

* * *

The train ride to Lucknow was a quiet affair. James felt helpless, which was an emotion he detested. Now not only was his brother missing, but two young women as well, at least one of which he felt directly responsible for. He walked the train corridor, too restless to relax in the confines of his own berth. The hour was late, and they were not due to arrive at their destination until the early morning hours.

The heat on the train had him loosening his tie and pulling off his cuff links. He put them in his pocket and wondered what Isabelle would think if he purchased himself a set of the native white linen attire so prevalent in the country. It was bound to be cooler. He shook his head. He could imagine such as much as he liked. The odds of him following through with it were slim.

A quick glance into a lounge car confirmed what he'd suspected; Colonel Bilbey was unable to sleep as well. His face was drawn into a pained expression that seemed to radiate itself throughout his entire body. The weight of the world appeared to rest on his shoulders as he stared, unseeing, into the black night.

"Sir," James said as he sat in a chair opposite the colonel.

"Ashby," the colonel answered, startled from his private thoughts.

"You will think it entirely odd, as I admit I did myself, but Miss Webb was privy to Kilronomos's private journal last night. There are some things, small things, we've been able to ascertain about his motives."

"Did Kilronomos show Miss Webb his journal?"

"Ah, no. That aside, however, let me tell you what we've been thinking." James pulled Isabelle's notes from his pocket and unfolded them. He told the colonel about the coincidences in the notes and the fact that he, Isabelle, Sally, Sparks, and Phillip had all stayed at the Pembroke in London.

"My wife also visited the inn," Bilbey murmured.

James nodded slowly. "She did. So we really don't know who he was hoping to see or who he was following. It could have been any of us, although the fact that he's gone on his own now leads me to believe he's trying to find Sparks and, therefore, the jewel."

"May I look at your notes?" Bilbey asked.

"Of course."

Bilbey perused the notes for a moment before his face slackened. He closed his mouth and swallowed, his throat working visibly. James grew concerned when the man's face blanched.

"Sir? What is it?"

Bilbey dropped the papers and stood, making his way slowly to the sideboard, where he poured himself a brandy that splashed liber-ally onto the polished surface of the bar. He raised the tumbler to his mouth with a hand that shook so badly he eventually lowered the glass without taking a drink.

James rose and picked up the papers. He walked to the bar, his alarm growing at the colonel's pallor. "Sir, what is it?" he repeated, looking down at the notes. He looked back up at Bilbey and saw in the man's expression anguish so fierce it gave him pause.

"Mr. Ashby," Bilbey finally managed, "I wonder if my daughter and Miss Rhodes aren't now in the hands of a murderer."

* * *

Sally and Alice sat huddled in a rattle-trap carriage and glared, the both of them, at Sergeant Lyle, who had made no bones about the fact that he had a firearm in the pocket of his greatcoat. He grinned at the pair of them, which tightened the skin around his eye that was even now beginning to show signs of red and purple where Sally had thunked him with a tightly closed fist. For her efforts, she had a red patch across her cheek that was a result of contact with the back of his hand.

"Too bad the Greek left me such 'splicit instructions," he said. "Otherwise, I might have a right good time."

Alice sniffed. "Explicit instructions for what? You've not told us a word—not on the train and not now in this wretched, dirty city."

"You'll fetch a pretty price," Lyle said, pausing to allow his pronouncement sink in. "His man in Egypt will pay well for you."

Sally gasped in outrage and launched herself across the carriage, her nails clawing deep scores into his face before he hissed in anger and shoved her hard back into her seat. He pinned her arms on either side of her and leaned into her face so that she felt his hot breath. "But don't push me too far," he growled. "I will kill you rather than continue to be abused. And if that don't scare you, I'll carve your pretty friend here to pieces while you watch." With a final harsh squeeze on Sally's upper arms, he sat back in his seat and gave the driver, who had stopped the conveyance, a curt command to continue.

Alice whimpered in dismay, and Sally could hear her breath come out in rapid panic. She reached over and clasped the other girl's fingers and squeezed with as much reassurance as she could muster. Up to that point, neither girl had shed a tear in fear, and she desperately wanted it to remain such, at least in front of Lyle. "I wouldn't worry, Alice," she said aloud, her gaze on Lyle. "Isabelle Webb is a Pinkerton spy. She will find us, and when she does, our friend here will never again see the sky outside his prison walls."

Sally knew a moment of satisfaction as Lyle looked concerned then scowled, his face contorting in heightened anger. She thought he might reach forward and strike her again, and as he straightened in his seat, she added, "And even if she doesn't, I don't see that any man would pay much money for bruised goods, do you?"

"Certainly not," Alice said, her voice not quite as forceful as usual. "I know that if I were a man, I would hardly want to look at a woman who had been hit."

Lyle gritted his teeth audibly and sat back in his seat, choosing to look out the window rather than at the two young women. Sally smiled grimly.

One small victory.

* * *

"Bilbey won't come out for breakfast," Isabelle said and sat across from James in the dining car. She snapped her napkin across her lap with a frown.

"Well, at least we know he's still alive," James muttered. "I was afraid he had expired. Did he say anything?"

"No, just that he wasn't hungry." Isabelle picked up her fork and speared a piece of fruit. "The only thing on that page he might have reacted to is the name and address in Bombay."

"Or maybe he was just stunned at seeing the address in London. Especially after he knew his wife had been there looking for Sparks."

Isabelle shook her head. "I don't think so. I believe he knows something about that person. The trouble will be in convincing him to divulge it. If he was as panicked as you say, he's not going to want to tell us."

"Well, if Ari is indeed a murderer, Bilbey is obligated to tell us all he knows." James picked at his food and wondered how much weight he'd lost over the last few weeks. His trousers were beginning to bag a bit at the waist. "Wretched food," he muttered and scowled.

Isabelle looked at him in some surprise. "I noticed you don't eat much," she said. "I thought it was because of your preoccupation with your brother's welfare."

"I cannot abide the curry," he answered. "I shall be most happy to return home to a solid plate of beef and potatoes."

She laughed. "I'm fortunate. I enjoy nearly everything edible. Sally teases me often; she says I should be as wide as a barn door." Her laughter faded. "I do hope she's still alive."

If James was surprised at her abrupt change of both mood and topic, he didn't show it.

"My mother is fond of saying we mustn't borrow trouble," he said. "We are going to believe Sally is well unless we learn otherwise."

Isabelle nodded silently and was rescued from further thought by the appearance of Colonel Bilbey. "Welcome, sir," she said. "Won't you join us?"

The man sat wearily at their table, which swayed gently with the continual movement of the train. "There are some things you need to know," he began, and Isabelle glanced at James. "I behaved most . . . oddly last evening with you, James, and I should explain." Bilbey took a deep breath, and Isabelle signaled for a server to bring him some tea.

"A woman who lived in Bombay," he said, his voice low, "was murdered last month by thieves. The authorities said that the home had been ransacked and that most likely this woman had interrupted him while he was looking for valuables in her home."

Bilbey nodded absently to the waiter who delivered his tea and took a sip before continuing. "She had a child, a young son, who was also killed in the attack." Here he paused, swallowing. "At any rate, the information you copied from Ari's notes is none other than this woman's name and address. It may be a leap of logic on my part, but I do not believe in coincidence. What possible business could Ari have had with this same woman?"

"What of the woman's husband?" Isabelle asked.

"She was a widow," Bilbey said. "Her husband died shortly after the birth of the child. Most unfortunate for her, really, because in India a widow is in the lowest possible realm of status."

"I will never understand that," Isabelle muttered. "As if her worth dies with him."

"I agree with you, Miss Webb," Bilbey said. "I do not believe a woman should be shunned and forced to beg for her existence because her husband has passed on."

"What of *sati?*" Isabelle asked him. "From what I understand it has been outlawed?"

"Outlawed, yes, but still practiced in remote regions."

"What is *sati?*" James asked.

Bilbey turned to him. "The practice of a widow immolating herself upon her husband's funeral pyre so that she might go with him into the next life and not live in disgrace as a widow."

James's mouth dropped a fraction. "She burns herself alive?"

"Indeed."

James sat back in his chair and looked out the window. "Forgive my disgust," he murmured. "My mother is a widow."

"Understandable," Bilbey said. "I find it abhorrent myself. But customs are hard to change, and when people believe something to be right or sacred, it's difficult for an outsider to change it, I suppose, or convince people that it should be changed. I support many Indian traditions and feel we ought to leave them alone. *Sati,* however, is not one of them."

Isabelle watched the colonel as he stared thoughtfully into his tea. There were lines about his face that she could have sworn were new since first meeting him. His brow was creased in contemplation, his eyes weary and sad. On impulse, she reached a hand to cover his, which lay limply on the tabletop.

"Sir," she said. "I am very sorry for your loss."

He glanced up at her, startled. "My loss?" he repeated, clearing his throat.

"Your wife. I certainly hope you reach word that she is well. And as for Alice, we will find her. I'll not stop until we do."

"Yes, thank you," he said. "It's my fault, really. All my fault."

"Sir, you must not blame yourself," James said. "You had no way of knowing Alice would come to harm on this trip."

Bilbey shook his head, lost in thought. "You don't understand the whole of it," he murmured quietly.

"Why don't you explain it to us," Isabelle responded, her tones matching his.

Bilbey's expression was remote, distant, as he watched the countryside speed by outside the window. "Miss Webb," he finally said, "India is a vastly large country. I want to share your optimism that we will find the girls, but . . ."

"Well, sir," Isabelle said, temporarily abandoning hope that Bilbey would divulge further secrets, "we don't really know that Ari is that clever. He maintains that he is familiar with India, but he may be stretching the truth. I suppose what I'm trying to say is that I believe your contacts will prove vastly more effective than his."

Bilbey shrugged.

"Perhaps the places he might think to hide the girls are places that will become readily apparent to us because you know of the same contacts as Sergeant Lyle. Probably more. Also, I wonder if there might not be a way to wire for help concerning learning details about Ari's past? Do you have sources that might begin searching for information regarding the man?"

Bilbey nodded slowly. "I do. I ought to have thought of it much sooner. As soon as we reach Lucknow, I shall wire my office in Bombay." The colonel thoughtfully rose and murmured his good-byes. James and Isabelle watched him leave.

"He's right, you know." Isabelle pursed her lips. "India is huge. How are we ever going to find them?"

"Do you not believe what you just told him? What you told me at the beginning of our journey?"

She lifted a shoulder. "I want to. I told him I wouldn't stop until we find them, and it's true enough. I find myself wondering, however, if that doesn't mean I'll spend the rest of my life here and die old and alone."

The answering expression on James's face could best be described as flat. "Miss Webb," he said, "during the course of our brief association, I've not yet known you to be maudlin or self-pitying. The drama does not become you."

Her mouth fell open in surprise, and she hastily clamped it shut. Before she could comment on his bluntness, he added, "Besides, you'll not be alone. I'll not leave either until we find the young women."

James turned his attention again to his food, giving it a dubious look. Isabelle felt her lips twitch, and her stomach gave a small flip. He really was growing more handsome by the day.

12

Isabelle sat on the edge of her bed, wishing she could go to sleep but knowing she would be unable to. Her body still felt as though it was aboard the train; the stillness of the land was almost unnerving. The accommodations in Lucknow were nicely appointed, as Bilbey had secured rooms for them in British officer housing.

What did she know? She asked herself the question repeatedly, reviewing the same details in her mind and divining nothing new. Lady Banbury had been in contact with Sparks, apparently with the aim of selling him information about the Jewel of Zeus. The Lady had need of speaking to Sparks, apparently after he had set sail for India, and she had attempted to hunt him down at the Pembroke Inn.

What had she wanted with him at that point? Isabelle knew the Bilbeys were short on funds, so presumably Lady Banbury was desperately trying to sell something to Sparks, something urgent that would have required her to seek him out at the inn after having communicated with him already. Yet Sparks sought Lord Banbury out when he and Phillip reached Bombay. Which meant that Sparks had not been aware Lady Banbury was still in London. Sparks confirmed as much by asking Bilbey where his wife was, as though he had expected her to be in India.

Isabelle wearily rubbed her eyes and wished they were back in Bombay. She needed to go through Lady Banbury's personal papers and correspondence. She would like to see firsthand the letters Sparks had claimed exchanging with her. Probably letters asking for information about the legend, most likely in exchange for money. But who was Sparks's money source?

And where did Ari fit into the scheme? He had been following one of them enough to know that they had either stayed at or visited the Pembroke. And then he booked passage on the same ship carrying several of the party in question to Bombay. He had conversed with Lady Banbury on more than one occasion—conspicuously enough to raise Sally's ire—and then followed the lot of them around India.

Isabelle lay down reluctantly on her bed and closed her eyes, attempting to relax her breathing and quiet her thoughts. *This will never work. I absolutely cannot sleep*, was the last thing she remembered thinking when she awoke the next morning.

* * *

Breakfast was a quiet affair. Colonel Bilbey, James, Isabelle, and Bilbey's two remaining sergeants, Linford and Weber, discussed their plans for the day between bites of food that none were inclined to enjoy. It was while they were seated in relative quiet that Bilbey was approached with a message that had just come across the wires. His eyebrows raised a fraction, then fell together in a frown.

"It seems Kilronomos is basically a man for hire," he said. "He has been known to act as a spy."

"Wonderful," Isabelle muttered under her breath. "One of my own."

Bilbey glanced up at her in some surprise. "I beg your pardon?"

She waved a hand at him in dismissal. "I wonder," she continued, "who has hired him, then. Someone who was willing to pay for information about one of us? The inn in London is the tie that binds us all together. But then, what of your friend, whose address was in his book . . ."

Bilbey shook his head.

"Colonel," Isabelle said, "I wonder if I might ask a delicate question about your wife."

"Certainly," he said in some surprise.

"Do you suppose she might have had any enemies? Anyone who would wish her ill?'

"I do not believe so," he answered, his expression open. "I am absolutely baffled. I do wonder, however, if I might have some enemies myself. I seem to be the one whose loved ones are coming to harm." He flushed. "Of course, I am not alone. You each have someone at stake in this whole business . . ."

"I understand," Isabelle said. "No offense taken." She absently tapped her fork against her plate, thinking.

"Perhaps Ari wasn't hired by anyone at all," James said. "Perhaps he's working entirely for his own ends."

"It is what we have assumed all along," Isabelle mused. "At this point I don't suppose anything would change if we believed he was hired by someone else. The fact of the matter is he still has the girls, and he's still looking for Phillip and Sparks."

Finally deciding little else would be gained by continuing to talk in circles, the small group finished their breakfast and began searching Lucknow's chawls and rooms for rent. Not only were Ari and the girls nowhere to be found, but nobody seemed to have seen them even in passing. Not even the railroad porters and attendants could recall having seen either Ari or the young women.

After an exhausting and frustrating day, Isabelle sat next to James in the small courtyard that was situated at the back of the officer's quarters.

"I don't think he's here," she said quietly, rubbing a finger across her forehead, trying to ease the ache that had settled there. "I think he's already in Delhi."

James sat back on the bench with a slight groan and stretched his long legs, crossing them at the ankles. He folded his arms across his chest and pivoted his head slightly around and from side to side. "This quest is fast losing its charm," he muttered.

Isabelle smiled in spite of herself. "You never believed it to have any," she said.

"I was trying to imagine it."

"Quite the feat for an unimaginative sort."

He scowled, the waning light of day casting shadows across his face. "I am not unimaginative. I simply avoid silly flights of fancy."

Isabelle laughed softly. "You, sir, are an incurable realist, make no mistake."

James grunted slightly and dipped his head in acknowledgment. "I suppose you are correct. I do have some capacity for imagination, however."

"Really. And what is it that you imagine?"

"I imagine a life where I might have met you under normal circumstances, that perhaps we might have been introduced at a society function or by a mutual acquaintance." His voice had dropped in tone and developed a husky quality that sent a heightened state of awareness through her senses.

Isabelle turned to look at him as the dusk continued to envelope the courtyard. "And what would you have said to me under such circumstances?"

James looked at her, the intensity of his gaze holding her fast. "I would have asked you for a dance and not relinquished my hold on you until the lamps were extinguished and the party-goers had all gone home."

Isabelle's mouth went dry at his comment, and she found herself searching for words in a mind that had suddenly gone blank. "I cannot imagine you troubling yourself to attend a ball," she finally whispered.

"It would be worth it to catch a glimpse of you, even if all I managed to do was watch you from afar. My gaze would never leave you. You would dance and laugh and charm everyone within your realm, and you would feel my gaze upon you continuously." He raised a hand to the side of her face and trailed his thumb softly across her cheek.

Isabelle closed her eyes at the thrill of his touch and gently leaned her face into his palm. His hand was large and warm, and she found herself wanting to crawl onto his lap and let him fold his arms around her, sheltering her from the world and even herself. "It would be so easy," she whispered.

"Easy to what?" he whispered in kind.

"To let you take care of me. And then I would be yet another on your list of burdens."

He shook his head, a smile playing about his lips. "The only burden would be attempting to keep my hands to myself."

Isabelle smiled, her eyes still closed. "Mr. Ashby, such talk."

"You must feel it," he murmured. "There is something . . . a connection . . . and I'm not a man given to believing in that sort of thing."

"A realist."

"A realist. With a real desire to never let you out of my sight." His hand slipped to her hair and traced it softly with his fingertips. "I rather like your hair unbound," he said. "Do you suppose you might venture out tomorrow with it down?"

Isabelle finally opened her eyes and laughed a bit. "You are determined to see me scandalized."

"You've seen much, Miss Webb. I doubt I could scandalize you."

"Ah, but unlike you, I am an imaginative sort. Lately I've scandalized myself."

He smiled. "I should like to hear more."

"But I fear I would scandalize *you*," she said and rose on unsteady feet. "I'm off to tell Lord Banbury that we ought to leave for Delhi in the morning. Should I remain here much longer with you, I would surely find myself compromised."

"You do understand that my mother raised a gentleman."

"Indeed. It's not *your* actions that concern me."

* * *

"I thought we were leaving for Delhi today," James said to Isabelle under his breath as they followed Colonel Bilbey down the street toward Lucknow's city center.

"He said he wanted to visit one other place. A place that saw significant action during the Sepoy Rebellion." Isabelle watched the colonel's back with a slight frown. "He's closed himself off more than ordinary," she mused. "It feels as though he grows more agitated by the hour."

After walking a bit, Bilbey's two men turned as the road forked and headed toward Qaiser Bagh Palace, at Bilbey's instructions. "We'll meet you there shortly," Bilbey called to them. James and Isabelle continued on for a few more minutes before Bilbey brought them to a halt before a collection of buildings that surrounded a larger brick home. The entire complex was unlived in, as evidenced by the gaping holes found in the walls. Isabelle pointed to one and gestured toward Bilbey, who nodded grimly.

"This was the British Residency. The shelling happened during the siege," he said. "Sir Henry Lawrence holed up here with all of Lucknow's British citizens. Once the Indian soldiers attacked, he expected to be relieved within fifteen days. However, help didn't arrive for eighty-seven days."

"So what happened to the British within?" James asked, eyeing the abandoned complex.

Bilbey sighed. "Well, by the time Sir Colin Campbell arrived, some two thousand people had died from either gunshot wounds or cholera and typhoid."

James tried in vain to think of a polite way to ask the colonel why they were visiting a site where the British had so obviously suffered. If Sparks believed the British had the Jewel of Zeus in their possession, surely they hadn't had it at the shelled-out residency. In the end, Bilbey must have read his mind.

"Retribution was swift and harsh," Bilbey said. "I believe that if Mr. Sparks believes the British army was in possession of that jewel, they used it to their advantage in this city when they ended the siege." For a moment Bilbey seemed lost in thought as he looked at the ruins. "It was . . . not pleasant," he said quietly.

"Were you here, sir?" Isabelle asked.

He shook his head. "I had just been transferred to a different post. My wife and Alice and I left mere days before the siege. Alice was so young . . . five years old. She likely would have died here. We were fortunate." He paused. "I returned to Lucknow months later—

arrived just behind Sir Colin. It was tragic inside, really," he said, gesturing toward the large house. "The women and children had been hidden down in the basement . . ."

James was at a loss as to how to respond to the man, who was obviously reliving unpleasant memories. "Sir, do you think we might find evidence of Sparks's presence here? Or Ari's even?"

Bilbey shrugged slightly and began moving toward the largest building. "I was told last night that a curator of sorts has been established here in the main house. I thought we might ask."

The interior of the house showed obvious evidence of its once-formal splendor in the beauty of the craftsmanship that adorned its floors and walls. James was loathe to admit, however, that the place echoed of pain and despair. He could almost hear the constant bombardment of shells and cries of fear and alarm.

"What are you thinking?" Isabelle whispered as Bilbey approached the young sergeant on duty.

"Imagining, I suppose," he admitted. He stopped from elaborating further when the sergeant nodded.

"Yes, sir, I remember him," the sergeant was saying to Bilbey. "Must have been nearly a week ago. He wanted to search the rooms upstairs and the basement. When I told him that not only was it not allowed but also that there was nothing to be found, he grew almost belligerent."

James moved closer to the young man. "Was there anyone else with him?"

The sergeant nodded again. "A young American," he said. "Stood nearly as tall as you, yourself, and . . ." The soldier paused in some surprise. "Why, he must be a relative, then? He was the very image of you."

James nodded. "My brother. Did he say anything at all?"

"No, sir. He seemed to be extremely fatigued."

James felt his heart trip. Images of his brother flashed through his mind in an instant, and James recalled every impatient thing he'd ever said to him. Phillip always took it in stride, smiling. He couldn't imagine a world where Phillip was frightened, where he didn't smile.

James nodded his thanks and moved to a corner of windows that looked out over the main courtyard while Bilbey continued questioning the young man and offering Ari's description. He felt Isabelle's hand on his back, and she rubbed gently back and forth.

"He was still alive and seen in public with Sparks as of a week ago," she said quietly to him. "And if Sparks wants him for the birthmark, which we believe he does, then we know Phillip will be safe from harm."

"Until Sparks finds the jewel," James said.

Isabelle's hand stilled, and James felt her gaze upon his face. He finally turned to her. "Have you taken leave of your senses?" she asked. "There is no jewel!"

He shook his head and opened his mouth to reply when he saw a young man in uniform enter the building and approach Bilbey with a paper. Bilbey read it, glanced at James and Isabelle, and said a quick thank-you to the young man who had been answering his questions.

"I need to speak with the both of you," Bilbey said, approaching them. "Why don't we go outside."

Once out on the front lawn, Bilbey led them to a shady spot and turned to them with a deep breath. "The legend of the Jewel of Zeus is not just a legend. There really is a jewel."

When Bilbey looked again at the paper in his hand and seemed disinclined to speak further, James said, "What is it you would like to tell us about this jewel?"

Bilbey took a breath. "It's been in my family for a few generations now. I own the Jewel of Zeus."

James heard Isabelle suck in her breath. "Is there a reason you've not told us this before now?" Isabelle said.

Bilbey tugged a bit at his collar. "It seemed inconsequential."

"*Inconsequential?*" James felt his anger mount. "Why don't you tell us the whole of it, sir, and if you please, leave nothing out."

Bilbey nodded.

"The jewel should be at my ancestral home in England now, but I suspect my wife may have removed it before sailing for Bombay.

"It has been in my family for years and is worth a fair amount of money, and yes, there is family lore claiming it is the ancient Jewel of Zeus. I have never believed it, my father didn't believe it, nor did his before him. It is superstitious nonsense that has come to nothing, and the jewel that is now under my care certainly has granted me no special powers, untold wealth, or knowledge. I should know," he finished in some disgust.

"This isn't about what any of us believe, though." Isabelle asked.

"No." Bilbey's shoulders slumped. "It's what my wife believes it to be that matters. She had never heard of the jewel or the legend when we married, but once my mother told her tales of the thing, it was all my wife could do to contain her excitement. She spent her time learning details of the legend and the curse, and she always maintained to others that she was on a quest to find it when in reality she believed it to be locked in a safe at home. It tickled her fancy to think that others believed her to be looking for it when she already knew where it was."

"Would she have found reason to sell it?" Isabelle asked, giving voice to the very thing that James had been thinking. How diplomatic of her to phrase it so when they both knew Bilbey was in severe financial straits.

"Yes," Bilbey admitted. "I told her just before she left for England to see our sons that we would need to find other schooling accommodations for them and that Alice would not be able to have a season." His face flamed with embarrassment, and James was uncomfortable for him. "So I imagine she fancied herself selling the thing to Sparks."

"Would she have known the value of the piece?" Isabelle asked.

"She did, and I suppose that point surprises me." Bilbey gestured in front of him and they began walking. "Having met Sparks, I don't imagine he had the resources to pay what the jewel was worth."

"You met Sparks, this is true," Isabelle said, "but I believe he can be incredibly convincing to one who wants to see something that may or may not be there."

Bilbey gestured toward the paper he held in his hand. "At any rate, the reason I tell you this now is because I've just received word that authorities in Bombay have conclusively linked Ari to Mrs. Hinshaska's murder. I don't have all of the details, but apparently he must have left evidence at the scene. I wanted you to know exactly what we're facing."

The three fell into silence as they walked the short distance to the palace to meet up with Linford and Weber. The combination of

Mughal, Persian, imperial, and other European influences was evidenced in every building they passed. Elaborate mosques with intricate carvings and arches stood near colonial homes and buildings similar in style to those James recognized in England.

The emotions James felt as they walked along were mixed, and he found himself feeling overwhelmed for a moment. He couldn't ignore the amazement his senses noted at the strange yet wonderful architecture and flora, but his worry about Phillip was engulfing nearly every thought. *I will be more patient with him,* he vowed. *If I ever see him again, if our lives ever again reside side by side, I will treat him with respect and allow him to live without my constant censure and disapproval . . . If . . . If . . ."*

The palace was at least as awe-inspiring as was the British Residence, although it was its polar opposite in architecture. It was largely in ruins, but the domed spires and arched balconies showed their former splendor. "When we retook Lucknow in '58," Bilbey said as they slowed to a stop, "we destroyed much of the outer pieces of this complex. There were sculptures of mermaids and cherubs. Now you can see that only two wings of the nawab's original residence are still here."

James looked at the obvious destruction, which clearly matched the place they'd just seen. "Looks like an eye for an eye," he commented to Bilbey.

"Indeed." Bilbey's face was grim. "I believe that was the theory behind it."

"You don't agree with the methods," Isabelle said, watching his face.

He winced a bit. "I didn't much have the stomach for it." He cleared his throat. "It was so horrible on both sides. It really doesn't bear discussion."

James caught movement out of the corner of his eye and gladly motioned his head toward Bilbey's two sergeants, who were approaching from the ruins. They were a welcome distraction.

"They were here, sir," Linford said. "I showed him the photograph of Mr. Ashby's brother, and they recognized it. They poked around the ruins but didn't ask any questions." Linford moved closer to the small group and motioned them in a bit.

"He had a weapon, apparently," Weber said, glancing at James. "The sergeant inside said that at one point the men appeared to be exchanging words. When your brother attempted to leave, Mr. Sparks pulled a revolver from his coat pocket and pointed it at him. He said something the sergeant couldn't hear and then put the gun away."

"Did nobody intervene?" James asked, prepared to question the sergeant himself.

Linford nodded. "When the sergeant tried to talk to the men and ask the young Mr. Ashby if all was well, Mr. Ashby brushed himself off and said he was fine. Then he and Sparks left together without incident."

"So he is keeping him by force," James said, largely to himself. "I suspected as much."

Bilbey nodded his agreement. "I am not surprised either, given his demeanor that day in my office." To Linford he said, "What of Mr. Kilronomos and the young women?"

Linford shook his head. "Nothing, sir. I am sorry."

"We are approximately three hundred miles east of Delhi, yes?" Isabelle asked Bilbey, who nodded. "Might I suggest we check to see when the next train departs?"

* * *

Isabelle sat on the edge of her bed in her night clothes, reading Ari's ransom note by the light of the lantern anchored to her bedside table as the train made its way down the track. *Meet me alone at Athpula, the bridge near the entrance to Lodi Gardens on South End Road.* She wasn't due to meet him for another two days. Her stomach clenched in knots when she thought of what he or Sergeant Lyle might do to the girls. Eyes burning, she closed them tightly and gritted her teeth together, offering up a prayer for help with a heart that was rusty from disuse.

Isabelle eventually opened her eyes and wiped at her tears, exhaling slowly and looking again at the note. She had to think like Ari. He wasn't necessarily intelligent, but he was cunning. He would tell her one thing and mean another. Perhaps her biggest mistake had been allowing him entrance to their small entourage. She had thought that by keeping him close she would be better able to keep an eye on his activities. Rather, it seemed all she had accomplished was to clasp the snake right to her bosom.

That night, finally falling into a fitful sleep, she dreamed of strange things—of a woman she hadn't seen in years. Why she would invade her thoughts now, even on a subconscious level, was beyond Isabelle's wildest imaginings, and she awoke confused and disoriented. Finally pulling herself together and readying herself for the day, she met James in the dining car.

He looked at his pocket watch as they sat. "Should be at Delhi in just another two hours," he said. Catching the look on her face, he added, "You look a bit bemused."

"James, as an orphaned young woman with no family to speak of, other than my sister, I attended the finest girls' school Boston could offer, and I had lived in Chicago until that point. Do you wonder how I did such a thing?"

If he was surprised by her topic of conversation, he kept it admirably from his expression. "Very little about you surprises me anymore, Miss Webb."

"I'm not certain I should be flattered by that statement, but nevertheless, I attended that school through the kindhearted donations of a woman who was known to me and my sister only as the Benefactress. We never knew her name, and we met her on only one occasion. She lived in Boston and said she had her own reasons for funding our educations. We had the smarts to accept her generosity if only to keep food in our stomachs and a roof over our heads."

"Were you literally living on the streets?"

"At that point, yes."

James quirked a brow. "And you were how old?"

"I was fifteen, and my sister was ten."

James drew in a breath and released it. "How did this woman find you?"

Isabelle shook her head slightly. "Her solicitor approached us one day as we stood in a food line. There was an older woman who lived near the abandoned home where we usually stayed—she fed some of us a few times a week when she had enough food left over. At any rate, the solicitor asked around until he found us—as it was, he said he'd been looking for three years."

"So you attended this school, graduated a finished and polished young woman . . . and became a spy for Pinkerton."

Isabelle smiled. "Follows all logic, does it not? I returned to Chicago. I was looking for . . . well, but therein lies a story for another day. My point with all of this is that last night I dreamed of the Benefactress." Here, Isabelle frowned. "She once told me, 'Things are not always as they seem.' Last night, I dreamed she was with me and she told me that again."

James looked at her for a moment before responding. "You know, my dreams never make much sense, and they usually involve outhouses."

Isabelle felt her mouth slacken. "Whereas I never surprise you, Mr. Ashby, I must say you constantly surprise me." She laughed then and was gratified to see one of his rare, dazzling smiles. "I admit to being highly curious, but for the moment I'll refrain from asking for details." Finally sobering, she added, "Truly, it was as though the woman was trying to tell me something. Obviously, it must have been about Sally."

"Has the woman passed on? Are you supposing she is visiting you from beyond the grave?" James continued to keep his expression blank, but she knew him well enough by now to recognize the signs of his disbelief. It was in the slightly arrogant tilt of his head, she supposed.

She smiled and continued, undeterred. "The last I heard of her, she was still alive and well in Boston." She shook her head and reached for the pot of tea that sat on the table. Pouring some into her cup, she said, "I could swear upon my very life that the dream went on all night long. I haven't thought of her in quite some time."

"Tell me again what she said."

"'Things are not always as they seem.' I simply do not know what to make of it."

"Belle, perhaps it was just a dream and nothing more. It may well be that you're reading more here than is really meant."

Isabelle nodded.

"You're not convinced."

"Of course not. I never have strange dreams and definitely not about the Benefactress."

"Very well," James conceded with obvious reluctance. "Let us suppose that this dream means something. Do you propose we somehow alter our plans?"

"No," she said, tapping her finger on the tabletop and looking outside the window. "I cannot help but feel we have all the pieces of the puzzle. They just aren't in the right places yet."

James cast a dubious look in her direction and bit into a mango. "This is unlike any puzzle I've ever seen," he said between bites. "The pieces are all a bit insane."

"I beg your pardon."

"Except for you, of course."

"Of course." Isabelle smiled. "Although I now believe in odd dreams. That may qualify me."

"Mmm. Insane but beautiful." He said it so casually she blinked in surprise.

"Beautiful, really?" she asked, feeling extremely vulnerable and beyond foolish for asking. The moment it left her mouth, she wished she could call it back.

He looked at her while wiping his mouth with a napkin. He finished chewing, still looking at her, and was silent for so long she had to fight the impulse to squirm. "So beautiful it hurts," he whispered.

She felt her eyes burn and mist, and for a moment she allowed herself to quietly, unabashedly return his gaze before his image blurred and a tear slipped over the side, trailing a path down her cheek. He reached across the table and wiped it away with his thumb. "Surely that's not the first time you've heard it," he murmured.

"No," she admitted, "but it's the first time I believe it was sincerely meant."

"Oh, I'm sure it was frequently sincerely meant," he said wryly, "and it makes my blood boil to think of it. It is most likely a good thing that I didn't know you a few years ago. I'd have found myself challenging many a poor fool to a duel."

She smiled. "I appreciate your attempt at levity."

"I'm not jesting." And he didn't appear to be.

"Ah." She cleared her throat and blinked back the moisture in her eyes. "Well, then. Where were we before I became all soggy and sentimental?"

"Enjoying this mango. The fruit in this country is exceptional when they refrain from adorning it with superfluous spices."

She laughed again, and again he smiled. Oh, that smile! What she wouldn't give to have it turned her way all day long. For a moment she genuinely resented their troubles for strictly selfish reasons, and she bit her lip in frustrated contemplation. Isabelle Webb was softening. Mysteries of the current sort usually lent her an air of excitement and challenge. Perhaps this time it was too personal from all sides, and it was intruding on yearnings she would have liked very much to pursue wholeheartedly.

"What are you thinking?" he asked after signaling a waiter for more fruit.

She shook her head slightly, her smile rueful. "Things better left alone. I suppose Zeus must be laughing himself silly over all of this."

"Zeus can go to Hades, for all I care," James muttered. "If I ever hear his name again, it will be too soon. I want to find my brother, find Sally and Alice, and go home."

Isabelle's heart skipped a beat. It would be over then, and how perverse of her to begrudge their missing loved ones their rescue! Her days with James were numbered, and the thought did not sit well. He told her she was beautiful, that he wished they might have met under different circumstances, but their lives were as different as night and day. He would return home to his mother and his community and his blacksmith shop. He would settle down with a nice, young, beautiful Mormon wife and have beautiful Mormon babies. Maybe he'd find himself two nice, young, beautiful Mormon wives. What did she really know about him anyway?

She knew he made her heart constantly trip over itself. She knew she loved his smile like she loved the sun and the moon and the stars.

She knew she admired his strength of character and his sense of responsi-bility. She knew he made her laugh with his dry sense of humor, and she knew she wanted to melt into his arms and never let go.

And it was all soon going to come to an end. She'd be better off distancing herself while she still had a heart beating in her chest. On that practical thought, Isabelle straightened her spine and stabbed at her breakfast. She'd let her guard down way too much for her own good over the past few weeks. Life had taught her better than to be so foolish.

13

The contrast between Lucknow and Delhi was amazing in terms of size. Delhi was streaming with people, conveyances, and animals, its streets full to bursting with vendors and carts. Isabelle looked with quiet despair upon the scene and wondered how they were ever to find the girls in such immense chaos, let alone Sparks and Phillip.

"One thing at a time, then," Bilbey murmured beside her and stepped forward from the train platform, directing their trunks to be placed on a waiting bullock cart. It wasn't long before they were all seated on the conveyance and winding their way through the streets. Once they had settled their belongings in officers' housing similar to that in Lucknow, they began their customary inquiries at boarding houses and inns that might house Sparks and Phillip. They also asked after Ari and the girls, to no avail.

It was well past the lunch hour, and Isabelle felt her stomach grumbling. "Perhaps we can find something to eat while we walk," she suggested and pointed to a side street that absolutely bulged with carts and shops with goods piled out the front doors and onto the street. Bilbey nodded his agreement and led the way to a food vendor who sold meat pies.

They ate and strolled at a slower pace, Isabelle eyeing the wares as they moved along. There were incredible cashmere shawls, jewelry, carpets, and materials threaded with gold and silver embroidery. There were brightly colored fabrics sold in smaller pieces or large bolts, some garments already sewn into clothing ready to wear. She ran her fingers lightly over wooden toys carved for children and wished she had room to buy one of each to take home.

Sally, have you seen any of this? she wondered. *You would adore this, all of it.* On impulse, she stopped and purchased a beautiful length of orange fabric embroidered with rows of elephants. She also bought a length of purple fabric sewed with brightly colored metallic silver thread and sequins. Digging again into her reticule, she pulled out enough money for two small carved wooden tigers and elephants. With a glance in Bilbey's direction, she quickly picked up a small carving of a British soldier being pounced on by a tiger and bought it with a smirk. She tucked it inside her other packages and made her way to James, who stood at the end of the street waiting for and watching her.

He took the packages from her arms without a word and touched a finger to the tip of her nose. "Your mother might like some of this fabric," she said with a gesture at the stalls and shops. "Or some of the spices, perhaps?"

"Heaven help me if my mother should ever decide to cook with these spices," he said. "Fabric and some jewelry she would like, however." He walked alongside Isabelle and chose a few brightly colored lengths of fabric and a silver bracelet inlaid with stones.

"You're a thoughtful son," Isabelle said with a smile.

"I'd be more thoughtful if I'd thought of this on my own," he said. "Must admit I feel a bit traitorous. Phillip's somewhere suffering, and I'm here shopping."

"We'll find him soon. We must be close—I can feel it."

* * *

The day passed uneventfully and frustratingly. The mammoth city was congested, every street so clogged as to make James's head spin. Perhaps the most disheartening of all was the city's poor, who lived in doorways and on the streets, sometimes selling small, crafted wares or offering to shine shoes. They were the untouchables, or casteless. They were lowest on society's rung and lived in ways that James would never have imagined.

He felt his stomach lurch at the sight of a woman huddled in a doorway. Beneath the red *sari* she wore, her hairline was visible. She had been shaved, and Bilbey told them it was evidence of her lowered status as a widow. Her teeth were mostly missing, her cheeks gaunt, her eyes despairing. Bilbey explained quietly once they had passed her that because she was a widow, her presence was unwelcome at family functions; indeed, the family paid her little heed at all. It was even considered bad luck to see a widow first thing in the morning.

James stopped and turned around, making his way back down the street to a vendor. There, he purchased some food and a long length of material. He returned to the woman and handed her the food, taking the fabric and tucking it about her legs. She pulled back at first but stopped when he looked her squarely in the face. His eyes burned, and he clenched his teeth together, continuing to secure the makeshift blanket around her.

She opened her mouth as if to speak but closed it and simply met his gaze instead. He looked into her deep brown eyes for a moment before her face blurred before him, and he was forced to blink. He nodded once, and she bowed her head in return. He stood and made his way to the others, where he heard Isabelle draw in a quiet, shuddering breath.

"I hope I haven't caused her more harm than good," he murmured to Bilbey as they began walking again.

Bilbey looked at him for a long moment with an unreadable expression. He finally said, "I don't think anyone was paying much attention."

"Will she be allowed to keep the fabric?"

Bilbey nodded with a slight lift to the shoulder. "I don't suppose anyone will check on her to take it from her."

"I've never seen anything so disgraceful in my life," James said, hearing the angry quiver in his voice. "I am utterly at a loss."

"She is one of thousands," Bilbey said. "The lack of quality in their lives almost makes me understand why a widow would choose *sati* over living. When a woman chooses *sati,* she is immediately revered and respected and treated like royalty for her remaining days.

She is worshipped after her death, her family constructing *mahi-sati,* or hero stones, in her honor."

James's throat tightened again, and for a fleeting moment he wished to be far, far away from such a strange place. He shook his head and thrust his hands deep into his pockets. Isabelle's hand crept to his elbow, and he moved his arm a bit to accommodate hers. She slipped it through his, and he hugged it close to his side.

He glanced at her only to find her gaze fixed on something in the distance, her eyes appearing as misty as his own. Isabelle had seemed distant since reaching Delhi, her usual good humor having slowly evaporated. He wanted to believe it was because of her worry about Sally and Alice, but the subtle way she avoided his glance, even his proximity, made him believe it had something to do with him. It was almost as though she had shut herself off from him, and he was baffled as to why. The fact that she now threaded her hand through his arm was the one bright spot on an otherwise wretched day.

Dinner was a quiet affair. Bilbey, James, and Isabelle sat together at a small table in a small restaurant, Linford and Weber at another. It was some time before Isabelle, who had been uncommonly quiet and pensive, spoke.

"Gentlemen, it occurs to me that our tactic in Delhi has been altogether wrong."

Bilbey frowned. "Wrong? How so?"

"To date, Sparks has no idea we're in the country, we can surmise. However, if we're not mistaken, he is here somewhere in the city, and he needs to be alerted to our presence."

James shook his head. "That might send him into hiding."

"Allow me to clarify. We don't what him to know who we are, merely that someone is in town at the behest of Lady Banbury and is in possession of some valuable information concerning the Jewel of Zeus. We spread the word and wait for him to come to us."

Bilbey considered her comments for a moment. "Spread the word where, do you suppose?"

"Wherever we know Sparks usually looks. The temples."

Bilbey drew in a breath. "That could prove difficult. We don't necessarily want to offend those who frequent the temples; they are not going to want to talk about the jewel."

"Perhaps not those who go inside, but what of others who may lurk close by? I've seen many young people who remind me of myself at that age; they must be street children. I would have spread the word about anything for a few pennies. I'm prepared to offer more than pennies," Isabelle said.

"You'll not be offering anything," James said. "He's my brother; I'll cover the bribery expenses. I think it is beyond time to force the issue. I agree wholeheartedly."

Isabelle smiled at him and his heart twisted. She hadn't smiled for quite a while. It made him realize how much he'd missed it. "Good, then," she said. "We'll go back to the temples we've visited and try for as many more as we can before nightfall. We will show people Phillip's picture, offer a description of Sparks, and tell them that anyone requiring information on a mysterious jewel should meet us at the bridge tomorrow evening at dusk.

Bilbey pursed his lips. "It's not foolproof, I admit, but I suppose little else has worked thus far. And as for Ari, perhaps he will hear and show his face as well."

Isabelle nodded. "If nothing else, I have an appointment with him the day after tomorrow at the bridge."

"I suppose the consequences for Sergeant Lyle will not be pleasant, once caught," James said to Bilbey.

Bilbey's face tightened noticeably. "His future does not look promising."

* * *

"I am telling you, you're a fool," Sally snapped at Lyle, who sat on the filthy cot with his head buried in his hands. "The sooner you turn us loose the better it will be for you. Ari hasn't shown his face in how long now? I think he's abandoned you and is continuing the search on his own. He's left you here as our jailor, and he's not coming back."

"You shut yer yap! I'm so sick 'n' tired of yer blasted Yank talk!"

"Ah!" Sally sucked in an indignant breath. "I am *not* a Yank!"

Alice spun around from her position at the small, filthy window. "This is absolutely unthinkable. We haven't been allowed to wash or freshen our clothing for days! We look as wretched as the people out there on the streets. Miss Rhodes has the right of it, you know. You're left here with us, and Mr. Kilronomos has gone on to find the jewel alone!"

"I said shut up!" Lyle began on a growl and finished on a roar. He came to his feet, red in the face. "The two of you are making me batty! Maybe ye're right, and he is gone. Maybe I'll just take care of matters myself!" He slowed and stopped, the look on his face suddenly speculative. "Maybe I will . . ."

Sally watched the sergeant warily. He was thinking, no small feat in itself, but she didn't like the apparent turn of his thoughts. Before she could formulate an objection, he spun on his heel and left the room, locking it behind him.

"Good," Alice huffed. "Maybe he won't come back."

"Not good," Sally said, rubbing her forehead and beginning to pace. "He's going to find a buyer by himself, without Ari's permission."

"A buyer for what?"

Sally looked at her. "Us."

* * *

Night was upon them, and Isabelle and James were secreted in a garden that hung with thick vines and foliage. It was an absolutely huge garden on the edge of the city that melted into the dense jungle. The air was filled with sounds of animals and insects—a backdrop of noise that was becoming familiar. They stood fifty feet from a bridge, the same that was to host a reunion between Belle and Ari the next night. The river that flowed underneath the bridge was tranquil and dark, deepening in color with each passing moment.

Isabelle was beginning to wonder if they had bribed the locals enough. They had made the rounds in the enormous city, stopping at holy sites and common tourist attractions in hopes of telling the right person the right thing. She transferred her weight from one foot to the other, tiring of standing still in one place for so long. "I'm trying to remind myself this was my idea," she said quietly.

James's intake of breath was swift. "That's him," he whispered. "It's Sparks."

Isabelle watched as the shadow of a man slowly walked onto the large bridge, looking furtively over his shoulder. The moonlight caught his face, and she glanced up at James to see if his assessment might change.

"That's definitely him," he said.

Bilbey, Linford, and Weber were situated inconspicuously at the gates of the park and would watch for Isabelle and James to leave. Isabelle felt her heart thud, and she hoped desperately that their plan would work. They figured upon following Sparks to his chawl and then watching the place until the time was right to either confront Sparks and bring charges against him or to sneak Phillip out.

"It may not be simple," Bilbey had warned. "Your brother is past the age of majority and began his journey with Sparks of his own free will. If Phillip will testify that he was afterward held against his will, we may have reason to hold Sparks; otherwise, he may go free. But we cannot just storm the room and arrest him. It becomes complicated. He is in India and is an American."

James nodded but was clearly frustrated. Now in the dark, Isabelle imagined she could feel the energy radiating from him. His every muscle was taut and seemed ready to spring; his face looked as though it were carved from granite. Isabelle looked back at the man who now stood in the center of the bridge and hoped James's cooler head would prevail. It was imperative that Sparks not see them or sense them as they followed him to his lodgings.

Sparks stood on the bridge for an additional ten minutes before thumping his hand once in aggravation on the railing and storming back in the direction he had come. Staying well hidden in the undergrowth, they waited until he was just out of sight before coming out of the dark and onto the moonlit expansion of the bridge.

Moving quickly, they soon caught sight of him again as he made his way toward the entrance of the park. Isabelle caught Weber's eye and pointed at Sparks, who still moved away from them in angry strides. Weber nodded once and melted into the crowd.

"I think we should separate," Isabelle said to James as they tried to keep Sparks in sight.

"Why?"

"Because Sparks knows the sight of you, not to mention the fact that you look very much like your brother. If he sees you and me with you, then he will know to watch for me in the future."

"I don't like it." James strained to see the man above the throngs of people. "Why are there so many people out tonight?" he muttered.

"It's a festival. Don't you remember Bilbey telling us there would be parades and celebrations into the wee hours?"

"Dashed inconvenient," James said.

"Or extremely convenient. We can follow so much more discreetly this way." Isabelle began to slowly move from James's side. He reached for her arm and held firm for a moment until she gently tugged, then insistently yanked and put some distance between them.

Her timing was excellent, for Sparks looked over his shoulder and locked eyes with James. Sparks stopped dead in his tracks, and Isabelle slid behind an elephant that was sporting pink, green, and white paint. Edging to the rear end, she saw Sparks open his mouth, his expression angry, and then his eyes widened. He closed his mouth, turned on his heel, and ran.

Isabelle sprinted behind him, hoping the bright colors of her *sari* would mark her as a native who was caught up in the rush of the celebrations. Lights from torches illuminated the city streets, casting a warm glow over the richly colored and adorned fabrics and decorated animals and conveyances. She glanced behind her and saw that Bilbey had caught James by the elbow. He was saying something to James, and although James didn't seem happy about it, he turned and walked quickly in the opposite direction.

Isabelle was relieved. He was most likely returning to their rendezvous point. Once Sparks realized he had shaken James, perhaps he would still continue on to his rented room. Mercy, but the man was fast. Isabelle's breath quickened, and she ignored the blossoming pain in her leg. Now that Sparks knew James was following him, she wondered what action he might take against Phillip.

She kept Sparks in her line of vision, just barely, and was gratified to see him continually glancing over his shoulder and then slowing his pace. He still moved quickly through the streets, looking to the left and right as if lost. He stopped and doubled back until he was nearly upon her. Isabelle lifted a shawl from a vendor cart and examined it, keeping her back to him.

She glanced to her right and spied Linford, who was dressed as an Indian native. He crouched in a doorway and examined some ivory carvings that were laid out for display. Bilbey and Weber were nowhere to be found, but she had no doubt they were close by. Even Bilbey was incognito, as Sparks would doubtless have recognized him from their meeting in Bombay.

Sparks passed behind her, and she heard him cursing under his breath. He approached the vendor next to her and brusquely barked out an address. The man behind the stall pointed to his right and spoke a few words in Hindi.

"I don't understand you," Sparks said to the man. "How far in that direction?"

The man spoke again in his native tongue, and Sparks dismissed him with an angry gesture. He ran a hand through his disheveled hair and made his way to the end of the street.

Isabelle slowly moved behind him, still examining jewelry and fruit on prominently displayed carts. She picked up a large looking-glass that was trimmed in ornate gold figurines. Holding the thick handle, she made a show of examining her face as she tiled the angle and studied Sparks unobserved.

He took a deep breath and smoothed his coat jacket. Wiping a hand across his brow, he hailed a passing rickshaw and repeated the address to the man who commanded it. At the driver's nod, Sparks climbed inside and sat back with another deep breath.

Isabelle replaced the mirror and pulled a pencil and paper from the pouch secured about her waist. She hastily scrawled the address and ran to Linford, who was meeting up with Bilbey and Weber. "Do you know where this is?" she asked Bilbey.

He nodded. "Well enough. It's a good two miles south of here. Why don't Weber and I go there now, and you and Linford can fetch Mr. Ashby from the rendezvous point. We'll meet you there in under an hour if you can secure transportation. Are you comfortable with these plans?" he asked her.

"I am," she said. Bilbey would have done well with Pinkerton, she mused. He included her in their plans yet sought to ease any discomfort. He was a good man.

Within minutes, Isabelle and Linford found James, who walked the platforms at the train station, seemingly fit to be tied. Isabelle rushed to him and told him what had transpired. It wasn't long before the three were in a dilapidated open carriage, winding their way through the crowded streets.

Their driver seemed sure of his instructions, and Isabelle tried to relax. Her stomach was in knots, however, and she could only guess at James's anxiety level. The minutes passed quickly, but the carriage did not. Isabelle was prepared to suggest they might be better on foot when the driver turned onto a side street and made his way in a serpentine fashion through a maze of streets and alleys.

She lost track of all sense of direction and began to wonder if they were ever going to find the proper address when the driver pulled the donkey up short and pointed. "This is the chawl," he said in halting English. James paid him, and the three alighted quietly, disappearing into the shadows.

"He went in and then left again, alone," a low voice murmured from the shadows. Bilbey stepped from a deserted doorway and motioned for them to join him. "We thought we'd wait for you, James, before entering."

James nodded. "How long ago did Sparks leave?"

"Roughly thirty minutes. Weber is following him."

James motioned toward the building. "Is there a landlord we should speak with before we try to find the correct room?"

Bilbey hesitated. "Ordinarily, yes. However, it is late, and I am not in uniform, nor do I have proper identification. Whereas under those circumstances I would be able to hold some sway with the landlord, I am now unable to prove my identity. I suggest we find your brother by stealth."

"Good enough."

Isabelle looked up at the building. "Someone should stand watch," she said. "I can whistle if Sparks returns. However, I'm not certain you would hear it if the room is on the back side."

"You're not staying out here on the street," James said.

"Agreed," Bilbey nodded. "Linford, you will await us here. Follow Sparks in, should he arrive before we come out with Mr. Ashby."

Linford nodded his agreement and situated himself more securely in the shadows of the doorway as the threesome moved forward toward the chawl.

Once inside the building, Isabelle stopped for a moment to accustom her eyes to the darkness. There were muted sounds coming from behind doorways, but the building was largely deserted as most of the inhabitants were enjoying the festivities in the heart of the city. She deftly began maneuvering simple locks with a thin pick she carried in her pouch. Opening only those doors where no sound escaped, they began eliminating the rooms one by one.

Climbing the stairs to the second floor, the three walked past a door that was wide open. An entire family sat within, some eating, many small children sleeping. "This is common," Bilbey whispered. "Whole families live in one room; the cotton and textile industry has brought many people from rural areas to the cities."

Isabelle forced her mind and her heart closed to the sight as she continued down the hallway. There would be time to ache later.

Door after door, and nothing. The last door on the left faced the street. Isabelle picked the lock, and upon opening the door, she noted that the small window facing the street allowed enough light to fall across the room and show a huddled form in a corner.

James squinted a bit at the figure. There had been other sleeping people in some of the rooms, but they had been distinctly Indian. This man was dressed in dark pants and a white shirt. Isabelle quickly followed James into the room as he approached the man and lifted his chin. The strangled sound at the back of James's throat confirmed her suspicions, and he clasped his brother to him.

Phillip awoke and began to thrash with a shout. He struggled to free himself from James's embrace, and James quickly released him but grabbed his shoulders.

"Phillip! Phillip, it is James!"

Phillip stilled his movements and stared at his brother. Isabelle realized that James blocked what little light came in from the window and that his face was entirely in shadow.

"Move slightly, James, so he can see you," she said, clearing her throat free of unshed tears. The sound of fireworks exploding downtown disturbed the silence. Otherwise, the room was hushed.

James gripped his brother and helped him to stand, and all the while, Phillip stared at him. "How did you find me?" he finally asked, his voice hoarse.

"We must get him out of here," James said, looking at Isabelle and Bilbey. To Phillip, he said, "I will explain later. Do you know where Sparks went or how long he will be?"

Phillip shook his head. "He said he was going to get some food, but I don't know how long he will be this time."

James glanced at his brother in concern as he kept an arm around his waist and helped him to the door. "Are you ill? How long since you've eaten?"

Phillip shook his head. "I don't know. A few days, perhaps. The idiot is running low on funds."

The small group made their way down the back stairs, out the front door, and onto the street. Bilbey called out to Linford, but the man didn't materialize. Isabelle looked with narrowed eyes to the doorway where the man had said he would wait. A dart of alarm shot down her spine, and she ran to the slumped form that blended in with the night.

14

"Sergeant," Isabelle whispered urgently. "Linford!"

Bilbey was quick on her heels and shoved at the unconscious man's shoulder. His head fell back, and his eyes rolled slightly, flickering. He opened them with some effort and clutched at Bilbey's forearm. "You must leave," he said.

Isabelle's nose twitched, and she smelled the sickening metallic odor of blood. Glancing down at Linford's abdomen, she saw his hand clenched across his midsection, covering the darkening stain that was spreading even as they watched.

"Who shot you?" she asked him as Bilbey cursed and tried to help his man to his feet.

Linford groaned in pain, and Bilbey eased him back to the ground. "Sparks," the sergeant said. "He must have seen me, though I don't know how." Linford gasped for breath and swallowed convulsively. "The window was open up there, I suppose he heard your voices . . . then he turned and saw me. If only I weren't wearing a blasted white tunic . . ."

"That was mere minutes ago," Isabelle said, taking the cloth from her head and wiping Linford's face with it. "He can't have gone far." She shook her head. "I thought I was hearing fireworks . . ."

"You must go." Linford gasped. "He may be watching. He'll kill you all."

Bilbey shook his head. "We're not leaving you here, man. We'll get you back to our quarters and send for the doctor."

"I won't last that long, sir," Linford said. Privately, Isabelle agreed with him. She'd seen her share of gunshot wounds.

James kept his attention on the street, continually scanning for signs of Sparks. His arm kept Phillip close to his side, and he seemed oblivious to Phillip's murmured utterances that he could stand upright without aid.

"I'm sorry to hurt you, Linford, but we must move you." Bilbey hoisted Linford up and put the wounded man's arm around his neck. Isabelle braced him from the other side, and with James helping Phillip along, the small group made their way down the street and toward the revelries at the heart of town.

* * *

"What is all that racket?" Sally asked Alice as the two girls crept from the small inn.

"It's a celebration of Vishnu," Alice said with a sniff. "The whole country is on holiday. Actually," she admitted, "it is rather exciting—when I was young, my father used to buy me trinkets and sweets, and we watched the painted elephants parade."

"Well, good," Sally said as she looked to the left and then the right. "Maybe there will be so much chaos tonight that stupid Sergeant Lyle will be delayed in looking for us."

"The whole inn is deserted," Alice commented as the girls made their way out into the night.

"That would explain why nobody came to see why we were screaming," Sally said. Her shoulder was likely bruised and would be for some time from the pummeling she had given the door. In the end, the girls had sat on a chair and kicked at the lock repeatedly until the wood splintered and gave way.

Sally glanced down the street and, grabbing Alice's hand, she steered her toward the noise and the lights. "Do you know anything about this city at all?" she asked Alice.

Alice shook her head. "Not much, I'm afraid. I suppose we shall just have to watch for men in British uniform."

"Oh, Alice, look at that!" Sally's eyes widened in amazement as she looked at the parades and shops spilling with the most incredible wares she had ever seen. "I want one of everything!"

Alice shook her head. "It is amazing. But I can't help but wonder what we will do if we cannot find anyone to help us."

"I don't care if we have to sleep on the street," Sally said firmly. "We are not going back with Lyle. If he comes upon us here, we will scream until we are hoarse. Are we agreed?"

"What if he should decide to shoot us?"

"Then we are freed from a life of slavery in the Orient. I'd sooner join my parents in heaven." Sally looked at Alice with one brow raised.

Alice nodded. "Agreed."

* * *

Linford was gone within an hour. The small group had come upon two hired hacks and made their way through the crowds back to the officers' headquarters where they were staying. Once they had put Linford on his bed and sent for a doctor, he had lost consciousness and never regained it. Isabelle sat on one side of his bed and held his hand, listening to his breath rattle out its final gasp. Bilbey sat on the other side, looking absolutely stricken. James and Phillip were off to one side, Phillip murmuring repeatedly that he was responsible for Linford's death.

Bilbey laid a trembling hand on Linford's forehead, prompting Isabelle to stand and motion James and Phillip from the room.

"That man died because you came for me," Phillip said when they were in the darkened hallway.

Isabelle shook her head. "He died because I suggested someone stand watch. It should have been me."

"Oh, for heaven's sake," James said and took Phillip and Isabelle each by the arm. He ushered them across the hall and into his room and closed the door. "We are not going to do this," he said and moved to light a lantern. "Sparks is responsible and nobody else. Neither of you shot him." He dragged a hand through his hair and looked at his brother. "We need to get you fed."

"Why don't we just go to the kitchens ourselves," Isabelle said. "The servants are already abed."

They made their way in silence to the kitchens where they fed Phillip food they found remaining from their dinner. The only sound was the clink of his silverware against the china.

"I hardly know where to begin," Phillip said as he wiped his mouth on a napkin and folded it. "I am . . . mortified . . . to have put you all in such a position. James, I am so very, very sorry." The younger man's eyes filled with tears, and Isabelle stood to give him some privacy with his brother.

"No, stay," Phillip said, rising. "James has told me what you've meant to his search, Miss Webb. I need you to know how very much I appreciate your help."

Isabelle sat back down and nodded. "It was my pleasure, Mr. Ashby. I am only too happy to see you safely back with your brother."

"Yet now your young friend and the colonel's daughter are missing. A man is dead. Again, I feel an immense responsibility." Phillip stared miserably at his hands.

Isabelle regarded him openly for the first time since the whirlwind rescue had begun. He was indeed the very image of his elder brother, yet with fewer worry lines around the eyes and mouth. She could see in his nature a penchant for the carefree, yet he was at the moment heavily burdened.

"We have yet to make the connection between Mr. Kilronomos and Mr. Sparks," Isabelle said. "As far as we know, the two episodes are entirely unrelated. You needn't feel so heavy on their account."

Phillip pursed his lips and nodded slightly. A tear escaped his eye, and he wiped at it impatiently. Isabelle glanced at James and saw him trying mightily to control his own emotions. In an uncharacteristic show of outward impulsiveness, James reached over and clasped Phillip's hand. "We'll speak no more of responsibility or regrets. I love you, brother, and I would do it all again to find you. I am sorry that I wasn't more able to convince you of your own worth to me at home. You might not have felt the need to go in search of something with Sparks."

Phillip stared at his brother for a moment before regaining his composure. "I hardly know what to say, James. I . . . thank you." Another tear escaped, and he slowly exhaled. "I was a fool. He spoke of treasure and adventure, and I believed every word because I wanted it to be true."

Isabelle cleared her throat. "Mr. Ashby, if I may ask, how long was it before you realized Sparks was up to no good?"

"Call me Phillip, please," he said. "And I suppose I had an inkling of the trouble I was in for by the time we left London. He told me he had mailed home some letters I sent to Mother and James, and I found them in his things. He maintained that he had just forgotten, but that was several days after he had assured me he had posted them."

"Phillip, you are not one to be bullied. I do not understand for the life of me why you stayed with him for so long," James said. "You are clever and certainly stronger by half."

"He threatened Mother. Told me that if I left before we found the jewel that he would make his way back home and do awful . . . horrible things to her." Phillip's face began to redden from the neck up. His fists clenched. "Even now I am afraid. I wonder if I shouldn't go back and play along with him for a bit longer."

James shook his head. "I'll send word through Bilbey's people immediately for the Steins to keep watch over Mother. That message will reach them before Sparks ever could, even if he should leave first thing in the morning, which I don't believe he will."

"Who are the Steins?" Isabelle asked.

"Our local sheriff and his family. Also happen to be close family friends and neighbors. He knows Sparks by sight and reputation," James said.

"I agree with you," Phillip said. "I don't believe he will leave by morning either. He hasn't yet found what he is looking for. He won't relinquish his hold on me easily, either. He believes I am the key."

"Because of your birthmark," James said.

Phillip looked surprised and nodded. "Because of my birthmark."

"Phillip, I must know, how on earth did Sparks come to know that you have that birthmark?" James asked.

Phillip's mouth turned up in half a smile, and he glanced at Isabelle. "Forgive me for being crass," he said, "but he happened to come across one of my pugilist matches. I was stripped to the waist and he saw the mark then."

"You're a pugilist?" Isabelle said, smiling. "How ever do you protect that pretty face?"

Phillip's grin was quick and engaging. Isabelle began to see the full effects of the young man's charm. "I'm fast."

James shook his head and sat back in his chair, crossing his legs at the ankles and lacing his fingers behind his head. "There are several of his friends who think fighting for sport is just the thing," he said to Isabelle. "Never understood it much myself. The fights I've encountered in my life have been less than pleasant."

"That's because they were true fights, brother," Phillip said. "Making a sport of it is altogether different."

Isabelle nodded slowly at James. "I'm beginning to understand some of the nature of your concern lately. You must have thought Phillip severely impaired, else he surely would have escaped Sparks by now."

Phillip sobered and nodded a bit. "I would have left, even penniless as I am, had he not continually threatened my mother." He clenched his teeth together and ran a hand through his hair in a gesture that Isabelle had seen many times from his brother. "I tried constantly to catch him off guard, but I swear the man never sleeps! Just when I thought I could escape the room or relieve him of the gun, he would stare at me with those green eyes."

"But he never dared hurt you," Isabelle mused, "because he needed you."

"Yes. He's just insane enough to make me believe he would take out his revenge on my mother, though. So I would threaten to leave, to turn him over to the authorities, to pound him into dust, and there would appear an expression on his face." Phillip's fists clenched on the tabletop. "I wanted to kill him, really kill him . . ."

"And you might well be justified in doing so," Isabelle told him gently, "but you must believe that the damage to your own soul would be far worse in the end."

James raised a brow at her, and she knew what she'd said sounded by and large religious. She shrugged slightly. "It is the truth. Until we arrived here, I'd not darkened the door of a church for a long time, but I've seen the effects of killing. One doesn't need to be a spiritual sort to realize that the taking of a life is not something to be considered lightly." She looked at Phillip. "You've a good, kind heart. I do not think you would ever be free of it."

He shook his head. "No. I suppose not. I wish you knew him, though. I wish you knew what he was like. Then you might understand."

"Oh, I understand," Isabelle said. "Without a doubt, I understand."

They sat in silence for a few moments. James finally broke it by saying, "We must send word to Mother immediately. She will be so relieved." He reached forward and clasped his brother's hand. "As am I." He squeezed Phillip's hand for a moment and released it.

Phillip nodded, his eyes downcast. "Thank you. Both of you."

Isabelle stood and smoothed her hand along the younger man's shoulder. In truth, he was but six years her junior, but she felt positively ancient. She smiled at him, feeling maternal, and left the room.

She then made her way out to the farthest reaches of the courtyard, sat on the ground, and sobbed. Sally was still gone, and there was no telling whether or not Isabelle would ever find her in one piece.

* * *

James splashed cold water on his face from the washbasin in his room and dried it with a towel. He looked at his reflection in the glass above the dry sink and took in the red-rimmed appearance of his eyes and the lines around his mouth. He blinked slowly, tired.

The relief he felt at having found Phillip was dimmed only by the fact that Sally and Alice were still missing, Linford was dead, and Sparks and Kilronomos were still at large. His heart skipped a beat while thinking of Isabelle, and he wanted nothing more than to whisk her away to the farthest reaches of the earth, where nobody would ever find them.

He glanced at his bed, his body yearning to fall onto it and sleep for a week. Of their own accord, however, his feet found their way to the door of his room and down the hall to Isabelle's room. The humidity was almost familiar now, and he rolled his shirt sleeves up and ran a hand across his freshly washed face. After a washing at home, his skin would nearly have dried before he reached for a towel. He wondered how Isabelle was faring—if she would miss the Indian way of dress she had taken to so well in the last few weeks. She had commented more than once on the comfort of the clothing.

He knocked on her door then frowned as several moments passed and he didn't hear any movement from within. Trying her door, he found it locked, and he might have assumed her to have already fallen asleep if not for the fact that he knew she slept lightly.

Turning, he made his way through the house and out into the back courtyard where the only light came from a partial moon that hung in the sky above trees that were strewn with moss and vegetation. The air was ripe with the scents of flowers and loud with crickets. He very nearly turned back to the house after giving the courtyard a cursory once-over when he saw Isabelle sitting in the corner by the stone wall that surrounded the officers' compound.

Briefly closing his eyes, he began walking toward her, his hands in his pockets and his heart hurting for her. He reached her side and tightened his jaw at the sound of her sad sobs. She cried quietly as though her heart might break, and he wondered if his heart might burst instead of hers.

James sank to the ground next to her and gathered her close, shushing her startled exclamation and gently guiding her head toward his shoulder. She leaned into him, soaking his shirtfront with her tears as he rocked slowly back and forth. He fumbled in his pocket for a handkerchief and handed it to her. She buried her face in it, her shoulders shaking with the effort to control her tears.

"We will find her, Isabelle. I swear it to you, we will not leave until we do," he whispered into her hair.

"You have a life at home," she cried. "You need to go to your mother. Phillip needs to go home."

"I will not leave your side. My mother is fine and my brother resilient. Isabelle," he said, placing his hands at the back of her head and her face, forcing her to look at him. "I love you. I will not leave you."

Her tears flowed afresh, and she looked at him as though she didn't believe him. She was vulnerable and hurting, and it tore at his insides. "Go home, James," she whispered on a sob. "You need to find a good woman and settle down. You don't know anything about me, about where I come from."

"I know your core, Isabelle Webb. I know your heart. The rest will come with time, and I want that with you."

"You don't know what you're saying." She shook her head, which he still held gently in his hands. "James, I am not traditional; I am not . . . normal."

He laughed softly and brushed at her tears with his thumb. "Then I must be abnormal as well. I am not concerned with traditional, Isabelle. I want you as you are. And you must stop your tears, because you are breaking my heart."

"I don't know that I can stop," she whispered. "I am terrified. Very few times have I ever been so afraid. I have no one, James, but Sally, and I love her so dearly."

James moved his hands to encircle her back and shoulders, and once again she laid her head in the crook of his neck. He rubbed her back softly as she wiped at her nose and eyes, and he whispered, "I will not leave you, and we will find her."

15

The following evening found Isabelle walking the length of the bridge and back again. How ironic that she stood at the very spot where Sparks had walked the night before. Of course, she and James had planned it that way, had found it fitting to use Ari's meeting place as the rendezvous point with Sparks, but now, as she walked restlessly, she could think only of Sally, of what she might be suffering.

There were a dozen British soldiers who had come along as reinforcement, who were hidden in the trees and undergrowth along the river. James, Phillip, Bilbey, and Weber as well, stood off in the trees along the riverside and watched her, prepared to rush Ari. She knew James particularly wanted to flatten the man, but they needed him in one piece so that they might find the girls

The sounds of a second night of festivities filled the air, and Isabelle absently noted the sight of fireworks exploding into the sky, rivaling the moon for attention. She wanted to be watching the display with Sally, not wondering if her charge were still alive and unharmed.

As for James's revelations the night before, she hardly knew what to think. She had wanted desperately to return his sentiments of love, but something within held her back, told her that it would pass, that he would find someone else more suited for him and move on without her. She was a practical woman, one who had carved a place in the world for herself, and her heart had taught her to trust very few. Her instincts maintained what she knew of his solidity, of his no-nonsense approach to life, and she would venture to guess that he did not declare such deep feelings lightly. There was a voice inside, though, that had dwelled there for as long as she could remember; it reminded her that her parents had left her and her sister utterly alone. Why on earth would a handsome, intelligent, witty man want to stay with her when her own parents had not?

She shook her head, trying to clear it and stay focused. A stab of panic she hadn't felt for some time shot through her system, and she gritted her teeth against it. She felt chilled despite the heat of the evening, and darts of cold fire raced up her neck, along her arms, and into her fingertips. Sometimes the feelings came with no warning, and she hated them. The fear, the panic, the irrational thoughts that her parents had left her intentionally, that they had not really died but had abandoned her. Her eyes burned, and she gripped the wooden railing, looking into the black water that reflected the warring moon and fireworks. She felt physically weak.

I am lovable, she told herself, biting her lip to keep it from trembling. *They didn't leave me. They died.*

On the eve of Isabelle's first day at the Boston girls' school, she had reluctantly expressed her apprehension to the Benefactress. The woman had quoted a verse of scripture that Isabelle somehow seemed to remember from time to time when situations seemed dire.

I can do all things through Christ which strengtheneth me.

The thought came to her now as she stood, digging her fingernails into the bridge railing and wishing she could disappear into the water below. Peace slowly stole through her body, calming her racing heart a bit and offering a measure of solace to her mind.

"I can do all things . . ." she murmured and loosened her grip. "I can do all things through Christ . . ." She didn't know much of Jesus, but she knew in that moment that she felt a bit better. Taking a deep breath, she straightened her shoulders. She would find Sally, and she would see what might transpire with James. She had one life, one chance, and the thought of not being with him made her want to sit down and cry all over again.

Isabelle was lost in her own thoughts and had just closed her eyes when the sound of muffled footfalls on the bridge had her snapping her head to the right. Ari appeared out of the shadows, and she turned her body toward him. Her pent-up emotions and fear of everything she was feeling served to fuel the fire, and her temper blazed with impressive acceleration. It was all she could do to keep from launching herself at him and clawing at his eyes.

"Where are they?" she asked him through clenched teeth. "You had better tell me they are unharmed, or there will be no place on this earth you can hide."

Isabelle had expected he would try to employ his usual charm or smugness. Ari appeared uneasy, however, and perhaps a bit angry himself. He was clearly agitated and matched her tone measure for measure.

"Where is the young Mr. Ashby?"

Isabelle tilted her head to the side. "You *are* working with Sparks," she said.

"You must have him. He couldn't survive long without money," Ari bit out.

Isabelle laughed. "Most of this country survives without money. Now we are at an impasse."

"And yet you would move mountains to see your Miss Rhodes again."

"If you kill her, Ari, you will surely get nothing from me."

Now he smiled. "Why would I kill her? That would be better than some alternatives, would it not? No, you will give me Mr. Ashby, because I can do worse things than death to Miss Rhodes."

Isabelle's arms went numb, and she fought to keep her expression bland. "Perhaps you might suggest an alternative, because I do not have Mr. Ashby."

Ari's face hardened, and he moved closer to her. "I'll not lay a hand on you, my dear Miss Webb, because I suspect well enough that your champions are likely hidden in the trees. Know this, however; we will meet here tomorrow at the same time, and you will produce the young Mr. Ashby or you will not see Miss Rhodes or Miss Bilbey again. Even now I have arrangements that will see them taken far away from your reaches or that of your remarkable Mr. Pinkerton."

Isabelle gritted her teeth. He *had* overheard her conversation with James that day in the tea gardens. Either that or Sally had filled his head with tales of her imminent rescue. "Answer me this much," she said. "Have you worked with Sparks from the beginning?"

"I don't see how it signifies," he said, "but Mr. Sparks and I are newly acquainted. We found we might be of some worth to each other."

"So you followed the plan we had all embarked on together, only you decided to beat us to Sparks and use the girls as your insurance."

"It seemed reasonable enough. You object?"

"It was my plan. Of course I object."

"Ah, Miss Webb. You envy me that I was able to locate Sparks first."

Isabelle smiled. "I don't think you did. You wandered around this city for nearly a week but failed. So you kept watch on the officers' housing until we arrived, because you in fact were *not* able to locate Sparks yourself."

"You are brave, here in plain sight of your supporters. Suppose we walk a distance together and continue our conversation."

"If I believed it would profit me something, I might do just that."

Ari's jaw worked, but he said nothing.

"But if you watched us, you knew as of last night that we had Phillip. You also would have known where. So what game are you playing, Ari?"

Ari glanced over his shoulder, and in that moment Isabelle knew Sparks lingered close by. "Why have you not told Mr. Sparks that you know where we reside with Phillip?" Her smile widened. "Too many aces up the sleeve will begin to find it crowded space. They might begin to slip back out."

"It is a dangerous game you play yourself, Miss Webb," Ari said, his flared nostrils belying his agitation.

"I am an American. Do you not know? It's what we do."

"A word from me, and Sergeant Lyle will dispatch the young women to places you will never begin to imagine."

"Then you will never have Sparks's jewel or whatever riches you might imagine yourself gaining."

Ari nodded slowly, almost as though to himself. "I can see we are indeed at an impasse. I think the young ladies have outlived their usefulness."

"Before you go, I simply must know—has Miss Bilbey given you the same amount of trouble that her mother undoubtedly did before you killed her?"

His face went slack, and Isabelle knew in that moment that not only had her bluff served to prove the truth, but that she had caught him off guard. "You do know too much," Ari said when he regained his composure. He slowly moved toward her, his hand disappearing into the folds of his jacket and withdrawing again. She caught the glint of light off of a wicked-looking knife. The blade itself was only a couple inches long but certainly substantial enough to do damage.

Isabelle backed up slightly, certain that if she ran, he would easily overtake her. She could imagine herself facedown on the ground with the knife buried to the hilt before the men in the trees could even fire off a shot. "You do know your life is forfeit if you harm me," she told him. "I want the girls, nothing more."

He shook his head. "You are mature enough to realize this has become far too complicated, Miss Webb."

"Then extricate yourself. Give me the location of the girls, and I will assure that you will leave this bridge unharmed."

"And beyond the bridge?"

"You would expect that I act as your protector for the rest of your life?" she asked. *Keep talking, keep talking* . . . "Suppose I arrange for Mr. Sparks to meet with Phillip Ashby. Where might I tell him to do so?"

Ari smiled. "Calcutta."

Isabelle blinked. She hadn't expected that.

"There are elements to this story you have yet to comprehend. Mr. Sparks was most interested to know that Lady Banbury was trying to reach him in London after he left. He was even more fascinated when I told him of her anger over the missing trunk," he said in a whisper as she continued to back slowly across the bridge. She noted that he kept the knife well hidden from view. "With your fertile mind, it's almost a shame to keep you in the dark as to his plans. You would find them most fascinating."

"Enlighten me," she said. "Certainly couldn't harm you. You plan to run me through."

"My mother would approve of you. You have all the feistiness of a Greek woman."

By the time Isabelle had reached the end of the bridge, she realized Ari had been using her as a shield. He turned and brushed past her, slamming his shoulder into hers and throwing her to the ground. He then melted into the trees at the water's edge and went crashing into the undergrowth.

Isabelle pushed herself upright and yelled into the trees, "Stay there! Do not come out!" As she looked back to the other side of the bridge, her suspicions were confirmed, and Sparks appeared. He looked her way for a moment, then at the spot where Ari had disappeared. Unfortunately, her valiant entourage was not inclined to stay hidden. It was with some shock that Isabelle recognized Colonel Bilbey as he tore into the underbrush after Ari. She wouldn't have guessed the man could move so quickly.

James ran for her, and she screamed at him to stay put. He paid her no mind, and she turned to Sparks, who stood indecisively on the edge of the bridge. "We do not have Phillip!" she yelled to him.

"You lie!" A flash of light and the sound of a shot quickly followed Sparks's outburst and Isabelle felt her heart leap into her throat when James grunted and fell beside her.

Movement suddenly swarmed from the trees as several British soldiers ran toward Sparks. He tore off in the direction of the garden entrance with no less than a dozen men on his heels.

"I told you to stay where you were!" Isabelle cried and grabbed at James. She tried to pull him close to her.

"It's just my shoulder," he groaned as she grabbed at him.

"I told you! Why didn't you listen to me? I knew Sparks was there! You should have listened to me and instead you all go running off like fools!" The tears came hot and fast, and Isabelle clutched at him, bending over him as though trying to shield him from the world. She couldn't keep her thoughts straight, couldn't formulate her next move.

Phillip's voice sounded quietly in her ear. "Miss Webb, Sergeant Weber and I will place him in the hack. We must get him back to the compound."

His words made sense, but Isabelle couldn't make her fingers relinquish their hold. She continued to cry, her despair causing her shoulders to heave.

"History is repeating itself. You must stop crying so, Isabelle," James murmured in her ear. "You will develop an awful headache."

"James Ashby, I am so angry at you," she ground out, her tears falling on his neck. "I am so angry at you."

"Isabelle," he said, "it's just my shoulder. We should go back to the house and summon the doctor. He will dig around with a metal stick, and after I have passed out from the pain, I am certain to recover."

She sat back slightly and looked at his face. It was drawn from pain already, but there was something else there, something close to humor and perhaps satisfaction.

"You are a deranged man," she said, tears trailing down her cheeks. "That you find humor here is absolutely deplorable."

He smiled a bit, wincing as she shifted and tried to extricate her arm from underneath his neck and shoulder. "I am merely thrilled to have confirmed something."

"And what is it, exactly, you think you've confirmed?" she asked.

"Oh, I think I'll hold that close to my steadily beating heart."

"You are wretched."

"Yes." James stood with Phillip's help and clutched his right shoulder with his left hand. "Weber, what do you suppose ought to be done about your colonel? His running off behind Kilronomos was not planned."

Weber nodded. "Colonel Stafford is just outside the gates. I'll inform him of Bilbey's actions and see what he suggests. I daresay we'll need to search along the river here for Colonel Bilbey if he doesn't show himself soon."

"Seemed awfully personal, the way he ran after the man," Phillip commented. "Of course, the Greek did abduct his daughter."

Isabelle exhaled slowly and walked close to James's side, trying to pull her shattered nerves together. Never in all her days working for Pinkerton had she ever come apart so completely, and the stress she had faced from Ari on the bridge had been minor. With some effort, she turned her thoughts to Bilbey's actions and gave them her consideration.

"The colonel knows that Ari was on board the steamship from London to India with us and spoke to Lady Banbury on numerous occasions. I believe he suspects Ari of killing her," she said sniffing and trying to discreetly wipe at her nose. Weber handed her a hand-kerchief from his pocket, and she accepted it with thanks. She paused, thinking. "There is more, however; he also believes Ari responsible for killing the woman and her child in Bombay."

James nodded as they quickly crossed the bridge. He glanced over at the river, searching the darkness. "Neither one of them will find his way in the dark," he said. "I hope Bilbey has the sense to return to the officers' compound if he's lost the man. Did anyone happen to see if the others assigned to following Ari managed to do so?"

Each replied in the negative. Isabelle followed James's gaze toward the river. The black of the night along the water and into the jungle was completely impenetrable. On the bridge and out into the city itself, along the streets and established neighborhoods, one could see the sky. In the thick of the jungle vegetation, however, there was no light, no direction. She shivered in spite of herself and raised her hand to clutch a fistful of James's coat jacket. She'd temporarily lost the possibility of finding where Ari had stashed the girls, but at least James wasn't dead.

He was still alive, still breathing. For the moment, it was enough.

* * *

"I must admit, this is much more comfortable than my clothing," Alice said to Sally as she plucked at the faded red Indian sari she wore. She leaned her head back against the wooden door against which the two girls sat and closed her eyes.

Sally nodded. Her own matching ensemble was equally comfortable, and she didn't miss the clothing she and Alice had traded with a young woman who had been laundering her own clothing in her small side yard. She examined Alice with a critical eye, and with a small, satisfied nod, leaned her own head back and closed her eyes.

Wearing their headscarves and keeping their faces averted, they might be able to stay clear of Sergeant Lyle. They had spied him the night before just after escaping from the inn and had taken great pains to put some distance between themselves and him. The only problem seemed to be that in doing so, they'd also distanced themselves from the British offices and officers' housing. Now that they knew which direction to pursue, they would have to spend the next day backtracking while avoiding capture.

"You know, though," Alice mumbled sleepily, "I should dearly love to get my hands on my trunk."

"Your trunk?"

"The one that never arrived with my mother's ship. It was full of beautiful things. She said she was going to bring me beautiful things." Alice sighed and drifted to sleep, her head tilted slightly to the side.

Sally watched her sadly. The day would soon come when Alice would have to acknowledge that her mother was most likely dead. Things could be worse, though. Alice still had her father. And the girls could still be the captives of that stupid Sergeant Lyle.

And where was Ari?

Sally felt a stab of anger and perhaps a bit of pain at the thought of the man she'd considered so handsome and charming. She'd even envisioned the day when he might ask Isabelle if he could formally court Sally. She shook her head and leaned back, tilting her head against Alice's.

Alice mumbled something in her sleep and fumbled a bit for Sally's hand, which she clasped tightly. Sally gave her a gentle squeeze and thought back to the moment a few weeks before when the two girls had met. Never in a million years would Sally have imagined striking a friendship with the girl.

Desperate circumstances caused strange things to happen, however, and now she clung to Alice with all her might. True, the girl was still a bit naive and rather useless when it came to survival, but she had all but lost her superior sniff and condescending attitude. Somehow, hunger had a way of humbling the haughtiest of people. Sally had been one of those herself.

Wishing she could sleep with one eye open, Sally pulled first Alice's head wrap and then her own more securely over their faces and gradually fell into an uneasy slumber.

16

James had been right about one thing—he did indeed pass out. Fortunately, however, the bullet had passed clean through the flesh of his shoulder, and the doctor was able to stitch together the pieces of torn tissue on the exit wound. He was pale from blood loss, and Isabelle sat clutching his hand and willing him to look his usual, robust self. Seeing his big form so still on the bed made her queasy with fear.

Isabelle reluctantly left his side when Phillip insisted she get some rest, but instead she found herself wandering the compound. Nobody had seen or heard from Colonel Bilbey, and she was growing increasingly concerned. Should he lose himself in the jungle, it might be ages before anyone found him.

The stillness of the night was eventually broken by the sound of hushed voices. Isabelle recognized two of the soldiers from the compound, and she approached them as they entered from the street.

"Have you seen Colonel Bilbey?" she asked.

"Yes, ma'am. We need to speak to Colonel Stafford."

Isabelle nearly groaned in frustration. "He isn't back yet either," she said. "Please, you must tell me where Bilbey is."

One hesitated then spoke to her. "We caught up with Colonel Bilbey alongside the river and followed the Greek through the park and back out to the city. We hung back a bit so he would think we were lost, and he eventually led us to a chawl. Bilbey ordered us to stand watch outside, and he went in. The Greek apparently went into his room and then out the window, though, because the screen had

been torn out. Bilbey came back to us outside and told us he was
going to wait for the man to return."

"So that's where Bilbey is now? Waiting in Ari's room?"

The soldiers nodded. "We came back here to tell Stafford."

Isabelle pursed her lips in thought. "Stafford is off chasing Sparks,
James is unconscious, and Phillip really is not safe outside the walls of
this compound. That leaves Weber, and the poor man is exhausted.
I'm the only one awake; you must take me to Bilbey."

The men looked at each other and then back at her, speechless.

"We do not have the time to argue about it. Take me there, and I
will accept full responsibility for it. You will have to trust that Bilbey will
expect nothing less of me at this point."

Her pronouncement was met with further silence.

"Every moment is precious," she said sharply. "Take me there or I
will wander around until I find him myself."

Finally, the older of the two shrugged. "This way then, ma'am.
We'll take the officers' conveyance."

* * *

James floated in and out of an odd reality where his shoulder was on
fire and then felt like ice. He thought he heard Isabelle screaming,
only to find it was Phillip, then his mother. He wanted to claw at his
shoulder, rip it from his body, so the pain would stop. He wanted
Phillip to stop blaming himself, and he wanted more than anything
to be far, far away with Isabelle.

She wasn't with him; he always knew when she was near. The very
air around him seemed charged with something that was uniquely her
whenever he was in her presence, and he felt her absence very keenly.
He wanted to believe she was in her bed getting some rest, but he felt
uneasy. Perhaps it was the laudanum he suspected the doctor had
slipped him against his wishes.

He struggled to open his eyes, but his eyelids weighed more than
he could manage. If he could just sit up for a moment, he'd be able to
find his shoes and go to her. He rolled onto his shoulder and saw an

explosion of white sparks. His whole body was on fire; he felt damp all over from his own body heat.

Phillip's voice sounded distantly as a cool hand rested briefly across his brow. "You're burning up, brother," he said. "I'll fetch the doctor." The voice echoed as though it was spoken through a tube. James felt desperate to stand up, to see if Isabelle was well. "Stay down!" The order was sharp, and James barely recognized Phillip's voice. When had his brother become the one to take charge?

Then Weber was there, telling Phillip something about the humidity and the jungle being dangerous to wounds. Telling him that infections were common.

* * *

Isabelle climbed the stairs to the second story of the chawl and couldn't help feeling a sense that she'd already been there before. The specter of the previous evening loomed large in her mind, and she shrugged off a stab of sorrow for the loss of Linford. The two soldiers from the compound stood guard, well hidden outside on the street, and had told her which room was Ari's. She silently walked the hallway to the farthest room. It looked out over a back alley; she had a good sense of how Ari had escaped injury from his second-story jump when she spied piles of dirty laundry and fabrics scattered in boxes and bins below.

Isabelle listened quietly at the door before turning the knob and cautiously opening it a crack. Bilbey stood near the open window with his eye on the door and a pistol at the ready. "It's Isabelle Webb, sir," she said softly but clearly.

The man exhaled. "I might have killed you, woman!"

She entered and closed the door behind her. "But you're not here to kill Ari, are you?"

He lowered his weapon and looked out the window into the night sky. "I don't know."

"Seems to me we need information from him. That won't be so easily obtained with him dead." She stood by his side and examined his face in the dim light that came in from the window. "Sir, you are absolutely exhausted. Two of your men are hiding outside, and we left word at the compound to send more. They can bring Ari in to the officers' house as soon as he shows his face." She glanced around the room. "Surely he'll return. All of his things are here, and from what I understand, he doesn't know for a certainty that you know where he's rooming."

"He must have known I followed—he went out the window. I want to speak to him personally. To think that I took that man into my entourage, while all the time he was the one . . . and now he has Alice . . . and where are they? The girls?"

It was a good question. Isabelle looked more closely at the room and could see that, clearly, the only inhabitant had been Ari himself. There was no evidence of another person, let alone another man and two young women.

Bilbey shook his head. "Something isn't right. He's played us for fools—there's been no sign of Sergeant Lyle anywhere in the city. As soon as we arrived, I sent word with our men here and wired every major city in the country that I am to be notified as soon as someone spots him. I've heard nothing yet."

"He must have them in another room, another chawl," she noted.

Bilbey shook his head. "You should go back to the officers' compound. When he returns, you will not be safe."

As though his words made the man materialize, Isabelle and Bilbey heard footsteps in the hall. Isabelle darted behind Ari's trunk and made herself as small as possible, thankful for the instinct that had prompted her, yet again, to wear the thin Indian clothing. Ari entered the room and gave a start when he saw Bilbey standing by the window.

"Well," Ari said. "So you did manage to trail me here."

"Where is my daughter?"

Isabelle peeked around the trunk to see that Bilbey had his pistol aimed at Ari's head. His hand was steady, his face hard.

"Where is Phillip Ashby? I have yet to see him outside the compound—is he holed up inside?" Ari countered.

"Keep your hands away from your pockets," Bilbey said. "And tell me why you need Mr. Ashby."

"Because Sparks insists and will not make a move without him."

"And why do you care what Sparks wants?"

"I do not owe you an explanation."

"I have a pistol aimed at your head. You have my daughter captive. You *do* owe me an explanation."

Ari sighed, sounding much like the dramatic man Isabelle had come to know. "It became clear to me that I would be able to locate Mr. Sparks much faster on my own."

"And what exactly were you hoping to obtain from him?"

"Well, as he was prepared to pay your wife handsomely for information, I decided to give him that information in her stead. She owed me money, and she did not intend to pay it to me. The money Sparks would have given to her was rightfully mine."

Bilbey's expression did not change, but his silence spoke of his confusion. Finally, he spoke. "And why, sir, did my wife owe you money?"

"She hired me to do some . . . investigating."

Isabelle felt the tension in the room rise a notch.

"Investigating?" Bilbey asked. "Of what?"

"A certain woman and child in Bombay."

Isabelle heard the smug tone in Ari's voice, and Bilbey's reaction proved what she had just begun to suspect.

"*You* . . ." Bilbey began, but anything further he might have said was silenced as Ari deftly slipped a pistol from his sleeve and fired.

Isabelle clamped her hand over her mouth as Bilbey fell to the floor with a single, circular hole in the middle of his forehead, his eyes wide open.

Ari stood still for several long moments before he finally turned and exited the room. Isabelle waited for the space of a few heartbeats before scrambling to Bilbey's side and placing two fingers at the side of his neck. She didn't expect to find a pulse and wasn't surprised when it was lacking. Bilbey's sightless eyes stared up at her in stunned horror, and she gently closed them. Oddly enough, her sorrow wasn't for him so much as Alice, who, when they did find her, would have to be told she was an orphan.

Isabelle stood, her heart heavy and stomach convulsing. It didn't matter how many times she had seen a person die; it never failed to come as a shock. One minute there, the next minute gone. Just like that, in the snap of two fingers, a life was snuffed out.

The sound of quick footsteps in the hallway had her bracing her hand against the large, open windowsill. Ari entered the room again, looking toward his trunk and moving to open it when he glanced up and spotted her at the window. He jumped back a bit and the startled expression on his face gave Isabelle a moment's satisfaction, but as he reached for his gun, she braced her palms on the sill and with a very literal leap of faith, vaulted through the window, falling toward the street. She twisted her body and landed on her back in a pile of fabric.

She scrambled off of the bin and stumbled, falling hard to her knees on the ground. A bullet whizzed past her head close enough to leave her ear ringing. Making her way hastily to her feet, she began running for all she was worth to the end of the alley.

Isabelle rather hoped that if Ari were inclined to give chase, he would take the stairs, but she heard him leave the room the same way she had. He landed with a grunt and a thud behind her just as she reached the end of the alley and turned onto another street. The way to the front of the chawl where the soldiers were was blocked by several large carts, so she turned and ran left instead.

Finding herself on a small street, deserted except for a few sleeping forms in doorways, she ran and zigzagged until reaching the end, trying to make Ari's aim on her impossible to hold for any length of time. He ran behind her, his footsteps growing closer, and the sound of another gunshot rang through the night.

She rounded the corner and spied a main street. She ran for it and was glad to see something familiar—the entrance to the gardens where they had met on the bridge. There was no way she would lose him on the streets. The revelries had finally ceased for the night, and with dawn approaching in a scant hour, the city was asleep and the streets quiet.

Fear lent her strength and speed, and ignoring the familiar pain shooting through her leg, Isabelle ran as she knew she could. She entered the garden and flew up the path, tearing across the bridge to put some distance between herself and Ari. She ran into the trees at the side of the river and tried to mark her progress as she went, wishing she could see where she was stepping.

She heard Ari crashing into the undergrowth several yards behind her, and she ran blindly, looking for a good place to lose him. He must have stumbled, because she heard him hit the ground and let fly a string of curses before he regained himself and gave chase again. By this time she had been able to put a fair amount of distance between them and spied a tree that hung with vines and moss, its branches sweeping and wide. It seemed to beckon to her with its open arms, and she leapt into it without second thought, climbing higher and higher.

* * *

In the darkness, James was high off the ground, looking around for a way to secure his footing. His head swam as he looked down at the ground. He had never liked heights. Why on earth would he be so far from the good, solid earth? He was warm, so warm! His skin was on fire, his shoulder burning and throbbing. A babble of hushed voices drifted in and out of earshot, bothering him.

Am I dead? I must be dead. So the afterlife is a dark place . . . I always envisioned it as one of light . . .

He couldn't be dead. If he were, he would see his father. Instead, he wrapped both of his arms and legs around a thick branch and hung on, watching as someone approached from beneath . . .

* * *

Isabelle held her breath and released it slowly, trying to calm her frantic breathing and pounding heart. Ari ran below her, stopped, retraced his steps, and then moved forward again. He had to have known she'd stopped, because he wouldn't hear her moving anymore or see further trampled foliage. She could barely see his outline in the black of the dense jungle.

Humidity bathed her in moisture, and sweat dripped from her forehead and down into her eyes. She heard a droplet fall to the leaves below and bit her lip in frustration. She lay on a thick tree limb, fighting to stay still on the moss, which was wet in some spots, dry and prickly in others. Both arms and legs were wrapped tightly around the limb, and she hung on for all she was worth.

Isabelle's clothing clung to her skin. She rubbed her forehead against her shoulder and tightened her hold with her legs when she felt herself begin to slip. Ari crossed the ground beneath her again and then let out a roar.

"I know you are here!" he shouted. "Show yourself or by the gods I will sell your charge into slavery!"

Her breathing was still labored, and she struggled to control it. She began counting quietly in her head.

"Do you know what happens to young girls when they are sold?" His voice turned to a near scream.

Breathe, two, three, four . . .

"I will have my money! I will not be stopped by a woman who has no idea what she has stumbled across! You should have died when Lyle pushed you from the train!"

Five, six, seven, eight . . . Sweat trickled down her neck and was absorbed into the damp green and yellow fabric.

Ari walked in circles, his pacing becoming erratic and his own breathing labored and coming in gasps. He stopped directly below Isabelle, and she put her forehead on the tree, closing her eyes in disbelief. What were the odds that he would hover below her very hiding place?

Isabelle felt the hair on the back of her neck rise, and she lifted her head to see two glossy eyes no more than a yard from her face. She sucked in her breath and held it, more frightened of the eyes than the gunman on the ground. She watched in horror as the smooth, yellow- and black-striped body behind the eyes slithered and coiled around the branch.

In that moment, all she wanted was to be away from the snake. Ever so slowly she began to inch her way back down the branch. Keeping her head still but moving her eyes downward, she spied a branch that was well within her reach. She gently swung her legs down and lowered herself to the limb below, gritting her teeth at the pain in her thigh and hoping the leg would not collapse.

Her movements seemed to pique the snake's interest, and it followed her, extending its body downward as she continued her steady descent, lowering her body from branch to branch until she was ten feet above the ground. The serpent matched her movements, and she felt a measure of horror that as she looked up into the tree, she couldn't see the end of the reptile.

She now hung by her hands from the tree, side by side with the serpent. There was nowhere to go but down. She ran the risk of startling Ari so badly he would turn and shoot, but the snake was watching her with its unnerving eyes and moving ever closer to her. Holding her breath, she dropped to the ground with a muffled cry at the fire that shot through her leg.

Ari spun around, gun raised and ready to shoot, when the snake brushed past his head and focused its attention away from Isabelle and on Ari instead, whipping its tail in excitement. Hanging from the tree and looking impossibly long, the snake studied Ari with interest. Ari's mouth opened, but no sound emerged; he stared for a long moment at the animal before stumbling toward Isabelle with a strangled shriek.

Isabelle couldn't back away quickly enough, and before she realized what was happening, Ari tripped and fell on top of her, taking them both to the ground hard. When they hit, she managed to grab hold of the gun that slipped from his fingers. She pulled the hammer back and jammed it into his forehead.

"Where is Sally?" she asked through gritted teeth. "Tell me, or I will put a bullet in your head and wander this country until I find her."

He shoved himself into a kneeling position over her and slowly stood, both hands raised in supplication. His breath came in gasps as he appeared to measure the greater threat; the one in front of him or the one that slithered close behind.

Isabelle rose to her feet and moved subtly toward him with the gun extended. "Tell me now, or I will shoot you just enough to let you live and let the snake finish you!" She inched closer to him, and when he remained silent, she backhanded him across his cheek with the butt of the weapon. "Tell me!"

"Calcutta," he spat out, the whites of his eyes visible in the darkness. "They are in Calcutta."

"Why!"

"Insurance," he said as she tightened her grip on the weapon. "So that I could reach Sparks and warn him you were looking for Ashby. I thought to make a deal with him."

"But why Calcutta?" she repeated.

"Because I knew I could get money for them if not from Sparks!" Ari's anger was beginning to show, and he seemed to regain some of his wits. He surprised her by quickly smacking at her hand. The weapon fired off wildly into the night, and he chopped again at her arm, causing her to drop the gun onto the jungle floor. It fell into a thick carpet of leaves and foliage, and for a second Isabelle debated which would be the wiser course—to try and retrieve the weapon or run for her life.

Ari made the decision for her as he clutched her throat and began to squeeze. She should have immediately run. Isabelle looked at a spot just over his right shoulder and forced her eyes to open wide, hoping her expression was one of horror. She stopped beating at his arms and pointed instead, and when Ari turned to look at what he thought was the serpent, she brought her knee up to make contact with his groin.

He doubled over in pain and released her. She gasped for breath and turned to run, only to catch herself on a branch that hit her at shin height. She fell to the ground, her face glancing against an enormous, jagged rock at the base of the tree. Her hair caught in the branches of undergrowth and she began to feel an urgent sense of panic. Her cheek throbbed where she had hit the rock, the pain causing tears to fill her eyes and obscure her vision. Shoving with all her might, she pushed herself to her feet and began to run forward. The moon was bright, and a small amount of light shone down through the thick canopy above.

Ari roared in anger. She looked back quickly to gauge the distance between them when she saw him stumble forward in an attempted pursuit and trip on the same branch that had caught her. His hands flew to either side of the large rock but his head hit it with a sickening crunch. He lay completely still.

Isabelle stared at the man in dumb shock. Her mouth slack, she stood immobile for a while. Even as she watched, blood seeped from his head and onto the stone, flowing in a red-black river onto the jungle floor. His sightless eyes stared at her much as Bilbey's had not an hour before. A movement from the corner of her eye caught her attention, and she noted the serpent. It slithered over the ground to Ari's foot, which still lay tangled atop the protruding root, and seemed to watch her as it moved. Further light showed her that the snake was nearly eight feet long, its body stretching back to the tree where she had found momentary refuge.

Deciding there was no further help for Ari, and not altogether certain she'd offer it if there were any, Isabelle turned and blindly ran back in the direction she'd come, limping heavily despite her determination not to. She followed the river until the thick vegetation cleared, and she saw the rendezvous bridge. Her shoes sounded loudly on the wooden planks as she ran across it. She made her way out of the gardens and back down the streets, the recesses of her memory showing her the way to the chawl where Bilbey lay dead.

When she reached Ari's room, she saw several British soldiers tending to Bilbey's body. The two guards must have finally received their reinforcements. They all turned at her approach and stared at her in shock, nobody saying a word. One of the men was Weber.

Heaving, she doubled over for a moment and then straightened slightly. "Kilronomos is dead," she said. "He's in the jungle gardens along the river on the east side. If Stafford wants you to retrieve his body, I suggest you make haste. The serpent won't leave much when he's done." She pointed to Ari's trunk. "Take that back to the compound. Take everything in here. Don't leave a thing behind."

She moved to Weber, who blinked at her as though coming out of a trance. "Miss Webb," he finally said. "Are you quite all right?"

Isabelle nodded. "Weber," she said, looking down at the body that was now covered with a sheet. "I am so sorry about your colonel."

He nodded, swallowing. "Ma'am, I should very much like to find his daughter. I will help you continue your search."

"I am so glad to hear it. We need to pack. We are bound for Calcutta."

He blinked again. "But Ari abducted the girls when we were in Barrackpore."

"Yes."

"Barrackpore is only thirty miles north of Calcutta."

"And that, my friend, is the most frustrating part of all."

17

"I most certainly did not steal this fruit!" Alice said hotly to the man who had come barreling around his stall in the crowded market.

"You did! I saw you take it!" the man answered her in English.

"I did not intend to keep it! I was examining it for . . ."

"Bruises," Sally supplied, linking her arm through Alice's.

"Yes, bruises. And I don't believe I will purchase it after all," Alice said and placed the fruit back on the stand. "It looks extremely substandard."

Sally stifled a groan and a roll of the eyes.

The angry merchant grabbed Alice's arm, which she hastily tried to pull free. "I am the daughter of a British officer!" she said.

"Ha! A likely story, dressed in those clothes."

Sally chewed on her lip, suddenly uncertain of the wisdom in abandoning their own things. She pointed behind the man and shouted, "Look! He's taking your fruit, and here you sit berating us!"

When the man turned his back, Sally yanked hard on Alice's arm and jerked her into the crowd. They tore past hands that, at the angry man's commands, attempted to grab them, and they zigzagged their way along the streets. Their pursuer was determined, however, and with a bark at his wife to watch their stall, he gave chase.

Sally looked back over her shoulder and was gratified to see that not only was Alice keeping pace, but that a young boy seated at the base of a statue alongside the street stuck out his foot and tripped the man, sending him sprawling on his face in the dirt. The young boy scampered off, and the fruit seller eventually got lost in the crowd.

Sally continued to run, and when she spied the docks, she pulled Alice along with her to hide inside a shack that looked near collapse. Breathing hard, the two fell to the hard-packed dirt floor.

"I know you're hungry," Sally whispered between gasps, "but next time, let me show you how to do it."

* * *

When James awoke, he had no sense of the time. The light in the room was dim; outside it might have been dawn or dusk. A single kerosene lamp was lit by his bedside. His door was open, offering additional light from the hallway. He was stiff and sore but blessedly cool. He raised himself slightly, wincing at the pain in his shoulder but otherwise able to maneuver. He leaned up against the headboard and rubbed his eyes and face.

He noticed Isabelle then, seated in a chair by his bedside and leaning forward on his bed. She slept on her folded arms, her face toward him. James narrowed his eyes and with a grunt sat up and leaned forward. He raised a finger and trailed it gently down the side of her face, touching a large bruise. Her hair hung loose and tangled down her back, and closer inspection showed her clothing to be torn and filthy. Her arms were covered with myriad scratches and cuts, some of which appeared to have trickled tiny streams of blood that had long since dried on her skin.

"What have you done, Belle?" he whispered. Muddled, confused memories of fear for her safety and images of darkness and danger returned with a vengeance, and his anger began to mount.

"Isabelle," he said a bit more loudly, shaking one of her arms. "Belle!"

She raised her head with a start, her red-rimmed eyes flying open in a panic. She groped for his hand and clutched it, moving to sit on the edge of the bed. She looked as though she had been through a battle and had come out on the losing side. "James, you finally look coherent! You can't imagine how insanely you've been babbling, and the fever has been raging for hours."

She placed a hand on his forehead, and he shackled her wrist with his long fingers, his shock at her appearance rendering him momentarily speechless. She winced at the contact, and he gentled his touch. When he finally found his voice, he asked, "What have you been doing, taking on the Greek and Sparks single-handedly?"

She seemed a bit irritated by his anger. "Not the both of them, no." She exhaled a bit and her shoulders sagged. "The story is a bit . . . complicated in the telling."

"I have no pressing engagements." He released her hand as she began to explain the events of the past night. Were it any other woman, he would have disbelieved the whole of it. Equal parts of fury and admiration flooded his brain, but the emotion underlying everything was fear.

"You were nearly shot several times and then almost bitten by a large jungle snake," he said and ran a hand through his own disheveled hair. "You fell and hit your face on a rock that mere seconds later killed a man. You jumped out of a second story window with no knowledge of what lay beneath the piles of laundry." He paused for a moment and looked closely at her. "You jumped out of a second-story window?"

She seemed surprised for a moment. "Yes, I did. Didn't even give it a moment's thought. It was the lesser of two evils, really. Perhaps my ghosts are exorcised."

He looked at her for a long time, and to her credit, she returned his gaze without stammering or blushing or looking away. "What was your intention when you left this place?" he asked.

"To find Bilbey and keep him from killing Ari before we knew where the girls were. I had hoped to find them in his room or at least in the same building."

"And you were certain Bilbey was going to kill Ari."

Isabelle nodded. "I've been wondering about Bilbey's connection to the murdered woman in Bombay. I think he may have had a romantic attachment to her. Indelicate of me to suggest it, no doubt."

James considered it for a moment and nodded. "Makes sense, I suppose."

"Even more scandalous, I also wonder if the child was his," she added, her voice hushed.

James exhaled a quiet sigh. "Would have shamed the Lady Banbury mightily if it were true," he said.

Isabelle nodded. "It would also explain why she hired Ari. She wanted information about the woman. I'm not convinced she wanted her dead, although we may never know what her actual instructions were. I plan to go through Ari's things as soon as Stafford allows me access. He has them all locked in an office down the hall."

James's lips twitched reluctantly. "I've never known you to be hindered by a locked door."

She didn't return his smile. "The truth of the matter is I was more worried about you. You've been delirious for nearly twenty-four hours. I haven't much cared for whatever Ari's assignment was or was not." Now she avoided his scrutiny and looked at the bedside lamp instead. "I feel desperate to get to Calcutta, but the thought of leaving you here, not knowing whether . . ." She shook her head slightly and pursed her lips, her eyes filling with tears.

"Sweet woman, your tears will be my undoing." He took her hand and rubbed his thumb across the back of her knuckles. "I am well," he said, his voice sounding hoarse, even to his own ears. "I will go to Calcutta with you on the next available train."

She shook her head. "The doctor said you shouldn't be moved for at least a week."

"For heaven's sake, it's just my shoulder."

"The fever, though—somehow being in the jungle makes it worse."

James laughed. "I was outside in the jungle for all of ten minutes after being wounded. I suspect it was that metal probe that made me sick."

Her eyes widened. "He used a metal probe? You were right then, you horrid man." She smiled, her lower lip cracking open a former cut. She ran her tongue along it with a wince. "Phillip tells me he's been praying for you."

James nodded.

Isabelle continued. "From what I hear, Phillip bodily removed the doctor last night while I was out. The doctor wanted to put leeches on your wound to suck out impure blood."

James laughed. "Phillip hates leeches. He fell into a pond full of them once as a child and hasn't been able to abide the sight of them since. Where is he now?"

"Eating supper with the soldiers in the dining hall."

"So it's that late, then."

She nodded, looking away again. "James, I . . ." she glanced back at him and then down at their hands. He turned her hand over and began tracing lazy circles on her palm with his fingertip.

"Yes?"

She sighed. "You're not going to make this easy for me. Fine, then. I love you, and I suspect you know that."

He smiled, taking in the whole of her disheveled, bloodied, and bruised appearance and thinking her the most beautiful woman he'd ever seen. "I do know that."

"I don't see how such a thing is possible, really, when I consider the fact that we've known each other less than one month's time."

"Much has happened in that one month. And we aren't children, Isabelle. I know what I like and what I want. I was beginning to doubt I'd ever find it."

She looked up at him again. "We are so very different."

"Thank heavens for that. I should hate to be enamored with a mirror image of myself."

She laughed. "I think you like yourself just fine."

His grin deepened, and he was supremely, smugly satisfied at her indrawn breath. It was his brother who usually garnered such a reaction. "One of me in the world is enough, wouldn't you agree?"

Her smile slipped. "And there almost wasn't one of you at all in the world, just because you wouldn't listen to me when I warned you."

He laced his fingers with hers and brought them to his mouth, closing his eyes. "Isabelle," he finally said, "watching you that night on the bridge . . . I thought my heart would stop. I was nearly paralyzed with fear. When I saw that man advancing on you and figuring he probably had a weapon or you would have stood your ground, I couldn't get to you quickly enough. It was as though my feet were stuck in the ground and couldn't move. When you fell . . ."

It didn't bear contemplation, really, thinking of what could have happened to her. Had he not been shot, he had no doubt he'd have run down Ari himself and torn him limb from limb. He shook his head. "All the forces in the world couldn't have kept me from your side. Your warning to me was laughable."

She scowled. "I was trying to keep Phillip safe, too. And you look so much like him—"

"Sparks knows the difference. He wouldn't have shot Phillip."

"You see? All the more reason for you to have kept yourself hidden." She waved her free hand. "It is done and finished. But I would like you to remember that I am not happy with you."

"Duly noted. I should like to state, however, that I am not happy with you, either. One night of unconscious delirium on my part, and you're off nearly getting yourself killed. This cannot continue. I'll do my best to heed your warnings in the future if you will agree to heed mine."

"You were unavailable for comment last night."

"You're being deliberately evasive. Furthermore, I don't believe it would have made a difference to you anyway. You were set on going, and you did."

Isabelle rolled her eyes. "Contrary to what you might believe, I do not enjoy finding myself in such a state." She indicated her face and arms.

James narrowed his eyes. "Let me see your neck."

Isabelle lifted her hair. "Why?"

"Are those *fingerprints*?"

"Ah, yes. That would have been from when he tried to strangle me."

His lips tightened. "And you're certain he is dead?"

Isabelle nodded.

"Pity. I should have liked to make him suffer." His words were mild enough, but he thought his blood might boil over. James wanted to pull Isabelle close, but the fact that she was sitting on his bed was enough to socially ruin her forever, despite the open door and the appropriate behavior from both lovers.

He took a deep breath and tried to calm both his anger at Ari and his fear for her. "Might I scandalize you for a moment, Miss Webb?"

She smiled. "I wish you would, Mr. Ashby."

"Well then, know this. There will come a day when I will pin you against the nearest wall and kiss you senseless. I dearly wish that moment could be now, but as I am recovering from a gunshot wound, fever, and feel as though a dead animal were residing in my mouth, and you look as though the fires of hell have swept down upon you and wreaked their vengeance, I don't suppose such a thing would be pleasant at this point."

Isabelle doubled forward on the bed and laughed, clutching at her midsection. "Oh, mercy," she said. "Your duty as my potential suitor is to tell me that I am all that is lovely and gentle in the world. You are to ply me with poetry and sweet words!"

He smiled and leaned forward, gently curling his fingers around the back of her neck and pulling her toward him to rest her cheek against his. "When the time is right for us," he whispered in her ear, "words will only be a hindrance."

He placed the lightest of kisses on her earlobe and pulled back to see her eyes close. She exhaled slowly and opened her eyes, and he saw in them flecks of gold and green. She smiled at him and shook her head slightly. "And you say your brother is the charmer," she whispered.

He kissed her forehead and gently nudged her back. "Go to your room and relax. I'm going to send for a maid to help you wash. Then you should eat something and rest. I suspect we will leave for Calcutta in the morning."

She frowned and stood. "James, I'm not altogether certain you should travel."

"We'll speak no more of it. I am fit as a fiddle."

She made her way to the door, muttering something under her breath. She paused and looked back at him, and he had to shake his head. She had been utterly beaten up and took it in stride. "You are beautiful," he said.

She blushed and left the room.

* * *

Night fell, and still Sally and Alice remained hidden in the safety of the dockside shack. It was full mostly of empty barrels, piled high and smelling of old fish. Sally looked out through the wide gaps in the planks to see that much of the hustle and bustle of the day had diminished. She mused over the possibilities of finding food while her stomach growled.

"Perhaps someone dropped some fruit in the street where the stalls were," Alice said.

"It wouldn't stay there for long," Sally said. "You've seen the people—they live in doorways and alleys and eat whatever garbage they come across. I've never seen so many poor people in all my life, and I lived through a war."

Alice sniffed, and Sally glanced at her. A tear stole its way down the girl's cheek, and Sally's heart twisted. "Now, now," she said and absently patted herself for a kerchief. When she saw what she was doing, she laughed, and to her relief, Alice did as well. "We will find some food, Alice, and in the morning we will find the officers' quarters. We're at the docks now; we must be close. Just think, a few more days of this and we'll no longer need corsets!"

Alice groaned and laughed. "You're incorrigible," she said. She wiped away her tear and shook her head. "I wish I were braver. You're so brave."

"No. Not brave, just . . . resourceful. I've done this before."

"You've run away from someone before?"

"No, I've starved before."

Alice's eyes widened. "During the war?"

Sally nodded. "We lost everything. Absolutely everything. My father was killed in battle, my mother sold everything of value in our home, and then she became ill. She . . . well, she died. And left me with three younger siblings and an empty house."

"What did you do?"

Sally smiled and felt a tear of her own gather. "Isabelle found me."

* * *

Isabelle examined the contents of Ari's trunk as the morning light shone through the window. She found clothing, a few receipts, and the diary she had found in his room in Barrackpore. He also had some receipts for train fare and a pouch with both Indian and Greek money.

Isabelle sat back for a moment with a train ticket in her hand. He had planned to go to Calcutta that very day. She walked out of the office and down to the dining room, Ari's notebook in one hand and the train ticket in the other. She examined the ticket as she walked, deep in thought.

She entered the dining room to see an officer speaking to Colonel Stafford.

"You're quite certain?" Stafford asked the man.

"Yes. Lyle was seen outside military headquarters yesterday. He was looking for a friend, according to the telegram."

"And he wasn't detained? Bilbey left specific instructions that the man was to be arrested on sight," Stafford said.

"No, sir, not that I'm aware."

Isabelle entered the room and acknowledged the men with a hushed, "Good morning," as Stafford stood. She sat at the table, her eyebrows drawn in thought as Stafford excused his man.

"I don't know how much you heard," Stafford told her, "but Lyle has been spotted in Calcutta."

Isabelle nodded. "It does follow what Ari told me, then. He sent Lyle off to Calcutta with the girls and came here to Delhi on his own, hoping to find Sparks."

Stafford shook his head. "I can't imagine what he thought he would benefit by doing so."

"Well, supposedly he wanted Sparks to pay him whatever he had been prepared to pay Lady Banbury for her information about the jewel."

"But did he have the information?"

Isabelle shrugged. "I don't suppose he would have been above fabricating something. He seemed to know a fair amount about the legend himself." She flipped through Ari's black notebook, paying closer attention to details she had been unable to find that night in the dark of his hotel room.

"Is that his journal?" Stafford asked, indicating to the book with his fork.

Isabelle nodded. "Unfortunately, much of it is in Greek."

Stafford looked surprised. "Ah, well, it is of no account—I have a soldier here who is quite literate in Greek."

"You jest."

"No, no! Truly, his mother is Greek. I've not heard him speak it much, but I know he reads many of the classics in their original form. Only allow me to finish my meal, and I will summon him. Shall we meet in the library in, say, twenty minutes?"

"Excellent. That should give me just enough time to finish packing my things."

"You leave at noon?"

"Yes."

18

Isabelle and James sat on a sofa in the library together, their bags packed and ready by the front door. She looked over James's shoulder as he slowly perused Ari's book.

"They never did find his body, did they?" he asked as he turned a page.

Isabelle shook her head. "No. Either he wasn't really dead or the snake made a quick meal of him. From what I understand, however, it was quite some time before Stafford sent men into the gardens to look for him. So either the snake really did finish him off or Ari came to and staggered into town."

"I should hope he never dares show himself again," James said and glanced at Isabelle, whose face was still slightly swollen and multicolored from scratches and bruises. "He will live to regret it. Provided I feel inclined to let him live."

"I shouldn't much like visiting you in a prison."

James turned another page. "No, I don't suppose you would. I should have to rely on Phillip for company, then." He ran his finger over a sentence written in Greek and stopped on the words, *The Davis*. "Why does that sound so familiar?" he mused aloud.

Isabelle squinted at the sentence. "Perhaps because it's the only thing written in English for pages."

They looked up as Phillip entered the room, followed by Stafford and a man introduced to them as Sergeant Christensen. As Stafford explained some of the particulars to Christensen, Isabelle rose and walked to a small table where she'd already placed some paper and a pen.

"If you don't mind," she said to Christensen, "I'll write as you translate."

The man nodded and moved to Isabelle's side, leafing through the book.

"Oh, first," James said, following him, "would you read this?" He pointed to the sentence he had been pondering over.

"It says, 'The lady's last trunk was placed upon the wrong ship. It will arrive in Calcutta on *The Davis*.'"

Isabelle nodded as James snapped his fingers. "That's it. Bilbey mentioned his wife's missing trunk, and at the London shipping offices I read *The Davis*'s schedule on the wall charts."

"Yes," Isabelle said. "I remember now also." She tapped the pen against her lip. "I wonder if it's already arrived." To Christensen, she asked if he would mind pulling up a chair and beginning his translation at the start of Ari's notes.

As the young sergeant began to translate, Isabelle scribbled anything and everything, listening for something that might help unravel the Greek's plans, but she was confused at some of the things Ari had in his diary. She noted Ari's page numbers on her translations, attempting to scrawl even the smallest details. Glancing at the book, she noticed that Sergeant Christensen had reached the page containing the dead woman's name and address. Isabelle's heart increased its rhythm.

"It says here, 'I have been retained by the wife of a British officer stationed in Bombay,'" Christensen said. "'She wishes for me to inspect the home of a woman and search for proof of her husband's indiscretions. She assures me that she will double my pay, contingent upon payment she receives from one who wishes to purchase valuable information from her.'"

Here Isabelle stopped writing and glanced up at James. "She not only didn't pay him double, but I don't believe she paid him anything," she said. "He thought to extract money from Sparks and then go back to Calcutta and await her trunk. She must have told him Sparks had a significant amount of resources at his disposal or he never would have bothered."

Phillip nodded from his position across the desk where he'd been watching the translating with interest. "Oh, yes. Sparks told her that he had received huge amounts of money from 'investors.'"

"Which wasn't true," Isabelle said.

"Of course not. He has barely two pennies to rub together. What he did have to begin with he received as an advance on his credit from a bank in California."

James looked down at the journal. He motioned to it and said to Christensen, "Would you mind skimming along to see if Ari mentions anything further about information he was trying to obtain on the woman?"

The sergeant nodded and looked ahead a page, then two. "Here," he said, his finger trailing along the text. "Just a simple passage: 'Obtained necessary information for the Lady. Found a letter written from her husband to the woman in question. Lady is in London, will search for her there and stay for the season. Search itself became complicated. Was interrupted.'"

James snorted. "I'd wager that's as good as a confession. Bilbey was correct—Ari killed Mrs. Hinshaska and her son."

Isabelle nodded. "And he must have decided to forego the London Season because he booked passage aboard our same ship back to India." She pursed her lips in thought. "What does he say on the dates we were aboard the ship, I wonder." She told Christensen the dates in question and waited while he scanned through the small book.

"Here we are. He doesn't say much, just lists an address in Bombay and this line, 'May use letter as leverage against the husband.'" Christensen glanced up as Isabelle scrawled his statement.

"And the address?" she said.

When he told them, she paused and looked up again at James. He nodded at her. "Bilbey's office," he said. "Ari planned to blackmail him with the letter he found at Mrs. Hinshaska's."

"Then the letter must still be in the trunk," she mused.

"Do you mind if I look in the trunk?" James asked Colonel Stafford.

"Not at all. We plan to send the contents to headquarters, however, so the original will need to remain here."

Isabelle sighed. "I suppose you'll be wanting the journal as well."

"Yes, but you may keep your copies."

Isabelle cupped her chin in her hand and wondered how she might bribe the colonel into letting her keep it. Christensen, meanwhile, had begun translating again, so she returned to her scribbling. She missed Phillip's thoughtful expression as he examined the scene.

* * *

The train to Calcutta sped along, and Isabelle began to wonder how many miles they'd crossed by rail in so few days. One thing was for certain—Sally had certainly received her wished-for adventure. James sat beside her in the lounge car and dozed, his head resting against the window and bumping with the movement. Phillip had secreted himself away in his and James's cabin, saying he was working on a project.

Isabelle wondered how she was going to pass the two days it would take to reach Calcutta without tying herself into knots worrying about Sally and Alice. She leaned back in her seat and closed her eyes, willing herself to imagine something other than the worst.

* * *

"I am certain it is considered a delicacy in some regions," Sally said as she and Alice examined the fish heads and tails they had found in a bucket farther down the dock. They'd grabbed it and ran back to the safety of their shack.

Alice looked at the contents of the bucket and inhaled. She promptly turned and ran for the corner of the shack where she proceeded to throw up the nothing that was in her stomach.

"Wonderful," Sally muttered. She looked at the bucket again. Perhaps there would come a time when she could convince herself to chew and swallow the contents, but it hadn't arrived yet. "It's only been two days, really," she said and set the bucket aside. "I'm hardly even feeling the pain anymore." She threw an arm around Alice's shoulders when the girl returned to her side and said, "I suggest we look for something else."

Alice had opened her mouth to comment when voices sounded outside the door. The girls turned and ran for the back corner, well hidden behind the stacks of barrels. They crouched down low and listened as someone entered.

Sally counted three voices engaged in conversation. One spoke Hindi, and the other translated into English for the third. "The barrels are to be transported to his other warehouse at that end of the docks."

"And how long do we have to do this?"

"He wants it finished by nightfall."

"And they are all empty?"

More Hindi, then English. "Mostly empty. Some are partially filled with textiles."

The men left the shack, and the girls looked at each other. "I suppose we should stop worrying about food and find the officers," Alice said.

Sally nodded, and after waiting for a time, they stepped from the shack and back out into the bright sunlight.

The streets were crowded again, and Sally was quickly losing what remained of her good humor as she spied the rows of food positioned on stalls and carts. Alice's feet seemed to gravitate toward the food, and Sally pulled back on her arm. "You saw what happened last time," she whispered to the girl. "If we steal and get caught, we're likely to lose a limb."

Alice let out a puff of air, and her shoulders slumped. Sally glanced up and down the stalls, surveying the scene. Picking the least attentive merchant, she slowly made her way over to his cart.

Just as she stretched forth her hand to quickly grab a piece of fruit, she glanced up and came face to face with Sergeant Lyle, who seemed as stunned as she was. Unfortunately, he regained his wits more quickly and grabbed her arm, his eyes narrowing and his grip tightening.

Alice screamed at him in outrage and stomped hard on his foot. When he bellowed and slackened his grasp, Sally yanked her arm free and ran, following Alice, who was heading back into familiar territory along the dock. They ran, dodging in and out of people, and tore into their shack, slamming the door shut behind them.

"I saw a man coming this way with a large, empty cart," Sally gasped. "I'll bet he is the one who is going to move the barrels. We can't stay in here." She eyed the barrels. "Unless . . ."

Alice nodded. "Yes! Quick! They'll move us to the other end of the dock, and Lyle will never know where we've gone."

They climbed into two empty barrels near the front door, each girl pulling her lid overtop. Sally heard the door crash open behind them and heard Lyle bellow like an enraged bull. With a wince, she heard him cross the threshold and begin shoving barrels over.

She began to think the game was up when she heard another voice yelling over the din. To her relief, it was the worker hired to move the barrels. He began a rapid fire exchange of angry dialogue with Lyle, who insisted that two young women were hiding in the shack. The worker must have had reinforcements with him, because before long, more voices joined the throng, and, by the sound of things, Lyle was forcibly removed from the building.

Sally breathed a sigh of relief as she felt her barrel being lifted with a grunt. Hoping against hope that the workers would think she and Alice were the barrels partially full of textiles, she clenched her hands and gritted her teeth as the barrel was thrown roughly into the cart, which began to move with a lurch.

* * *

It was nearing evening of the second day aboard the train, and Isabelle sat in the lounge car, trying without success to read a novel. She was beginning to wonder if Phillip was going to show his face before they reached Calcutta. He had been holed up in his cabin, working on his project, and Isabelle was becoming irritated by her own curiosity. That James had become privy to the secret did nothing to improve her mood.

Finally, Phillip emerged looking much like a harried professor, his hair disheveled, his clothing rumpled. On his face was perched a pair of spectacles, giving him a very scholarly air indeed. Close behind him was James, who entered with an amused glance at his brother. James sat in a chair next to Isabelle as Phillip extended her a black book.

"What's this?" she asked him as she took it.

"A replica."

She looked inside the book and realized that Phillip had copied, verbatim, Ari's diary into a blank journal. She looked up at the young man, amazed, and began to laugh. "You've been copying that diary all this time? Phillip, you wonderful thing!" Isabelle rose to her feet and hugged him. His arms closed around her, and he gave her a squeeze. When she pulled back she saw the look of tenderness that crossed his features.

"It's a small enough thing, given all that you've done for me. I know you wanted that diary. So I . . . borrowed the original. With the intent to return it, of course."

"Of course." She smiled at him and rubbed her hand along his arm. "Thank you so very much."

When she sat back down, she was caught by surprise at the scowl on James's face. "I'd have copied the blasted thing for you, had I known it meant that much."

She laughed out loud, absurdly pleased by his jealousy. "Of course you would," she said and placed a hand alongside his cheek. "You're equally wonderful."

Phillip sat opposite them, looking pleased with himself. "It's nice to have finally beaten you to the task, brother," he said. "That would be a first for me."

James shook his head. "You're always the perceptive one." He turned to Isabelle. "Last year for Mother's birthday, I gave her a new set of pokers for her fire. Phillip gave her a new dress, a bonnet, and a bouquet of roses."

Isabelle laughed again and winked at Phillip. "Cherish your gift," she told him. "Someday you'll have a wife who will worship the ground you walk on."

James shook his head and motioned to the book Isabelle held. "Why did you want the original so much?" he asked.

"I don't know, really, other than that I think there may be more here than meets the eye. I feel as though I've missed something."

"But much of it is in Greek."

"True enough. I just . . . I don't know."

* * *

As Isabelle looked through the journal later that night, she paid special attention to Ari's most recent entries. He had notated places in Delhi where he thought he might locate Sparks. He'd taken pains to make certain he knew where the British officers' compound was.

Her brow wrinkled in thought when she came to the very end of Phillip's copied notes. Deep in thought, she absently wandered from her cabin and knocked on the one next door. James opened the door some time later after having covered his nightclothes in a robe.

"You do make a habit of nocturnal visits, don't you," he said.

"Is your brother awake?"

At this, he leaned against the doorframe with his shoulder and tilted his head. "And why, late at night, do you want to see my brother?"

She looked up from her book and brought herself more fully into the present. He filled the doorway with his large frame and looked utterly appealing. A slow smile spread across her face, and she folded her arms over her chest. "Well, I don't see where that's any business of yours, now is it."

"Mmm. You know, the thought has crossed my mind that the two of you are closer in age than are you and I. Were I the gallant sort, I ought to step aside and concede to the more appropriate man."

"It might interest you to know that my tastes run to the older sort."

His eyes narrowed fractionally, and she had to work to keep from laughing. "I'm not entirely in my dotage just yet," he said.

"Not entirely."

"And in requesting an audience with my brother, might I be allowed to attend?"

"I should hope so. I'm not looking to spend time with him alone. Were you under that impression?"

He rolled his eyes. "You wouldn't be the first."

At that she laughed. "He is rather charming. And handsome."

"I think I've heard enough."

"And he is the very image of his elder brother."

He inclined his head and stood, allowing her access. "Very well. You may come in. He's in the next room."

Isabelle entered the tiny sitting room that adjoined the sleeping berth. Phillip stood, and she waved him back down. "Sit, really," she said. "I've just come to ask you something quickly about these notes here at the end of your copy."

"Certainly." He rubbed his eyes as though he'd fallen asleep reading.

"I'm curious about these notations here. I don't remember Christensen translating them." Isabelle pointed to the last page on which Ari had written something.

Phillip shook his head. "Christensen didn't translate that—those notes are from the telegrams."

"Telegrams? What telegrams?"

Phillip's brows drew together in confusion. "You know the ones— you were reading one of them in the office after Christensen finished."

Isabelle shook her head. "No, I was reading the letter Bilbey wrote to Mrs. Hinshaska."

Phillip's jaw dropped open. "You haven't seen the telegrams?"

Isabelle and James both shook their heads. Phillip jumped up from his seat and retrieved Ari's original diary from his newly purchased satchel. Flipping to the back of the book, he brought it close to Isabelle and said, "You can see there's an envelope of sorts back here attached to the cover. It's rather hidden—it opens toward the spine. If you're not careful, you'll miss it. Inside, I found these telegram receipts. I was certain you had seen them."

Isabelle took the receipts, and James placed a hand on her back as he read over her shoulder. "These were all sent from Delhi and are addressed to Sergeant Lyle. 'Keep valuables under close watch.'"

"The girls?" James asked.

"Probably," Isabelle said. "This one was sent the day he died. 'Cairo's Promise. Midnight. Mr. Ramses.'" Isabelle frowned. "And then today's date. What's happening tonight at midnight? And what is 'Cairo's Promise?'"

James shook his head and Phillip shrugged. "Almost sounds like a ship," James said.

"A ship that leaves tonight at midnight. What time do we arrive in Calcutta?" Isabelle asked.

"One o'clock in the morning," Phillip answered her.

Isabelle's heart thudded hard in alarm. "We're going to miss them by one hour," she whispered.

James rubbed his hand along her spine. "We don't know it's a ship," he said. "It may be a restaurant or other establishment where he'd planned to meet Lyle and this Mr. Ramses. As soon as we arrive, we'll ask some questions."

Isabelle nodded. "I feel sick."

* * *

Sally felt the tears run down her cheeks and tried for all she was worth to stifle her sniffles. She and Alice had been trapped inside the barrels for hours, and she was numb from the waist down. They hadn't been able to climb from their hiding spots because at least two guards had patrolled the warehouse since their arrival.

She knew Alice was close by; shortly after their arrival, she had heard her friend's complaint from within her own barrel. Sally had dared a quick, "Hush!" but then later had tapped softly against the side of her small prison and had been glad to hear Alice tap back.

Just when she was about to burst out of the barrel and throw common sense to the wind, she heard Lyle's voice.

It can't be! They cannot have let him in here! He was still insisting that the young women were in the warehouse, his voice growing angrier as their footsteps grew closer. Sally was light-headed with fatigue and hunger; she wasn't sure how far she would make it if she tried to run, and she knew for a fact that Alice wouldn't last long.

Once again, she heard him being forced away, and as he went, he shouted, "I will be just outside this door! You can't make me leave the dockside, and you'll see! There are women in here!"

"That man is crazy," she heard another worker say. She then heard several men enter the building and begin to talk as they moved things around. She heard snatches of conversation that indicated the barrels were to be moved again.

"Alice," she hissed, hoping the conversation around them was loud enough to drown her out.

"What?" came the miserable reply. The girl had clearly been in tears.

"I think we should stay where we are. If Lyle is outside, we can't chance leaving now or hiding somewhere else in here, because he will find us."

"Yes." Alice sniffed. Providence was smiling upon them; she sounded as though she were right next to Sally. "And then wherever they put us next, if Lyle isn't around, I think we should get out and try to talk to whoever is there."

"I agree," Sally said. "We probably should have tried to talk to someone today. Perhaps even now we can reason with one of these men."

"I don't know, Sally," Alice said. She sounded absolutely wretched. "I'm so afraid. If we show ourselves, they will realize he was right all along, and suppose he's been telling them we're in his care or some such? If they believe him, they'll turn us over to him."

"So we don't move an inch, then," Sally said, but stopped when voices grew closer. She winced as her barrel was lifted and carried from the warehouse. Shouts and orders continued, commands to empty the warehouse; everything inside was going. They were rushing; an authoritarian voice was yelling that time was short, someone or something was leaving . . .

Sally knew the moment she was outside and set down on the dock. The very air felt different, and she was so anxious to be out of the barrel that she would have welcomed just about anything. Shouts came from another direction, and again she heard Lyle's angry voice. She closed her eyes, knowing she would hear that voice in her sleep for a long time to come. She couldn't suppress a shudder at the sound of his bellowing.

A cacophony of voices rose in the night, and then she was again hauled up and carried over a distance before being set down. She heard the sound of feet on creaking wood and hoped against hope that their next warehouse would soon be abandoned enough for them to make their escape. The sounds of the dock were loud against her ears, and she was trying to mark how long it was taking for her to be carried from their former location to their new one when she felt her barrel slipping.

One of the men carrying it muttered something that must have been a curse, and then the barrel hit the ground hard. Sally's breath expelled in an enormous *whoosh,* and her head hit against the side of the barrel. As quickly as a snap of the fingers, her world went black without time to formulate a coherent thought.

19

Isabelle stood at the dockside, frantic and looking out at the black sea. "What do you mean, it's gone?" She was very near collapse, and she had never been one for fainting.

"Memsahib," the dock master said, "she left port over two hours ago. I am most sorry."

"And the ship is headed *where?*"

"Egypt. Cairo."

Isabelle clutched James's arm with fingers that were bloodless. Weber, who had accompanied them from Delhi, stood at her shoulder and looked at her with great sympathy.

"Miss Webb," he said "It is entirely possible that the girls are not on board. We should check in with the officers here to see if Lyle has been seen. In the morning we can question the dock workers who helped load the ship. They might remember seeing either him or the young women."

Isabelle nodded, numb. James put a tight arm around her shoulders and helped her toward their hired carriage. Phillip's face was white and drawn in the moonlight.

If only the train had been ahead of schedule, she thought. *If only I would have stayed in our room that night rather than pawing through Ari's things. If only I would never have brought her here . . .*

Perhaps Ari had not intended to put the girls on the ship. It was possible he and Lyle were to get on themselves and leave the girls in Calcutta. Isabelle's head throbbed, and she rubbed her temples as the carriage made its way over the uneven road.

Not much time passed before they arrived at the British compound. As Calcutta was currently the British capital, the compound was impressive. Stafford had been sure to notify the officers of their impending arrival, and their rooms were ready for them.

The thought of sleep was laughable, and Isabelle stood in the center of her room, rooted to the spot and terrified. Once she had known for a surety that the girls were in the city, she had harbored a foolish optimism that she would find them. Never in a million years would she have imagined that Ari would have had them spirited away on a ship bound for Cairo of all places.

She sank to her knees, suddenly gasping for breath. It was too much to bear, and she was exhausted and spent with worry. Her entire body was still a mass of scratches and bruises from her encounter with Ari, and her spirit felt equally beaten.

She lowered her forehead to the floor, her hands beside her head in fists. She cried, then, and felt as though her heart was broken. *Oh please,* she thought, *please protect her. Please, I beg of you, keep her safe and take me to her! If you're even there, please take care of her. Don't let anyone hurt her.*

After a few moments, a feeling of peace stole over her mind, and her breathing slowed. She exhaled quietly, breathing in and out and feeling a measure of control for the first time in days. She crawled over to the bed and climbed up into it, fully clothed. Falling into an exhausted slumber, she dreamed of the Benefactress. *All will be well,* the woman told her. *You needn't fear.*

* * *

James quietly closed Isabelle's door and frowned in thought. She was exhausted and beside herself with worry over Sally's welfare. The sooner they found Lyle and could question him about the girls, the better.

James made his way down the hallway and toward the officers' quarters. Despite the late hour, there were voices. Following the sound and rounding the corner, he was surprised to see Weber approaching him.

"Sir," Weber said, "I am going out with some of the men on a second shift to see if we can't find Lyle. I don't suppose you'd like to come along?"

"I would indeed."

The night was balmy, the air thick with humidity. The docks were quiet—an extreme contrast to the usual noise and bustle of the daylight hours. "We think he's hiding here in one of the warehouses," an officer told James. "The men we're replacing say they lost him somewhere in this region."

After splitting into teams of two, James and Weber found themselves combing building after building, looking in corners and crates to no avail. They were outside considering which structure to enter next when James spied a dark shadow from the corner of his eye. The shadow slipped into a building several yards down the wharf. James's instincts went on high alert, and for no other reason than sheer impulse, he motioned to Weber and ran toward the building.

He had seen the flash of red on the man's uniform—he could have been any of the other officers—but something in the way the shadow had moved and darted seemed suspicious. James pointed Weber to one entrance and then circled around to the back side of the building. He entered as quietly as possible, allowing his eyes time to adjust to the darkness.

The building was filled with wooden crates stacked shoulder height. James began slowly making his way through the maze, cautiously approaching a corner and peering around before proceeding. He followed the narrow passageway, turning his shoulders and inching along, carefully avoiding disrupting the piles.

He jerked his head to the right at a crash and muffled exclamation from a voice he recognized as Weber's. A movement from the shadows at his left showed a silhouette taking some stairs along the far wall. The stairs led to a loft overhead that was partially filled in with wooden flooring, the rest of the structure consisting of bare floor joists.

James ran to the stairs, hoping the figure would believe Weber to be the only one in the building. As if on cue, Weber called out, presumably hoping to draw attention away from James. As James took the stairs two at a time, Weber yelled, "Lyle, the game is up, my man. If you come with me now, it will go better for you."

The answering laugh from above was curt and without humor. "Weber, is that you? You would turn on your old friend?"

"You're not the friend I believed you to be," Weber called up as James made it to the loft. "I can't imagine that you thought the Greek was someone to be trusted. We disliked him from the start!"

"His money was more than I'd make in a year in 'er Majesty's service!"

"He never had the money!"

"And how was I to know that?" Lyle exploded from the corner of the loft. "The bloke was such a fancy nob." He broke off and muttered something to himself that James couldn't hear.

James inched his way toward the corner of the loft. There were crates stacked there as well, and as his shoulder brushed against one, he noted they were empty. He caught it as it teetered in place and closed his eyes briefly. He felt sweat gather under his clothing and trickle down his back. The heat in the loft was oppressive, and he wiped his sleeve across his forehead.

"Listen to me," Weber was saying from below. "I will leave now and give you some time to consider your options. You must believe me, old fellow, it will be better for you if you turn yourself in. I'll not rush up there and take you by force."

James inched his way toward the corner where he knew Lyle was hiding. He heard Weber below, opening and then closing the front door. He was very nearly to the corner when Lyle stood up with a sigh and saw him.

"You!" Lyle exploded and raised his hand. James barely had time to register the fact that Lyle held a gun. He dropped and rolled to the side as Lyle squeezed the trigger, sending a bullet flying where James had been standing.

James scrambled to his feet and ran; then he crouched to a defensive position behind a stack of crates. As he heard Lyle approaching, James lifted a crate from the top of the stack and hurled it at the man. It hit Lyle square in the face and shoulders, stunning him long enough for James to run at him and take him with a thud to the floor of the loft.

Lyle recovered his wits and began to roll with James, throwing punches to James's ribs and midsection. James turned until he had Lyle flat on his back then began grappling to shove the man's hands to the floor. He repeatedly slammed Lyle's gun hand to the floor until the gun clattered to the side.

"I'm coming, James!" Weber yelled from below, and James could hear a shout outside the building, accompanied by the sound of running feet.

Lyle's eyes widened slightly, his fear reflected in his face. With strength that must have been born of sheer desperation, he heaved himself slightly upward and to one side, throwing James off balance just enough for Lyle to roll again and attempt to pin James on his back, all the while reaching for the gun that had landed a few feet away.

Using the other man's momentum, James kept rolling until he realized, his heart thumping once, hard, that they had reached the end of the flooring and were nearly on the rough beams. Releasing Lyle's arms, he flung his own around a beam and kicked to free his legs. Hugging the beam with both arms, he succeeded in wrapping one leg around the thick, wooden piece as well.

Lyle rolled over him, clutching at air as he slipped through the widely spaced joists, managing to snag a fistful of James's suit coat. He held on for a split second before losing his grip on the fabric and falling through the air with a crash as he hit the crates below. A swarm of soldiers was upon him before he could let out a groan.

With muscles that were beginning to protest their fatigue, James twisted and pulled himself above the beam and crawled his way back to the flooring of the loft. He stood and stripped his coat from his shoulders, shoving a hand through his sweat-soaked hair. Rotating his head around on his neck, he grunted as Weber clasped him in an exuberant embrace.

"Mercy, Ashby, I pegged you for a dead man!" he exclaimed.

"I was beginning to wonder myself," James said.

* * *

James stood outside the prison cell of one very hostile Sergeant Lyle. Morning had come quickly, and despite his fatigue, James found himself too restless to sleep. James now stood, unconsciously flexing his sore muscles and leaning against one of the bars as he listened to another officer question Lyle, who was belligerent in the extreme.

"I don't know what ye're talking about, and I'm tired of all these questions!" he barked at the man. Lyle's face was mottled and bruised, and one eye had swelled completely shut. James couldn't help his satisfied smirk. *You should see the other fellow,* he imagined telling his brother. "I don't know where those girls are. Ari Kilronomos has them."

"The woman who runs the inn where you were staying verified that they were with you for several days," the officer said.

"What woman? Ye're lying!"

"Ari gave you up," James said quietly from outside the bars. Both of the men inside looked at him. "He was caught in Delhi and laid all the blame at your feet. Said this whole thing was your idea."

Lyle's face became angrier, the veins in his neck standing out. "It was all *his* idea! He used me from the beginning!"

"So where are the girls?" James asked. "Once they're found, things will be much easier for you."

Lyle hesitated, indecisive.

"Or if they stay missing, you'll go to prison for kidnapping and murder."

"They're in a warehouse; or they were," Lyle finally said.

At this, the man questioning him interrupted. "The warehouse where you were arrested?"

Lyle nodded. "I know they were, I saw them go into the one before the ballast was transferred. They were hiding in some barrels."

"All of the barrels were placed on board a ship," James said.

"You see, I don't know where they are. I have no idea which ship they were put on."

"They're headed for Cairo." James watched Lyle's expression closely and wasn't surprised at the disbelief he read there.

Lyle laughed then and was soon doubled over. The officer questioning him became angry, and Lyle eventually brought himself under control.

"Ironic, isn't it?" James fought to stay calm, to keep from grabbing the bars and trying to break his way into the cell. "They're on the very ship you were supposed to put them on, per Ari's instructions."

Lyle nodded, his face contorted with ill-concealed satisfaction. "And were you going to join them?"

"Both of us were going to," Lyle spat. "We were supposed to use the Bilbey chit to claim her mother's trunk and then set sail last night."

"You didn't think it through very well, did you?" James said, his voice flat. "Alice is underage—they wouldn't have given her the trunk. Only her father would be able to claim it."

"Not if he was dead."

James's brow rose a notch. "What makes you think he is dead?"

"Ari planned . . ." Lyle suddenly shut his mouth.

"And how did you plan to get two screaming young women aboard a ship bound for Cairo?" James asked.

Here, the officer answered James while still looking at Lyle. "We found ether and laudanum in his belongings. I suspect they had plans to heavily sedate the girls."

"You can't prove anything!" Lyle burst forth again. "I was being blackmailed!"

James turned and left the cell after a nod of thanks to the officer inside. He made his way out of the jail and across the compound, wondering if Isabelle was awake yet. Phillip met him halfway across the grounds to tell him Isabelle was in the breakfast room.

After witnessing the state of her nerves the night before, James was uncertain as to what her condition would be. To his surprise, she looked rested and much like her stronger, former self. He was curious, but personal questions would have to wait. She was seated with several officers who all listened intently as she related the events of the past several days.

Isabelle looked up at him as he entered, and her face softened. He was glad she seemed to find a measure of peace in his company, and he sat in a chair opposite her at the table. Sitting next to her was impossible, he noted wryly, as every available chair anywhere near her was taken.

He was anxious to tell her what he'd learned from Lyle but didn't want to share Isabelle with everyone else in the room. They would all hear of Lyle's half-hearted confession when the questioning officer returned from the cell. He wanted to save his conversation with Isabelle for a private moment.

"We only just learned this morning," one of the men was telling Isabelle, "that two of the porters aboard your steamship agreed to help Ari Kilronomos dump one of Lady Banbury's trunks overboard. One of the men confirmed that Kilronomos told him her body was inside. There is a trunk here," he continued. "It arrived last week for Lady Banbury. We were going to send it on to their new cottage to be with the rest of their belongings which arrived last week."

Isabelle nodded noncommittally, and James could see the wheels in her head spinning. He fought and failed to suppress a smile. She wanted to see inside that trunk. He shook his head slightly and took a sip of the drink that had been placed before him. He wondered if they'd be making an unexpected detour by the room where the trunk was. It was funny—a few weeks before he would never have believed he would have looked on such a thing as an acceptable occurrence.

Once Isabelle was finished with her breakfast, he motioned to her with his head, and she nodded, making her good-byes to the others in the room. He motioned likewise to Phillip, who was still trying to replenish his starved body's nutrients every chance he could. He stuffed a buttered scone in his mouth and followed them out the door.

When they were out on the grounds, James pointed to a bench under a shade tree. He told Phillip and Isabelle about the things Lyle had said. "I also wonder, though," he said when he finished, "whether or not the girls really are on that ship."

"You missed it before you came in," Phillip said. "One of the officers said he and two others had been combing the dock since sunrise and found a worker from the warehouse who verified that he saw one of the girls in a barrel."

James whistled under his breath.

Isabelle nodded and swallowed. "He said he was in the warehouse getting ready to haul a barrel out to the gang plank when the lid lifted slightly and he saw someone peeking out. He was going to shout out but said that the girl looked very scared and pointed at the door where they were taking Lyle out, kicking and screaming."

Isabelle's hands were knotted into fists in her lap. Phillip continued for her. "Apparently, Lyle had been hanging around all day causing a disturbance and insisting there were two women who were in his care hiding in the warehouse. Of course, everyone thought he was crazy, and because this one particular man took a disliking to Lyle, he took pity on the girl and didn't say a word. He says that he, personally, helped carry the barrel that contained her."

"I wonder which girl it was," James mused.

"The man said dark hair and blue eyes. That would be Alice," Isabelle said.

James looked at Isabelle for a long moment. "Do you believe they are aboard?"

She returned his gaze then nodded. "I do. I believe they are."

"We've been told that they couldn't be in better care," Phillip said and laid a gentle hand on Isabelle's fist. "The captain is a personal friend of the commander here and is an English gentleman through and through. Once the girls make their presence known, they will be well cared for."

"Then I suppose our next move must be to find the soonest ship to Cairo. Phillip?"

Phillip nodded. "Absolutely. I'd not miss it."

Isabelle looked from one brother to the other. "I can't ask it of you," she said.

James shook his head. "You're not asking. Nor are we asking for permission. We'll go together to Cairo to find them."

Isabelle swallowed and finally nodded. "Thank you," she said. "I should hate to be looking for them alone."

* * *

It was dark and quiet when James and Isabelle stole into the locked office containing Lady Banbury's trunk. Isabelle made quick work on the trunk's lock after James made certain they hadn't been seen, and by the light of a single lantern, they began to sift through the items.

"Clothing for Alice," Isabelle whispered. She carefully placed aside each article and quickly made her way through to the bottom of the trunk. Once there, she retrieved a box that measured approximately five inches square, along with a small notebook.

She opened the notebook first, noting the fine, feminine script. It looked to contain mostly addresses and a few personal notes next to names. Toward the back, she saw Ari Kilronomos's name and an address in Bombay. Lady Banbury had also written the name Siri Hinshaska and the now-familiar address, also in Bombay.

"Look at how the script here changes," Isabelle said, pointing to the woman's name. "The hand becomes heavier, angrier." She turned a page and saw a few sheets of paper folded within. Withdrawing them, Isabelle saw them to be receipts of items paid for and to be sent to Mrs. Hinshaska's house, and they were signed by Lord Banbury.

"Do you suppose Lady Banbury assumed her husband in love with this other woman because she found some receipts he had signed?" James asked.

"She had to have had other reasons," Isabelle said. "Changes in the marriage, perhaps? Rumors from other women? The gossip-mongers can be ruthless. And so she hired Ari to find out for certain if it was true, and he ended up killing the woman and her child. When he told Lady Banbury about it aboard the ship, she panicked and demanded an audience with the captain, presumably to turn Ari in."

Isabelle set the book aside for the moment and looked at the box. It was tied tight with twine that she began to delicately disentangle. When it finally came free, she glanced up at James and lifted the lid.

The stone inside was beautiful. It was a deep purple and shaped like a large egg. Very gently, she lifted it to the lamp, noting the translucent quality as the light shone through from the other side. "Do you suppose this is it?" she murmured to James, who took it from her and weighed it in his palm.

"I hope not," he muttered. "We'll probably be struck dead by morning."

She smiled. "I wonder if Lady Banbury believed this to be the real Jewel of Zeus."

"You know," James said, "I don't know if she did believe it, but she was desperate enough to sell it for what she believed could be a large amount of money."

Isabelle took a breath. "It rightfully belongs to Alice and her brothers. I think we should take it with us."

James looked at her, a slow grin spreading over his face. "Of course we should. For the good of the family."

Isabelle nodded, her grin soon matching his. "For the good of the family. And to keep it far away from Thaddeus Sparks." She paused for a moment. "How do you feel about making a quick visit to the Bilbeys' new home?"

His brow arched. "Now?"

She nodded. "It's just across the compound. The officers here told me they'd just finished unpacking the Bilbeys' things when they received word of his death."

"What are you looking for?"

"Lady Banbury's diaries."

Isabelle was grateful James didn't ask any more questions but followed her out into the night. Once at the Bilbeys' cottage, they went around to the back of the building, and Isabelle picked the lock. She was nervous about lighting a lantern, so they were forced to rely on the light of the moon once they located Lady Banbury's personal items.

"I feel a bit strange," James said as he looked around the bedroom.

"As do I," Isabelle said.

"Is this really necessary?"

Isabelle continued her search through the armoire and dressing table. "I admit, part of me is curious about this whole affair," she said, "but secondly . . ." She straightened and looked at James. "I want to be able to try to explain things to Alice. When she discovers what has happened."

"Perhaps she doesn't need to know exactly what transpired."

Isabelle shook her head, feeling strangely sad. "She will eventually learn the truth. People always do."

"Wouldn't it be a kinder thing to leave her to her ignorant bliss for as long as possible?"

"Until when? A society mama sees fit to lower Alice because her own daughter isn't as pretty? I believe she should know now. Knowledge is power."

James nodded reluctantly. "It will be a hefty amount to absorb at once."

Isabelle agreed. "I will be gentle. Ah, here we go," she said and opened a small, unpacked box on the floor. Finding a small book within, she carried it to the window and opened it to see script that matched the diary she'd already found in the trunk.

They quietly left the house the same way they'd come and, at James's suggestion, walked away from the officers' compound and toward the waterfront. They made their way past rows of buildings along the edge of the water where people worked by day, doing laundry and bathing. Eventually, they came to a spot of beach that lay quietly beckoning in the bright moonlight. James removed his coat and spread it so that Isabelle could sit on the sand. She smiled at his gallantry, and they sat side by side beginning to leaf through Lady Banbury's diary.

Isabelle's eye fell upon certain telling passages, and she felt her heart grow heavy in sympathy for a woman who was losing the love of her husband.

I cannot abide his actions . . . he denies everything, but I know in my heart . . . How can he do this to me? What will people think? I am mortified. I know it is common, but I never anticipated it . . . I am not so beautiful now as I once was . . . I must know for certain. I have hired a man to look into the matter.

The Bilbeys' money troubles were also alluded to in the diary's passages.

He tells me we will be forced to sell the ancestral estate. Sell the ancestral estate! I had planned to leave him here to his pursuits and return home. Now I can no longer do even this. I have nothing left, and the boys will be forced to leave school. Alice will not have a proper season . . .

Wonderful news! I have been approached by an enterprising American with some wealthy benefactors who has sought me out for my knowledge of the jewel. Perhaps our money woes are about to become a thing of the past . . . I am so looking forward to my holiday in London. I believe I will even see if I can't make arrangements for the jewel to be sent to me in London. The American may find it easier to reach his funds while still in London as opposed to being in India . . .

James sighed. "And the rest is history, of course."

Isabelle nodded, closing the book with a frown. "Perhaps I will wait a bit before divulging the whole of it to Alice. There are details in here she may be better off without until she is older."

James placed a hand alongside her face, and she turned into it. The look in his eyes was tender, yet carried with it a sense of urgency she had come to recognize in his gaze. He leaned forward, touching his lips to hers, gently at first, and then insistently, as though he had held himself in reserve long enough. Isabelle sighed and closed her eyes, and when she was able to form a coherent thought, she realized that James had been right. Words would have been a hindrance.

* * *

Sally and Alice stood at the railing of the ship, their faces toward the sun. Fortune had indeed smiled upon them, as their captain was a good British gentleman who happened to also be carrying a small party of passengers in addition to his cargo. When he had realized he unwittingly carried two helpless young women aboard his ship, he had been all that was solicitous and kind.

He had procured them temporary clothing that, while not entirely of the best fit, was clean and presentable, and he had placed them under the care of an elderly woman who had been a governess in India for many years to a British family. She had fussed over them and made them feel much better about their current circumstances.

Sally had lain unconscious in her barrel for a good two hours after they had been placed aboard the ship, by which time they were well underway. When she realized they were out to sea, she had tumbled from her barrel with a sharp cry of pain and once stretched, began groping around in the dark of the hold for Alice, who had similarly extricated herself upon hearing Sally.

"Why didn't you say something to someone?" she had cried to Alice. "Do you realize we're probably in the middle of the ocean?"

"We agreed to keep quiet!" Alice had cried back. "And you weren't saying a word!"

"I was unconscious!"

"How was I to know?"

And so it went until a crewmember heard the ruckus and came upon them. And now they stood together in the sun under the watchful eye of their temporary guardian, with assurances from the captain that once they reached port and had rested for a bit, they would be returned to Calcutta, no worse for the wear.

A gentleman they had seen in passing over the last several hours approached them and, with a smile, took his hat in his hands. "I understand the two of you have had quite a scare," he said with an engaging smile.

Sally answered his smile with one of her own. "And you, sir, are from the States, if I'm not mistaken."

"I am indeed. You sound much like a Southern belle if ever I heard one."

"My name is Miss Sally Rhodes. This is my friend, Miss Alice Bilbey."

He nodded his head again. "The pleasure is mine." His gaze lingered for a bit on Alice. "I do believe I've met your mother, Miss Bilbey, and you must believe it is a compliment when I say you resemble her."

Alice stiffened a bit, and Sally put a hand on her back. "My friend has recently lost her mother," she said. "Perhaps you hadn't heard."

"We don't know for certain where she is," Alice said. "I'm sure we shall hear from her soon."

"I am so sorry to hear," the man said. "I do hope you will soon receive word from her."

"Sir, we don't yet know your name," Sally said.

"Forgive me. My name is Mr. Jones."

"A pleasure, Mr. Jones. And where are you from?" Sally asked.

"New York City. But I do travel a fair bit."

The man had unusually green eyes, Sally noted. An exotic green color that she was certain she'd never seen before. He was handsome enough, she supposed, but much too old to be considered appropriate suitor material. He must have been nearly forty, after all.

One of the crew members approached them and said to Mr. Jones, "You need to report below decks." He smirked a bit and added, "Time to earn your keep with the cook."

Sally flushed a bit for Mr. Jones. He obviously was working to pay his passage to Cairo, and from the look he shot the crew member, he didn't want anyone else to know about it. He excused himself, and the girls watched him leave.

"Strange eyes," Alice murmured. "And how does he know my mother?"

"I don't know. But I do know one thing," Sally said. "I'm having a grand adventure, and although I've been nearly scared witless, I've made a good friend, and I'm glad you're with me, Alice Bilbey."

Alice looked askance at Sally. "I hated you at first, you know."

"As did I. I wanted Ari's attention to myself." Sally shuddered. "Odious man. I hope that when Belle finds him, she gives him the thrashing he deserves."

"She has probably found him by now," Alice said. "I wonder where they all are. I miss my father." She was quiet for a moment. "I don't treat them . . . well. My parents."

Sally sighed. "I didn't much either. I was rather selfish."

"Do you still miss them?"

"Terribly. But the ache lessens a bit. I can now speak of them without crying. Isn't that something?"

Alice smiled. "That is something. And I'm glad to be your friend. I've never had one. But do you suppose everyone has been able to find Mr. Ashby's brother? And do you suppose we will make it back to Calcutta? And once we're there, how will we stay away from Sergeant Lyle?"

"I'm not sure about anything, other than the fact that Isabelle will not rest until she succeeds."

"You have so much faith in her."

Sally nodded. "I do. She has earned it."

Author Notes

The railway system was fairly new to India in 1865, and I have my characters traversing nearly the whole of the country in this book. At that point, the tracks weren't as extensive as I would have the reader believe. I used a little bit of creative license here.

The Victoria Terminus Railway Station was completed in 1888 but was in use starting in 1882. I used it in this book because it's incredibly beautiful and, well, I just wanted my characters to see it.

The Sepoy Rebellion of 1857 was a real event that has been used in fiction before and I found it particularly interesting because it really was, in my opinion, a true attempt at Indian independence. I take a few shots at imperial Britain in this book, but I certainly mean no offense. India has a fascinating history and has been shaped by so many different cultures. The British Colonial period is such a fascinating study—such an amazing attempt to blend the Western world with the East. Or superimpose the West upon the East, I suppose, depending on whom you ask.

About the Author

N. C. Allen is a prolific and award-winning author. Her Faith of Our Fathers series won the Best of State award for fiction in 2004. She loves research and is meticulous in her efforts to be accurate and fair. She also loves a good story.

The author is a graduate of Weber State University and lives in Ogden with her husband and three children. *Isabelle Webb: The Legend of the Jewel* is her ninth book. Please visit online at www.ncallen.com or write to her in care of Covenant Communications, 920 E. State Road, P.O. Box 416, American Fork, UT 84003-0416.